Goldhead

Jaeme Haviland

Published by:
Southern Yellow Pine (SYP) Publishing
4351 Natural Bridge Rd.
Tallahassee, FL 32305

www.syppublishing.com

This is a work of fiction. Names, characters, places, and events that occur either are the products of the author's imagination or are used fictitiously. Any resemblance to actual persons, places, or events is purely coincidental.

The contents and opinions expressed in this book do not necessarily reflect the views and opinions of Southern Yellow Pine Publishing, nor does the mention of brands or trade names constitute endorsement.

ISBN-10: 1-940869-81-1
ISBN-13: 978-1-940869-81-0
ISBN-13: ePub 978-1-940869-82-7
ISBN-13: Adobe eBook 978-1-940869-83-4
Library of Congress Control Number: 2016951300

Printed in the United States of America
First Edition
October 2016

Dedication
For my father...

1
~~Tampico, Nueva España~~
12 Agosto 1523

The torrid sun glinted off the polished steel of the soldiers' armor as they walked single file down the dusty street. Their colorful uniforms contrasted wildly with the drab adobe walls of the native village. Striding through the warren of mud and thatch huts, the short haughty man who led them looked almost comical as he marched stiffly through the squalor around him, but there was no humor in his face or his mission. Children and adults scattered before him, and dogs barked at the procession from the safety of darkened doorways. As far as Comandante Gregorio was concerned, Tampico was just another gritty cesspit in a long line of hellholes he had encountered in this new world. The sooner he collected his prisoner and got back to the ship, the better.

Stopping at a small, rock-lined well in the middle of a broad, barren courtyard, he peered down into the shaft, looking to see if his captive was still alive. The morning light did not quite penetrate to the bottom of the blackened pit, but he could see a human form slumped against the wall.

"Bring him," was all he said.

***

Claudio sat cross-legged atop the frigate's fo'c'sle with his journal in his lap, watching the shoreline as he cut a new quill point with his dagger. The salt air was already thick with humidity, and he shuddered as the sweat rolled down his spine. Gaining strength with the rising sun, the heat sent wave after wave of familiar odors—wood, pitch, and canvas—to his nose. Over many months at sea, they had become the reassuring smells of home. They were not as sweet as the emanations that wafted from his mother's kitchen back in Spain nor as refreshing as the breezes that played through the orange blossoms that bloomed in the plaza of the pueblo where he grew up, but they held the promise of security, a modest income, and some degree of fame.

It had been four hours since sunrise, and the ship had to sail with the tide or stay in the bay until the next morning. The current was already slack, and the waters at the mouth of the Rio Panuco roiled as they met the Mer de Mexico. Pushing down from the bluffs of Hidalgo, the muddy river conveyed its charge of silt near to the point where they were anchored. Relieved of its load, it mingled with the Gulf, creating an invisible force that would help launch the *Mano del Rey* on her homeward voyage to Havana.

The *Mano del Rey* was a treasure *frigata*, heavily modified for the sole purpose of transporting the booty of New Spain to the old world. Even though she was armed with some twenty-five guns of various sizes, she would be joined by at least one larger and more formidable galleon on the return trip across the Atlantic. Such a rich prize was too often an irresistible target for English privateers and other pirates. Terrifying storms and potentially mutinous crews added to an already dangerous passage, but it would be well worth the risk if they were successful in eventually returning to Andalusia—Southern Spain.

Yet Claudio Hernandez had not signed on to fight or even to handle the ship. One glance at his sensitive brown eyes and flawless complexion was enough to recognize he was not a professional *soldado* or *marinero*. Nimble fingers and hands free from calluses also hinted at a more genteel life than most of his shipmates. He was one of the few men on board who was literate. His artistic skills as well as the fact that he was fluent in Latin, Arabic, and Portuguese had won him a position as a midshipman. Official chronicler of the voyage, Claudio was also popular with the crew for his musical talent with the lute and recorder.

He hoped to publish his account once he was back in Cadiz, bolstering his reputation as an adventurer and adding to the small stipend he had been promised for his service on this voyage. At any rate, Claudio had no desire to stay in Havana. Life there was too

6

tenuous, too political. He had seen many *caballeros* pass through striving for power, fame, and wealth by committing acts of genocide and rapacious greed.

For the last three months, they had struggled to subdue the Mexica who lived between the gulf and the mountains three leagues to the west. Brutal and mostly lopsided battles had watered the plains with the blood of both Christian and savage. Under the banner of Christ and King Carlos, Comandante Bernardo Gregorio de Seville had managed to eliminate one tribal army after another until a grim silence that passed for peace settled onto the region. Now nine strongboxes lay in the hold, full of freshly minted silver plate and gold bars, looted from the Mexica treasury. The only task remaining was to retrieve the most recent captives. The Comandante would return soon with the local *cacique*, Yaotl. The *indio* had waged a vicious resistance campaign with tactics that included beheading and eating his Spanish prisoners. Comandante Gregorio was especially determined to make an example of him.

A movement on the beach caught Claudio's eye, and he straightened his back to get a better view over the rail. Gregorio stood in a longboat, encouraging the oarsmen to pull harder against the low-rolling surf. Trailing behind them was a narrow punt, tied to the gunwale. In it sat the *cacique* wearing a yoke of heavy timber, his wrists manacled to each wooden arm as if crucified. In front of him knelt another new slave, cuffed hand and foot in iron chain. In the rear crouched an arquebusier, his weapon trained on the chieftain. Even at a distance, the dark countenances of the prisoners were plain to see, along with newly inflicted brands burned onto their faces. Each now wore the King's crown on one cheek and the arms of the house of Gregorio on the other. Their eyes glittered with hatred.

The first slave was hauled roughly aboard and dragged down into the hold, but the *cacique* was hoisted over the side by means of rope and block, his rigid ankle irons preventing him from even the most feeble use of his feet. Whether by confusion or by intent, he was left hanging in midair for a few minutes, a living crucifix, before he was cruelly dropped to the deck. Three or four *soldados* picked him up and lashed his yoke to the main mast, passing a loop of the coarse hemp rope around his neck, so he was forced to stand upright or slowly strangle if he slumped forward in his bonds.

Braced against the starboard rail, Claudio watched the Anahuac *cacique* for nearly a quarter-hour, trying to take the measure of the savage. His face depicted no emotion at all now—no hate, no pain, no sorrow, or fear. His eyes remained fixed on the receding shore, as if memorizing it for all eternity. Claudio couldn't help but harbor a large portion of respect for the aboriginal. Even now, manacled and branded like a beast, Yaotl's horrific reputation still had the power to strike fear in men's hearts. The *soldados* kept their distance, and the other *marineros* averted their eyes as they performed their tasks, unwilling to meet his gaze. Surely, he had the power of the evil eye. Perhaps he was a *brujo*.

Beginning to write, Claudio carefully and methodically recorded every detail of what he just witnessed.

> *How many men,* he wondered in his journal, *has he killed with those huge, rough hands. His coarse, jet black hair, which was swept up into a top knot as is the normal style for the Anahuac, falls down across his face and over his shoulders, partly masking the brands of slavery still blistering and smarting from the red-hot iron. His mahogany-colored skin bears witness to the wounds of many battles, and it is greatly tattooed, as is their custom, in all manner of fantastic shapes and designs. This is no ordinary* indio.

***

In the long shadows of his cabin, the Comandante sighed, relaxing his shoulders ever so slightly, as if laying down a great weight. In the privacy of his inner sanctum, he could relinquish at least a small part of the iron persona he projected to the world. Unbuckling his rapier, he laid it on the chart table along with his heavy leather gloves and unconsciously smoothed back his thinning black hair. Glancing into a small silver mirror, he removed his ruffled millstone collar and briefly tended to his graying spade-shaped beard. A timid knock came at the cabin door and his *grumete* slipped in to help him remove his breastplate and other armor. Underneath it all, Bernardo Gregorio was an unprepossessing figure, somewhat rangy and aging fast. What war and deprivation had not taken from him, the tropical sun and climate were now attempting to. Like most of his men, he was of average height, almost small—a characteristic he compensated for constantly with a rigid and arrogant personality. The product of a lifelong military career and schooled in the art of politics, Gregorio had a wife and two children in Spain, a mistress in Cuba, and no friends. Even his allies were cautious of him and with good reason. His ambition was notorious, his ruthlessness infamous. Where political power and vast wealth were concerned, he would not be denied.

Under his feet, he could feel the ship begin to move and shift, as if stirring from sleep. The wooden masts creaked and groaned softly as they took on the weight of canvas and the energy of the wind. The soft lapping of waves against the hull was replaced with the tiniest trickling sound of water rushing past the sides of the *frigata* as they got underway. Now it would be just a month's sail to Havana, where he could count his money and lie in the arms of his mistress once again.

2
~~Cedar Key, Florida~~
June 6, 1959

The half-clad figure sprawled across the double bed slowly stirred as the sea breeze blew through the jalousie windows. Outside somewhere, the faint tinkling of a glass wind chime mingled with the murmur of tourists down at the marina to create a soft, pleasant noise that told the young man in blue boxers it was time to get up. If the breeze had started, it was already after nine a.m. He was late for work. Rolling sideways, he gradually remembered it was Monday. No work today. The shop was always closed on Mondays. Nothing in Cedar Key was ever open on Sunday, and very few boats went out at the beginning of the week. As soon as his feet hit the hardwood floor, he was already making the bed, his basic training still deeply ingrained twelve years after his last day in the military.

Ben Wheeler had been a very young, Navy salvage diver during the forties. While the war raged all around him, he never saw much more than the machine shops and the dry docks of Key West. His only war wounds were a persistent case of insomnia and a bad case of the bends just before he had mustered out. He usually got by on about five hours of sleep, sometimes staying up till almost dawn. Fortunately, a couple of beers last night around midnight did the trick, and he had rested better than usual.

After carefully shaving, he noticed with some displeasure that his clean face showed the little bit of weight he had gained over the past few years. Maybe to compensate for it, he had grown his hair long enough to be styled in a pompadour. He had always been particular about his hair until he met up with Uncle Sam's barbers. His first act as a new civilian had been to rebel against the buzz cut and grow his hair out again. A quick splash of Aqua Velva completed his toilette. Dressed in khaki shorts, a madras shirt, and canvas deck shoes, Ben went in to make coffee. He made his strong and drank it black, usually with a slice of white bread wrapped around a cold chunk of oleo margarine. Dunking it in the powerful brew always left an oil slick, but that didn't bother him. He was already accustomed to stale java and fried doughnuts from his Navy days.

From the kitchen windows, he could see most of the town since the building he lived in was one of the few in Cedar Key that was two stories. Across the alley were the rear entrances of the bank, a shoe store, and the florist. In the next street, he could see the facades of a beauty salon and a small grocery. The whole island was only about two square miles and the habitable space about half that. The rest was tiny mangrove- and juniper-covered islands—anchoring sand bars—and the whole area was just ten feet above the Gulf of Mexico's normally placid waters. The last bad storm had been Hurricane Easy, nine years ago, that had only damaged the marina and First Street. Unfortunately, that's exactly where he lived now, over the tackle shop he ran for a man in Gainesville. Another big blow might mean the end of this job and set him homeless again. Well, that was the way it was when he got here, and he could manage to do it all again if need be.

The rest of his morning routine usually included a smoke on the landing at the top of the wooden stairs leading down to the alleyway, but he had smoked his last cigar Friday night. He double-checked. Sure enough, the old ammo box where he usually kept them was empty. Ben picked up his keys and his tortoiseshell Ray-Bans. The drugstore was only about four blocks away, but he felt like a little cruise down the strip. His ride was a blue 1953 Cushman Eagle scooter, beefy and heavier than a lot of motorcycles. He was able to keep it in the warehouse at the back of the tackle shop, out of the sun, the rain, and salt air. Constant polishing kept the tank and frame from oxidation. The dark spot on the floor underneath it was from frequent greasing of the flywheel and axles. In short, the bike was pristine.

Ben stomped on the pedal starter twice before the little two-stroke engine sputtered to life. The fat tires absorbed the bump over the slight

11

curb at the street, and a noise like flatulence erupted as he gunned the engine. The scooter was not particularly easy to drive with its rear brake pedal on the right and the clutch pedal on the opposite side. It had the reputation of having a "suicide shifter," since the driver had to brake, press the clutch, and use their left hand to shift a lever into first, second, or third. The motor was too small and the belt drive too weak to slow the scooter effectively by downshifting, so riding in traffic was always hard on the brakes. Fortunately, in a town as small as Cedar Key, any real traffic was rare. A hundred years ago, the place was booming—the railroad shipped lumber, salt, and fresh seafood to Jacksonville. Before the war, it was a hotspot for sponging and the oyster business, but like most other things, once the sponge beds were emptied and the oyster harvest died off, there wasn't much left to do. Now it was a ghost town. Only about seven hundred and fifty people lived on the island year round. Not many people wanted to be in the middle of nowhere except those who were running from something.

In the drugstore, he checked the boxes behind the counter for his favorite smoke. Cuban Crooks were clear Havana cigars cured in rum, small and dark. Distinguishable by a square, pressed shape with a peculiar hump that gave them their name; they had become his trademark. People commented on the aroma and had begun associating him with the odd little cigar. He bought two packs and lit one immediately, now immensely satisfied. Returning to the waterfront, he could hear the jukebox in the bar down the street. Without air-conditioning, the interior was cooled with ceiling fans, and the front door stayed wide open.

***

Pulling into the warehouse, he put the Cushman on its kickstand. The minute he shut off the engine he heard a familiar voice behind him.

"Not bad, pal."

Ben turned to look at the silhouette in the doorway.

"Well fer chrissake, Dollar Bill!"

Dollar Bill Walden had worked the tender for all the divers in Key West during the war. It was Dollar Bill who took care of him when he got the bends on that one dive. Ben gave him an enthusiastic handshake. The last time he had seen Bill was a decade ago in St. Pete. A few years older than Ben, he always sort of looked on the younger man as a kid brother. Bill had kept his curly, light brown hair fairly short, and it was turning blond in the summer sun. He was still trim but not muscular. Usually clean-shaven, a day-old stubble covered his weather-worn face.

"I see you're smokin' rope now," he teased Ben.

"Want one?"

"No, I'll stick with my coffin nails. Say, you got a few minutes?"

"Sure."

"Let's go next door and have a beer."

"Yeah, that sounds good. You on a fishing trip, or are you visiting someone?"

"You could say it's sort of a fishing trip. I came up here looking for you."

Ben followed his old friend down the street and into the bar, which was now thankfully quiet. Apparently, whoever had been playing the jukebox had run out of nickels.

"Have a seat. The beer's on me." Bill motioned to a table in the corner. Returning shortly with a pair of drafts, he hunkered down opposite Ben and lit a Pall Mall.

"Still diving?" he asked.

"Once in a while, shallow stuff. Mostly snorkeling, spear fishing. Why?"

"I know a guy in Miami. He needs a couple of experienced divers."

"For what?"

"Recovery. Probably thirty feet or less."

Ben wiped the gathering condensation off his beer mug, pursing his lips in thought.

Bill continued, "I thought maybe you could use the money. He's paying big bucks."

"Where?" Ben asked finally.

"Somewhere on the Gulf coast. He didn't tell me where exactly."

"Sounds shady," Ben murmured into his mug, then sipped his beer.

"I think the guy's on the level. I checked him out. His name is Noble Fischer. He's from New York, and he's loaded."

There was a long silence before Bill spoke again. "Dan says he's in if you're in."

Ben looked up. "Hamster Dan?"

"Yep."

Dan Hampshire, "Hamster Dan," had been the other diver on the team in Key West. Perpetually cheerful and round-faced, his nickname seemed to fit. Skilled but often over-cautious, he was usually a spotter or safety man when he went down. Nonetheless, he was rock-solid and had become a good friend. He stayed in the Navy a few years longer than nearly everyone else at the base. Ben thought for sure he was going to be a lifer, but last he heard, Dan was married and operating a dive-boat operation out of Key Largo.

Ben turned over the ramifications of the offer in his head. He would have to get someone to step in and run the tackle shop while he was gone or quit his job, one or the other. Guess he could start paying rent to keep his place. Maybe he ought to move anyway.

"How much is he willing to pay?"

Bill drained the last swallow from his mug before he announced, "A hundred bucks to sign up, then five C notes a month until the project is over."

A hundred bucks was more than Ben made in two weeks, not counting the fact he lived rent-free.

"How long is this project?"

"Unknown."

Ben stared at his friend's face to see if he was holding back something.

"What the hell is he trying to recover?"

Bill shrugged his shoulders. "I didn't ask. I don't care really. I've had a bad streak of luck lately and I need the dough."

In fact, Walden had lost his house and his girlfriend due to gambling, mostly at blackjack. All he had left was his clothes, his diving gear, and an aged 1947 Chevy Woodie, in which he often slept. He had been in every campground and trailer park from Fort Myers to Zephyrhills, including the 'Glades during the last few years.

"All right," Ben finally agreed. "Ya gotta give me time to square away everything here first."

"Can you meet me in a week?"

"Sure. That's plenty of time. Where?"

"The filling station in Chiefland, where Highways 19 and 27 meet. You know it?"

"Yeah, it's on Main Street. Red and white building…, Texaco, I think."

Suddenly, the old Dollar Bill was back.

"Welcome aboard, shipmate," he said as they shook hands again.

Ben watched his friend cross the street and waved as he drove off. He wasn't sure if this was a good deal, but at least it would get him out of town for a while. The money was good, too good maybe. It was a cinch that whatever this guy was looking for was worth a helluva lot. That was the real thing that made him nervous. People start acting stupid when a lot of money is involved, even people you think you know.

3
~~Golfo de Mexica~~
15 Agosto 1523

The morning was gray with a high overcast obscuring most of the sun, making the surface of the sea look like mercury. There was little breeze, and the ship was only making four to five knots, even with the current. The track was north by nor'east, hugging the shoreline as they made the great circle toward Havana. By now, they had passed north over the Trópico de Cáncer headed for the delta of the Rio de Santo Espiritu. For the next hundred and fifty leagues, there was the danger of shifting sandbars and shallow water if they came too close to shore. Even half a league out, the bottom might suddenly rise from five fathoms to a single fathom without any warning except the color of the sea. One could only discern the change in color from the lookout on a sunny day. On a gray day like this, it would be almost impossible to spot until the ship grounded. Even so, Comandante Gregorio was anxious to make as much headway as possible. At noon came the order to add bonnets to the sails, increasing the canvas aloft. It added a few knots per hour, but far less than he wanted. Arrogant enough to think he could command even the weather, he stood with his chin in the air, right behind the helmsman on the sterncastle. His pose was as imperious as his attitude.

Claudio wrote in the journal:

With silent prayer and resolute in the promise of God's salvation, the Comandante seems to move the ship by his will alone. Many of the men have been whispering that the cacique lashed to the mast is mala suerte, calling El Diablo to curse us and this ship. The unrest grew almost to mutiny near sunset when the wind all but ceased. Finally, Comandante Gregorio had him taken down, lest the marineros cut his throat during the night.

Yaotl still has not spoken a word in our presence, yet I overheard him speaking in low tones to another slave, the shorter one brought with him, the one they call Chorotega. They spoke in their own language, which is foreign and unintelligible to me. Perhaps they were plotting how best to make good their escape, which is all but impossible save with the intercession of whatever savage deity they pay homage to.

Shortly after sunrise, the breeze picked up once more, but it seemed to be changing quarter frequently from northeast to northwest. Low, puffy, gray clouds scudded across the sky while higher overhead another bank of clouds passed through on the opposite track. The navigator was obliged to tack from time to time, battling the inconsistent wind. By the sextant, the *Mano del Rey* should be just off shore from the mouth of the Rio Escondido. The Comandante was well acquainted with the area. His *soldados* had pacified this region the year before and helped establish the mission at Cacos. Confirming their position with the spyglass, he finally seemed satisfied with their progress.

Soon they would need to change course to the northeast, still following the coast of the vast unknown land they had barely begun to explore. The Mexica told bold stories of many golden cities in a place called Cibola, beyond the territory of the Navajo. The Apalachee spoke matter-of-factly about large towns and powerful chieftains who lived among great mounds far up the Rio de Santo Espiritu. But even now, four years after the most skilled navigator Alonso Alvarez de Pineda had compiled the best maps of the northern coast of the great Mer de Mexico, it was still *terra incognito*. No Christian knew what actually

17

lay beyond the strands and marshes. When the ship did begin to turn, the sails finally filled with the prevailing wind. On a bearing now of thirty-five degrees north–nor'east, the *frigata* picked up speed, slipping through the water as she was designed to do. As the sun and shadows shifted place on the deck, a small shaft of light briefly reflected from Yaotl's eyes, gleaming like polished obsidian in the darkness.

***

In the middle of the afternoon, Claudio put away his journal and retrieved his recorder from below. Seated on the hatch cover amidships, he began to play a dance tune with a lilting exuberance to distract the *marineros* from the monotony of their work. Calloused bare feet and chapped hands took up the beat, pounding the rough wooden deck in time with the melody.

Absorbed in the music, no one noticed Yaotl slowly lifting his head to look up through the grated hatch, trying to determine the source of the sound. In the darkened hold, he listened intently. This was not the droning noise of the priests, chanting their prayers. This was more like an Anahuac song. With his yoke removed, Yaotl was fettered to a chest fully laden with iron shot. Like the other slaves, he was also restrained by cuffs on each ankle, leaving just enough slack to shuffle his feet. He prayed silently to Tlaloc, the water god, asking him to drown the bearded ones in a huge storm, even if it meant sacrificing his own life. After a time, he looked at his fellow Anahuac and pointed with his chin.

"Why do they call you Chorotega? Is that not the name of your people?"

"The whites did not understand when I told them. I will carry the name of my people with honor." Chorotega paused. "In my home, I am called Iccauhtli."

A miniscule smile worked its way around Yaotl's face.

"Well, little brother, stay close to me. Tlaloc will send a storm to sink this water house and destroy the whites. I have received a vision."

Yaotl lapsed into silence again. He seemed not to notice his bloodied wrists and ankles where the cast-iron manacles were eating away his flesh. Seated on the end of the chest he was chained to, his posture was once again that of a *cacique* on his dais.

18

***

The *Mano del Rey* covered a hundred leagues in two weeks, even with the often fickle winds. Headed due east now, they were well out into the Gulf. They had run into some small rainstorms, but nothing like the squalls Claudio had seen on the voyage from Spain to Cuba. The *frigata* seemed seaworthy enough that he put it out of his mind completely. After all, they were nearly halfway back to port. Each day, there was more sunlight than the day before, and the mood on board had begun to settle back into the usual regimen of life at sea.

The *marineros* made oakum from hemp and soaked it in boiling pitch, pounding the sticky fibers into the deck to prevent leaks. The masts had to be greased and sails mended. Rope needed to be wound and spliced. The work was tedious, but necessary. *Soldados* used their time aboard making lead shot and sharpening their blades. Bolts had to be crafted for the crossbows. They were all small cogs in the great wheel of conquest, the *máquina invencible*. After many campaigns, they worked in concert, like a team of oxen plowing rough land into civilized ground. Each took a share of the spoils. All took a share of the risk. Every one of them had come to the edge of the known world to go home rich.

The lookout in the crow's nest atop the main mast had been ordered to be alert for any sign of another ship. Pirates did not usually prowl the Gulf, preferring instead to work from the Caribbean. The entire expanse of ocean between Lucaio and Havana was dotted with rocks, *arrecifes*, and small atolls that would rip out the hull of a large ship such as the *frigata*, or shelter the smaller and faster boats of the pirates. Nevertheless, the west coast of *La Florida* had many inlets and bays capable of hiding privateering schooners.

In the perpetual twilight of the hold, the *indios* maintained silence until the small hours of the morning. The night watch heard them speaking to each other in their native tongue, Nahuatl. Few on board had even a rudimentary knowledge of the Mexica language. Comandante Gregorio and the *soldados* depended on captured Anahuacs to interpret their demands and edicts.

The only thing that attracted the *indios'* attention was the soft notes of Claudio's recorder. It acted as a temporary distraction from the vile stench of their prison. The reek of human urine and feces, mingling with the waste from the livestock below, wafted from the hatch during the heat of midday. Occasionally, the *marineros* would throw buckets of seawater on the prisoners in a feeble attempt to wash the smell away. It only made matters worse as the water turned rank and septic, leaving the slaves to stand, sit, and sleep in a slurry of their own waste. Straw was thrown down and scattered to absorb some of the watery filth, but it did little to mask the effluvium. In the end, the hold stank like a floating stable.

> *Insomuch as God has so far granted us a smooth passage,* Claudio wrote, *the Comandante has consented to pause briefly near the Anchon de Braxos to search for such food as may be found and fresh water.*

The Anchon de Braxos was still some seventy-five leagues distant, more than a week's sail. Until then, they would eat more or less the same thing the *esclavos* ate—corn mush, dried beans, and smoked fish. Occasionally, the *soldados* also received a ration of boiled goat and onions. Once a week, the entire ships company received fruit—limes or naranjas and papayas. On the last Sabbath of the month, the whole crew feasted on a pork stew containing the fiery peppers of the Mexica. It was a strong incentive to attend Mass. Once the animals on board were consumed, however, they would have to make do.

The shallow bay where they sought anchorage was in the middle of the Yustaga chiefdom. Their king Uzachile was known to be antagonistic toward the *caciques* of the Apalachee to the west. This did not mean he would welcome the Spanish. By now, all the Atimuca had heard horrifying stories of the devils from Cuba. The other main chief they might have to contend with was Caliquen of the Potanos. He, too, would take a landing by Christian soldiers with alarm. Comandante Gregorio was gambling that if any savages were in the area, it would be the local *indios* under the *cacique* Uriutina. They were less likely to attack, preferring to avoid any contact.

4
~~Chiefland, Florida~~
June 13, 1959

Ben gunned the blue Cushman to nearly fifty miles an hour as he crossed the last bridge onto the mainland. From here, the two-lane blacktop cut a straight line through miles of Gulf hammock. Gallberry bushes and palmettos lined the sandy, low shoulders, backed up by pines and sable palms in the drier areas. The red cedars that had once been the lifeblood of Cedar Key stood in the waterlogged mud and shallow swamps.

Dressed in a white T-shirt, long khaki pants, and his favorite boat shoes, Ben rolled along with a cigar in the corner of his mouth. The last tune he had heard coming from the bar's jukebox as he left town was stuck in his head. Trying to occupy his brain and dump the repetitious tune, he wondered if Dollar Bill would actually show. He was usually pretty reliable, but this was an oddball situation.

With his breakfast of stout black coffee and a couple of BC Powders starting to take effect, it didn't seem like a long ride to the main highway. Heading north toward Chiefland, Ben kept trying to fit the pieces together in his mind. It had to be either something big or something valuable for the head honcho to want three experienced divers. It was somewhere in the Gulf. What had gone down in the Gulf during the war? A tanker, maybe a freighter or two. Anything worth salvaging had been raised and brought back to Key West during the forties.

***

As he approached the intersection where the gas station sat, he didn't see Bill's car, but a new, bright yellow Ford pickup was parked at the edge of the lot near the highway. He pulled in close to the building, and as he dismounted, Dollar Bill came around the corner. Hamster Dan followed just behind him.

"Hey, Ben, good timing! Buy ya a beer?" Bill gestured with the beer bottle in his hand.

"No thanks. Dan, you're looking good."

Dan Hampshire had always been a heavy guy, and peacetime life only accentuated that. Slightly overweight now, that irrepressible round face of his was even more affable

"Ben, it's good to see you," Dan murmured with genuine warmth. He still sported that constant smile. With his clean-shaven face and businessman's haircut, he looked every inch a successful entrepreneur. The sleeves of his white shirt were rolled up to his elbows and his collar open as if he had just ditched his coat and tie. He wore plain black shoes under his charcoal-gray slacks and seemed comfortable in it all.

Meanwhile, Bill gestured toward the pickup.

"Look at this! Dan's done pretty good for himself!"

Ben took a stroll around the truck, admiring the sleek lines.

"Pretty nice, Dan. How much did this set ya back?"

"About twenty-two hundred dollars, but I needed it for my business."

Ben made a face and slung his hand as if he had hit his thumb with a hammer. He was beginning to understand why Hamster Dan was in on whatever this job was.

"Where's your car, Bill?" he finally thought to ask.

"I left it at Dan's place. We rode up here together. Got to talk about old times."

"Yeah, telling stories about the war," Dan agreed with a grin.

More like making up stories, Ben thought.

"So, what's the poop, Bill?" he asked directly. "What is all this hush-hush stuff?"

Bill lit a cigarette and perched his beer bottle on the rear bumper of the pickup.

"I don't know any more than you do. We were all supposed to be here to meet a guy who's going to be the ramrod. I bet that's him now."

Bill nodded toward a man pulling up in a Navy surplus Jeep. All the decals had been painted over, but it had been one of Uncle Sam's Willys all right. It still had the flat, Navy-gray paint job and the worn vinyl seats. The man who got out was tall and thin, almost gaunt. He was older, probably in his mid-forties with the bearing of a man who was used to being in charge. His dark brown hair was slicked back into a duck-tail, and he had a Clark Gable mustache. His eyes were hidden behind aviator sunglasses, and there was no hint of a smile on his face as he approached. The combat boots he wore made loud crunching sounds as he strode across the gravel lot.

"Good morning, men. Is one of you Bill Walden?"

Bill halfheartedly raised his palm.

"That's me. You work for Mr. Fischer?"

The man nodded. "I'm Luke Duprez. People call me Lucky."

Dan reached out to shake the man's hand, but the stranger either did not notice or purposely pretended not to. He did not extend his.

"I'm Dan Hampshire. This is Ben Wheeler." Ben kept his hands in his pockets.

"This is your sign up bonus," Duprez continued, reaching in the hip pocket of his military-style dungarees and handing each of them a sealed envelope. Ben found two, crisp fifty dollar notes in his. So far, so good.

"Monday morning at 0800 we need to meet back here. I'll have a deuce and a half waiting for you. The driver is a nigra called Jimbo. Just put your gear in the back and get in. He'll take you to the base camp. Once you get there, I'll brief you on the expedition."

Bill spoke for the team, "We'll be here."

"Good." Duprez nodded and walked back to his Jeep.

For once, the smile disappeared from Hamster Dan's face as he chewed his lip.

"Somebody needs to tell him the war is over."

"And we're not in the Navy anymore," Ben added.

Bill just flicked his cigarette butt into the street and swilled his beer.

"Let's go ahead and get everything squared away," he belched.

Ben was already square. He had written to the owner of the store a

23

couple of days ago and let him know he was moving out. In the end, the choice had been an easy one. The apartment had come more or less furnished, so most of his personal stuff fit in a heavy wooden footlocker. He packed his clothes and diving gear into his old sea bag, but the most troublesome problem was what to do with his scooter. He finally talked one of the regulars at the tackle shop into letting him store the Cushman in his garage indefinitely. Ben gave him twenty-five dollars and the deal was done. Now all he had to do was leave the apartment key on the kitchen counter Monday morning.

***

Monday dawned clear and warm, just like the day before and the day before that. Dollar Bill showed up in his old station wagon exactly at 0600, and Dan was rousted from a catnap to help Ben load the footlocker into the cargo bay. Dumping his duffel bag on top, Ben slid into the back seat.

"Morning, men."

"Oh, shut up." Dan yawned.

"Off yer cocks and grab yer socks," smiled Bill, poking Dan in the arm. "We're shoving off."

"Aye, aye, captain." Dan saluted wearily.

Ben farted in response.

"I thought we'd be riding in Dan's new truck."

"I'm not leaving my new truck in the middle of nowhere for somebody to steal."

"You're a very cynical man," Bill commented. "Very cynical."

Before leaving Cedar Key, they stopped into a small cafe on the edge of town to coffee up. No matter what was going to happen, caffeine would make it better.

"A cuppa Joe and a coupla sinkers, takes me back," Ben mumbled.

"You miss the Navy?" Bill asked, slowly stirring his coffee as if it was a Zen exercise.

"Not really," Ben said with his mouth full. "But it wasn't a bad life."

In 1947, Ben left the Navy as an E3, just below Bill's E4 or Petty Officer 3rd class.

"Dan, I thought you were gonna be a lifer for sure," Bill said, then sipped his coffee.

"Me, too." The Hamster sighed wistfully. "When I got passed over for promotion in forty-nine, that was pretty much the end of it."

"Well, we'll make you an honorary PO3." Ben clapped his hand on Dan's shoulder.

"G'wan," Dan responded.

They ate in silence for a few minutes. Then Bill stood up, tossing out enough money on the counter to pay for everyone and still leave a good tip.

"Let's weigh anchor," he announced.

The ride to Chiefland was short and quiet, with each of them absorbed in their own thoughts. At the gas station, Bill went inside to talk to the owner about leaving his car around the side while Ben stood on the corner and lit a cigar. Just before eight a.m. he saw a Navy-gray, two-and-a-half-ton, eight-wheeler coming down South Main Street toward them.

"Bill," he called over his shoulder. "I think our taxi is here."

Dan joined him curbside as the huge truck squealed to a stop to let a car go by before turning left, screeching again as it halted on the shoulder.

"Jesus," Dan swore softly. "This guy must have bought out every Army-Navy surplus store in the state."

Bill was already unloading gear from the back of the station wagon.

"Come on, swabs. I'm not gonna carry it for you!"

"Christ," Ben muttered. "I swear I don't remember re-enlisting."

The REO deuce and a half was a gasoline model, so at least they wouldn't have to breathe the acrid diesel fumes some poured out. A tan canvas cover over the bed kept the sun off them and they sat on a long, hard wooden benches—strictly regulation. Even with the canvas wall rolled up, the back was hot. Ben and Dan claimed the area behind the cab and reclined against their duffel bags on the floor. Bill opted to sit on the driver's side bench to see the driver in the long, door-mounted, rearview mirror. The black man named Jimbo had a broad face, narrow-set eyes, and a shaved head. His hands on the steering wheel were huge, and Bill estimated he was probably between two hundred fifty and two hundred seventy-five pounds. Periodically, they caught each other's eye. Bill was always the one to look away first.

Rolling back north, it took a bit more than twenty minutes to reach the Suwannee River, where Dan performed an acapella rendition of "Way Down Upon the Suwannee River," at the top of his lungs. Bill noticed that Jimbo seemed to be cursing to himself in the cab.

"Hey, Dan. Stow it, will ya?"

Beyond the river, the truck headed west toward Cross City. The next time it slowed down to make a turn, Bill spied the road marker that told him they were on State Road 51.

"We're headed for the Gulf, boys," he surmised.

"It's about time," Ben groused. "We've been in this damn thing almost forty-five minutes."

"Let me know if you see a Stuckeys," Dan added.

Live oaks, red cedars, and pines on either side of the road created a coastal hammock, with miles of tangled brush. Palmettos, gallberry bushes, and greenbrier covered the forest floor. Occasionally, the white flowers of a blackberry thicket showed themselves along the shoulders of the road.

Bill kicked Ben's foot. "Isn't the Steinhatchee River around here somewhere?"

Ben thought a minute, trying to get his bearings. "Yeah. Couldn't be too far. Think that's where we're going?"

"No," Bill answered, weighing the chances.

The truck slowed to navigate the small burg. From the town's main streets, they could see the river now. Steinhatchee had started out as a military post during the Seminole Wars, but it eventually grew big enough to boast a salt works and a booming timber industry. When the same hurricane that spelled the end of the pencil factory and lumberyards of Cedar Key hit the area, commerce died off, just like their neighbors. The residents were reduced to fishing and subsistence farming for nearly half a century. As the local fishing business began to grow, the spongers arrived. Before the war, hundreds of sponge fisherman in small sailing vessels routinely clogged the harbor. In the 1950s, the sponge fleet was all but gone, replaced by dozens of fishing camps along the river.

Just out of town, the truck made one final turn onto a dirt logging road. After about fifteen minutes, the pines gave way to masses of saltbush and stunted, windblown junipers. Eventually, the road ended in a wide, sandy clearing. When the truck engine was shut off, the silence was almost deafening. There was nothing but the sound of the sea breeze moving over the dried sedges in waves and the buzz of insects. As the men climbed down stiffly from the truck bed, they could see a cabin cruiser anchored about ten yards offshore in the Gulf.

Jimbo climbed down from the cab and slammed the door. They all looked to see what this man who had driven them into the middle of nowhere looked like. He was a giant, broad-shouldered and six feet tall.

"Damn that's a big buck," Bill whispered.

"Good, we're all here now." A vaguely familiar voice drew their attention.

Lucky Duprez strode toward them, dressed exactly as he had been two days ago. Apparently, it was a uniform of sorts for him.

"Gentlemen, welcome to Dead Man Bay."

5
~~Anchon de Braxos~~
24 Septiembre 1523

God granted us a steady wind for seven days and seven nights without stopping. We made such speed, we arrived at Anchon de Braxos two days earlier than expected. Even now, with the sun directly overhead, the golfo is disturbed by this zephyr to make modest swells, causing the ship to wallow at anchor. After prayers of thanksgiving, Comandante Gregorio landed a small troop of soldados on shore, armed with pikes and accompanied by two arquebusiers. They were immediately swallowed up by the forest and disappeared into the interior. We have heard no discharge of weapons or cries of alarm, and we pray now to the Holy Family for their safe return.

It was late in the afternoon before the landing party emerged, carrying with them a deer they brought down with a pike, two rabbits who met their demise at the end of a halberd, and several live tortoises in a canvas sack. The water barrels they carried with them were still empty. They found no fresh water.

"When the Comandante heard that there was no water to be had within a day's march of this place, he remarked that we should pray to our most merciful God to send rain, so we should not perish from thirst

At first light on the next day, it appeared that their prayers had been answered. The sun never rose over the horizon, but hid behind a solid thatch of lead-gray clouds, creating a tobacco-colored light that waned quickly into a second twilight. Ominously, the sea had become glassy, and the sails hung slack without so much as a breath of air to stir them. The air was thick, and after an hour, it also became hot, adding to their misery.

> *Conditions became so intolerable that the Comandante was obliged to bring the slaves on deck, lest they die within the confines of the hold. Even though they were native to this climate, they were weak and glistening with sweat. The soldados allowed them to sit with their backs to the main mast, restrained only hand and foot with manacles. They were fed spoiling fruit, which they still consumed greedily. Buckets of seawater were poured over them to cleanse and revive their bodies.*

Yet it refused to rain. Misfortune and miscalculation had led them to anchor in the one place they should not have. The computations of the navigator confirmed that they had re-crossed into the doldrums of the horse latitudes, an area of the subtropics infamous for the lack of any sustained winds. Spanish ships becalmed here ran out of food and water often, resulting in the slaughter of the armada's horses for meat. The *marineros* knew it already from bitter experience. The stifling air and the stillness of the sea were unmistakable. Even the anchor rope floated just under the water as the ship hovered immobile. With no wind or current, the tide would only beach them. They waited, sulking in heaps on the deck.

> *Whispers, then audible shouts rose from the crew, demanding that Comandante Gregorio throw the* brujo *Yaotl overboard or strand him ashore. Only the presence of the* guardia *intimidated them enough to prevent mutiny.*

Dusk came early, but brought no more relief than a warm breeze. In the east, invisible lightning colored the horizon pink and orange, exposing huge castles of cumulus clouds. The thunder generated was inaudible, but it was clear that ferocious weather was making its way up from the Caribbean. As twilight faded to darkness, lanterns were lit on the sterncastle and the officers' quarters. Again, for fear of what might happen under the cover of darkness, Gregorio had the sergeant-at-arms take a detail to secure the slaves down in the hold. Bread and cheese were distributed to the crew and only a double ration of wine cheered their uniformly sullen faces.

During the second dog watch, a freshening cool breeze came in strong enough for the *Mano del Rey* to slowly start swinging on the anchor line. Eventually, the line became taut, and the resulting jar was immediately noticeable. The air sweetened, promising rain. Gradually, the tympani of rolling thunder reached them, guaranteeing a downpour.

With little notice and a great deal of doubt among the officers, the order came to make the *Mano del Rey* ready for departure. The anchor was retrieved from the sandy bottom and every sheet was deployed to take advantage of the rising northeast wind. Sailing at top speed in the dark this close to shore was risky, but Comandante Gregorio was determined to use the energy of the approaching storm. True to his reputation, he was always ready to sacrifice the lives of others in the name of his single-minded pursuit of gain. It was often said he mistook madness for daring.

The night was pitch black with no moon or stars to aid navigation. Only the phosphorescence in the surf and the echo of the waves as they lapped the beach kept the helmsman from drawing too close to shore. Fighting the tide and current, Comandante Gregorio ordered a course more southwesterly to take the ship farther out. Heavy rain lashed the deck intermittently so the command went out to batten the hatches and close all ports.

***

As the hold now became even darker than the night, Yaotl began to chant the death song. Tlaloc had come. At any moment, Chalchiuhtlicue might open a whirlpool to suck them all to the House of the Owl Man.

"Our beloved sun has disappeared. We are in darkness." Yaotl prepared himself. Praying to Mictlantecihuatl, the Lady of the Land of the Dead, he asked for guidance through the underworld.

***

On deck, the wind rose till the rain fell sideways. Whitecaps climbed the hull, threatening to overtop the rails. Neither the helmsman nor the navigator knew where they were or how far off course they might have drifted. The astrolabe was useless in the storm, and the compass only showed which way the ship was pointed. Permission was given to shorten the sheets to prevent damage to the sails and the masts as the wind increased to gale force. They dared not furl them all. If the ship had no forward motion, the rudder would have no effect and they would be at the mercy of the wind and tide.

Soon the storm began to batter the ship in earnest. Large waves broke over the deck almost faster than the scuppers could drain them away. In the crew's quarters below, Claudio swung in his hammock as the ship pitched like a living thing. The lantern in the center of the compartment waved even more violently, casting eerie shadows on the bulkheads. Around him, the *marineros* not on watch could be heard softly praying. *Santa María, Madre de Dios, pray for us sinners, now and at the hour of our death.* Someone in the gloom grumbled that the Comandante had sailed the ship directly into a *huracán* and they would all surely drown.

No sooner had the words been uttered than the loud, terrifying sound of splintering wood was heard and felt throughout the ship. All hands, including Claudio, climbed up to the deck, stumbling like drunken men toward the sterncastle. The roaring winds had finally snapped the mizzenmast. A tangle of rope and canvas lay on the wheel and the helmsman was nowhere in sight. Immediately, the *marineros* began to cut away the rigging, jettisoning the boom and shattered mast. The damage broke the lantern stays, knocking the ship's stern lamp into the churning water. While they worked, the wheel spun back and forth, answering to the stress on the rudder. The entire steering system was working in reverse, with the ship in control of the wheel.

In the midst of all the chaos, Claudio spotted Comandante Gregorio emerging from his cabin and turning to look at the damage. His bearing, his manner, nothing suggested he was particularly concerned. After a few minutes, he retreated, as oblivious to nature's fury as he was to his men's growing fear. Eventually, the lieutenant took the wheel, steering the ship back to a southeasterly heading. Lashing the wheel in a neutral position, he abandoned the sterncastle and sought refuge below. It was up to God now.

Back in the crew's quarters, Claudio began to think that they might lose the ship. The only thing that was irreplaceable among his meager possessions was his diary. Rolling it into a cylinder, he placed it in the leather tube he always carried to keep it from rain. Looking around, he slid his recorder into the void left by the rolled up manuscript. Then buckling the cap on the end, he looked around for an empty keg to stash it in. The wooden barrel would at least float and help keep the journal from damage. Even if he did not survive, perhaps the record of their journey would.

The ship gave a long, low groan, then a thump. Claudio could feel the *frigata* turn sharply to port. It began to wallow like a palm log riding the swells. They had lost the rudder. The rain drummed on the timbers overhead as the wind howled like demons through the rigging. At any moment, they could capsize. Claudio made the sign of the cross and waited. Like a nightmare he could not escape, time was distilled into one long terrifying moment.

"¡*Tierra*!" someone on deck yelled. "Land!"

A *marinero* crept up the wooden steps and lifted the hatch to peer out.

"There is land on the starboard side. Not far away." The alarm in his voice was evident.

The crew scrambled about, making ready to abandon ship, stuffing keepsakes and gold nuggets into small leather pouches hung around their waist or neck. Claudio could already hear the commotion on deck as a hundred men struggled to escape the belly of the *frigata*. It would be impossible in the face of hurricane winds to launch the long boats.

Panic was setting in. The officials shouted, "Calm down!" over the din. Comandante Gregorio was still in his cabin. Before the *sargento de armas* could fetch him, the ship abruptly stopped, throwing the entire crew to the deck. Some washed overboard immediately. Grounded on the muddy bottom, the *Mano del Rey* slowly listed starboard, tossing even more men into the heaving ocean. Those who could swim struck out for the shore, a hundred yards away. Those who could not vanished beneath the angry sea.

As it became every man for himself, Claudio hung on to the cask and prepared to jump overboard when it occurred to him that the *esclavos* were still chained below. His Christian conscience troubled him to think they were deserting those savages, condemning them to certain death. They may have been the enemy to Comandante Gregorio, but Claudio understood, perhaps naively, why they resisted. If he freed them now, maybe they would see God's grace and embrace His infinite mercy. By saving their lives, he might also save their souls.

He had no idea where the keys to their irons were or even if he could find them, but he did remember seeing a hatchet on the sterncastle when they were cutting away the broken mizzenmast. With unsteady legs, he managed to make the wheelhouse. The hatchet was still there, stuck in the wooden deck. Wrenching it loose, he tried to stay on his feet, crossing the slippery deck, holding the cask under one arm and gripping the hatchet with the opposite hand. Making his way cautiously down the ladder to the hold, which was by this point nearly knee-deep in bilge water, he looked for the prisoners.

It didn't take long for Yaotl to slog toward him. Their eyes locked for a minute, Claudio's showing his apprehension, Yaotl's full of quiet defiance. Claudio slowly raised the hatchet in his hand then gestured for Yaotl to hold his hands out. He knew immediately what Claudio meant. Bracing the chain of his manacles on a timber, hands on either side, he nodded at Claudio. The chain was not thick and was made of soft cast iron. It took just a few well-aimed blows to cut a link, freeing the *indio*.

The one called Chorotega emerged from the rising water, seeing what had happened. Claudio hesitated then handed the hatchet to Yaotl, not knowing if he would use it to kill him or free the other *indio*. Yaotl seized the tool and turned to free his fellow prisoner. Claudio used the moment to disappear up the hatchway. It suddenly occurred to him the enormous consequences of his good deed. If it was ever discovered that he freed those slaves, especially given Yaotl's notoriety, he would be summarily hanged. That is, if he survived.

A rogue wave, larger than the others, slammed into the crippled ship's hull, pushing it further into the sand. The timbers creaked as the ship finally careened onto its side, snapping the remaining masts in half. They were now stranded, without food, water, or weapons.

6
~~Dead Man Bay, Florida~~
June 15, 1959

The camp was arranged with four tents in a semicircle. A small tan wall tent was on the north side with the sides rolled up to catch the Gulf breeze. Inside on the straw floor, a cot was already made up. A steamer trunk sat at the back. Clearly, someone had already claimed the tent. The larger, tan wall tent next to it looked empty. A drab, olive command post tent, or 2HQ as it was known during the war, was next around the circle. Ben had seen the Seabees work out of a portable canvas hut like this. Finally, on the south end, a large, tan pyramid tent also had all sides rolled up. The floor was made of plywood sheets, and a couple of picnic tables, and a grill was made out of a fifty-five gallon drum cut in half which stood just outside.

"You three will be bunking in there," Lucky said, pointing to the larger wall tent. It was big enough for twice that many people.

"Stow your gear and claim a cot. At 1200 hours, we'll have chow. Then I'll brief you on what we've got here."

"Back in boot camp," Ben muttered under his breath.

"Think of it as summer camp with beer and cigarettes," observed Dan, with his trademark hamster smile.

"There's no place in the Navy for complainers." Bill was only half-serious. Dan threw one of the heavy wool blankets from the cots at him.

"Kiss my foot," Ben added.

Rolling up the back wall made the temperature inside the tent more

35

tolerable. Ben was a bit happier when he realized a big drapery of mosquito netting was folded up and attached overhead. When he let it down, it formed a canopy big enough to cover all three cots. Bugs loved him for some reason. Every time he went fishing, he came home with welts from mosquito bites and those damn no-see-ums. Even with the breeze coming through, the tent still smelled like new canvas, sisal rope, and straw.

Dan looked around at the space between the tent wall and ground.

"We might be able to keep out the bugs, but there's nothing to keep out the snakes," he announced.

"We can put out some tobacco dust or sulfur flour," offered Ben.

Bill looked at both of them like they were crazy.

"Where the hell do you think we're going to get tobacco dust or sulfur out here?" he demanded.

"It was just a suggestion," Ben murmured, shrugging his shoulders.

"Sleep with a machete if you're worried about snakes." Bill looked at each of them.

Dan lay back on his cot with his hands behind his head.

"Yeah, we're probably more likely to get a shark bite than a snake bite."

Chow call was a simple affair. Ben noticed that Jimbo sat by himself at one of the tables, while a newcomer was seated at theirs. They ate in near silence, waiting for Lucky to stand up and start the briefing. At length, Duprez got up and walked over to the table where the giant sat alone. He withdrew a small pad and a pencil from his shirt pocket and began.

"Gentlemen, I think first we need to introduce the team. You all know me. This...," he gestured toward the black man, "is Jimbo Rogers. He's our mechanic and driver."

When Jimbo looked up at them, Ben noticed that unlike every other negro he'd ever met, Jimbo's eyes were a steel gray. He was altogether intimidating.

"The man sitting with you is Lonnie Baker. He owns the boat out there."

Lonnie turned to his table mates.

"Hey, y'all," he said in a distinct Alabama drawl.

"Lonnie, these are the divers and your first mate—Ben Wheeler, Dan Hampshire, and Bill Walden.

Each of them leaned over to shake hands.

"Just call me Dollar Bill," Walden said with a forced smile.

"Now," Duprez continued. "Let me tell you why you're all here."

"You mean besides some rich Yankee paid us to?" Ben interjected.

Duprez ignored him.

"Noble Fischer, the man who's paying for all this, recently bought a seventeenth century manuscript that is a genuine, handwritten copy of the journal kept by one Claudio Hernandez in fifteen twenty-three. His ship, the *Mano del Rey*, went down in a hurricane in October of that year."

"Oh, Jesus. We're going treasure hunting," Dan whispered to Dollar Bill.

Bill spoke up, "Most of the missing ships in the Spanish Plate Fleet went down in the Caribbean or the Atlantic. Everybody and his brother has been looking for the *Atocha* and *Margarita.*"

"We're not going after the Plate Fleet," Duprez explained with some irritation in his voice.

"The *Mano del Rey* was returning from Mexico to Havana with gold, silver, and slaves. There were about forty sailors and a detachment of soldiers on board when it foundered. The wreck should lie in shallow water under the mud somewhere between here and Bowlegs Point."

Lonnie whistled through his teeth. "You're talking about better than thirty-five square miles."

"That's right."

Duprez let them think about it for a minute.

"Come 'ere, I got something to show you." Lucky led the group to the command tent and opened the flaps. On the ground, near the entranceway, was something that looked like a rocket with an elephant's trunk attached. A long length of cable intertwined with coax was threaded inside a rubber hose coiled on the ground beside it.

"Know what you're looking at?"

"Yeah," Bill replied matter-of-factly. "It's a flux gate magnetometer."

"Good. Then some of you may be familiar with it."

37

"This guy Fischer must have a wad of dough," Ben speculated, voicing the obvious.

"Walden, give Jimbo and Lonnie a hand getting this thing out to the boat." Duprez went on, "Once we get it rigged up, this thing will pick up anything metal underwater—especially iron. Cannon, shot, weapons, the anchor.... It may take a couple of weeks, but this will make it easier to find what we're looking for."

"What about gold or silver?" Dan asked the million-dollar question.

Duprez hesitated, taking in a deep breath and releasing it, almost like a sigh.

"We may find some gold, silver, maybe pearls, or gemstones, but there's probably not much down there."

"Then why are we looking for it?" Dan queried.

"Because we need to know where the ship actually lies so we can figure out where we need to look next."

As Dan, Lonnie, and Jimbo wrestled the magnetometer out into the surf, Bill and Ben walked slowly back to their tent.

"This is bad business." Dan shook his head.

Looking back at Duprez, Ben agreed. "He knows a whole lot more than he's saying."

The rest of the afternoon was spent configuring the magnetometer and making a few test readings. While Lonnie and his crew cruised up and down the immediate shoreline, Duprez disappeared into the command tent, leaving Ben and Dan to sit on their cots and check their diving gear. Beyond the drone of Lonnie's occasional pass in front of the camp, everything was quiet. Too quiet to Ben's mind. There were no buzzing flies, no birdcalls in the distance. Just the small lap of gentle surf, and the periodic stir of the sea breeze.

"Have you noticed anything strange about this place?" Ben finally asked aloud.

With sweat dripping off his nose, Dan glanced up from the gauge he was calibrating. "You mean besides Captain Ahab and Queequeg?"

"They're odd ducks all right, but I meant about this place."

"The camp?"

"Yeah. Listen." Ben touched Dan's forearm to make him quit moving.

"I don't hear anything," Dan responded after a few seconds.

"Exactly. No birds, not even gulls. No other boats have been by. No planes overhead."

"Just means that we are truly in the boondocks." Dan shrugged, going back to his work.

Ben couldn't dismiss it as easily. Something was wrong.

Later, in the heat of the afternoon, it was too warm in the tent to do much of anything. They rolled up the sides of the tent to admit more air, but it was still hot. Bill was out on the boat with Lonnie and Jimbo, while Duprez was nowhere to be seen. Dan lay on his cot reading a *Superman* comic book as Ben drifted into a light sleep. He dreamed not of his Navy days nor his blue scooter, but of Elena. He had not seen her in months.

***

Elena Giannopoulos was the only daughter of a retired sponge diver and sometime shrimper in Tarpon Springs. She was a second-generation immigrant, as her mother and father were both born in Greece. She and Ben were about the same age but from widely different backgrounds. Elena was born in the US, but she spoke Greek and English fluently. She could even read and write in her parents' language, having been raised in the Greek Orthodox tradition.

Ben, on the other hand, was from a small town named Hahira in Southern Georgia, just forty miles or so from the Florida border. Disowned at seventeen by his estranged father, Ben joined the Navy at Mayport, Florida. Religion had always escaped him, especially the ritualistic services and ecumenical rigidity of Greek Orthodoxy. When pressed to claim a religious preference during enlistment, he opted for "Protestant" over "none." Having been an occasional Baptist, it really didn't matter to him as long as he had a decent funeral if something happened to him in the Navy. Now that he was out, it mattered even less.

They met in 1948 when Ben was living in Dunedin with Dollar Bill. Elena was a waitress at a local seafood shack near Lake Tarpon. He could still see her in the peasant dress she wore, her dark brown hair curling down around her shoulders. She had Mediterranean olive-

39

colored skin, smooth and flawless with hazel eyes that always seemed to be smiling.

They dated off and on, mostly Saturday morning walks and a picnic lunch on the beach at Clearwater or Sunday dinner at her parents' house after church. To avoid being asked to go to the cathedral with the family, Ben had lied to all of them, saying he was a Presbyterian and a lay reader at that. He figured if he was going to tell a lie, it might as well be a big one.

Elena's parents were strict and overly protective of her. They probably had good reason to be. She was an attractive, vibrant young woman in a world that was rapidly changing. Old World values and morals were getting harder to come by in post-war America. Combat had changed the young men who went to fight overseas, and not for the better. Many came back shattered, disillusioned, broken, and bitter. Now calloused and cynical, they were beginning to challenge what they saw as naked hypocrisy entrenched in the fabric of American culture. Worse, an equal number wanted to cling to the past, a rosy picture of life before the war. Once faced with the reality that they could never go back, they set about recreating memories of things as they never were, a place where children never lost their innocence and father always knew best.

For as much as they enjoyed each other's company, Ben figured out early on that things were not going to work out. He got the impression her parents felt he wasn't good enough for her. In hindsight, maybe they were right. Elena was the type of woman who wanted a stable home life, a house, kids. Ben was having trouble supporting himself, much less a wife, children, and a mortgage. Nevertheless, he had always regretted leaving that part of his life behind. He would probably always wonder, "What if?"

***

Waking slowly from his bittersweet dreams, Ben was startled into full consciousness by a hulking silhouette standing at the front of the tent, blocking out the sunset. Immediately, he realized it had to be Jimbo, and if that had been all it was, he would have been able to slow his heart rate, but the man had a long machete in his hand. Ben fumbled for his diving knife, but before he was able to do much of anything, he watched Jimbo raise his weapon and strike the ground less than a foot from his cot.

"What the hell are you doing?" Ben practically screamed. "Dan! Bill! This crazy Bumbo is trying to kill me!"

He rolled off his cot toward the outside edge of the tent and escaped under the rolled up canvas wall. By the time he got to his feet and stormed around to the front, Jimbo was picking up something with the tip of the machete. Ben paused a minute, breathing heavily. The black giant turned to show him what he had scooped up. Stretched across the flat part of the blade, still writhing, was a small brightly colored snake, its body nearly severed.

"Red on yellow, kill a fellow; red on black, friend of Jack," Jimbo explained in a booming bass voice. "And the name is Jimbo, not Bumbo."

It was a coral snake, small but lethal. Ben remembered the rhyme from basic training, used to quickly distinguish a harmless king snake from its venomous cousin. Dan's worst fears were confirmed. They would have to check the ground now before getting up.

Dollar Bill came strolling up behind Jimbo and was about to ask what all the racket was about but stopped short as Jimbo displayed the dead snake again.

"Hey those things are deadly poisonous," he began, as if preparing a lecture.

"No shit." Ben was still sweating from the exertion and his agitation. "Good thing Jimbo saw it. I would've stepped right on it."

"You're a lucky bastard at that. You ought to be thanking Jimbo and your lucky stars you're not dead right now."

Ben swallowed hard and looked up at the man's face.

"Thanks, Jimbo. I mean it. Oh, and sorry about the...well, you know."

Jimbo tossed the dead snake into the palmettos at the edge of camp, then turned and fixed his steely eyes on Ben.

"No problem, white man," he finally said at last. Erupting into a rich, deep laugh, he walked back to his own tent, still swinging the machete.

"What was that all about?" Bill asked in a stage whisper.

"You had to be there," Ben explained.

Dan appeared a few seconds later, walking across the pitch with a beer in his hand.

"Hey! What's going on?"

"Nothing," Ben and Bill responded simultaneously.

Ben took the beer can out of Dan's hand and drained it. "You need another beer," he belched.

7
~Somewhere en La Costa de la Florida~
26 Septiembre 1523

Daylight brought little succor to those who lived to see it. The rain now fell periodically; the wind blew only slightly less violently. It was a wet, blustery day, occasional gusts slamming into the palms with such strength their fronds twisted into knots, clattering like wooden shutters. The quick and the dead lay together on the beach, some half in and half out of the surf.

Claudio awoke to find himself above the tidal line, shivering in the wet sand. As his eyes slowly focused, he saw a speck moving slowly up the beach, examining bodies with a tap of his boot. He reached and rolled some of them over to check for the pallor of death. As the figure moved closer, Claudio recognized the shape as that of Comandante Gregorio. He appeared detached, unmoved by the grisly spectacle before him. When he came near, Claudio stiffly gained his feet, his legs cramping in the cold, damp wind. The Comandante had a bemused look on his face, as if surprised to see another living soul.

"God has shown us compassion in our time of distress," Gregorio finally spoke. It came out in a patronizing tone, as if he was still evaluating the benefit of that small miracle.

"*Ave Maria, gratia plena.*" Claudio's chattering teeth made his Latin almost unintelligible.

Together, they made the sign of the cross.

"Are there many more alive?" Claudio asked, squinting against the rain that stung his face.

"Thirty-five, maybe forty men...some are dying as we speak. They have made a shelter about a half league north of here at the edge of the jungle." Gregorio turned and glanced over his left shoulder. "Rejoin the crew. Let them know I will return in a little while."

Comandante Gregorio turned and trudged on with the manner of a gentleman on a morning walk along the seashore. Claudio estimated that if only two score of his shipmates made it through the storm, then fully two-thirds of the ship's company had drowned or been mortally wounded.

He found them camouflaged under a tattered remnant of sail propped up with broken spars and pieces of salvaged planks. Those who could had retreated to this makeshift tent in the lee of a large dune. There was no fire or fresh water save the pooling of the intermittent rain that ran off one corner of the dirty canvas. Nothing was dry and the men were huddled against one another for warmth, as well as to comfort the injured. Food was non-existent. They were without so much as a cup of wine to help ease their misery. Many had crushed extremities and shattered bones. Others had sustained horrifying blows to the head or were cut open by debris. Exposure had already claimed several lives, despite the meager shelter they had cobbled together.

One by one, the incessant coughing of men with lungs half-full of seawater were silenced by the sweet release of death. There were no clerics alive to hear confessions. Claudio moved from man to man, saying the *Ave Maria* for them. Every time he paused, an undercurrent of soft sound from the group came to his ear, the murmuring of many labored voices whispering the *Actus Contritionis* in a mixture of Latin and Spanish before the death rattle closed their throats forever. It would have been heart-breaking had Claudio not already been shocked into numbness by the nightmare.

The Comandante returned at dusk, as weary and ragged as Claudio had ever seen him. Without prologue, he announced that there was no sign of any Christian habitation to the south, only wilderness. They were alone, at the vagaries of the weather and whatever *indios salvaje* that may be nearby. His announcement done, he lay down with his back to a mound of sand and appeared to go to sleep. He offered no hope, no message of encouragement. To those who had served under him the longest, his misanthropy was to be expected. The Comandante only chose to lead when it suited him.

Slumber eluded Claudio as the night wore on. He was constantly alarmed by sounds coming out of the blackened forest. Several times, he heard the cry of a panther, once very close by. Praying his rosary with shivering hands, he couldn't block out the rustle of rats in the dead palm leaves a few feet away. It was as if he could feel the *ángel de la muerte* moving among the group, snatching the souls of the dying with its cold hands.

***

When light returned, it brought clearer skies and a welcome warmth. The breeze had finally waned to something that approached normal. As the orange ball of the sun rose higher, the more able-bodied of the crew began to struggle to their feet, staggering and squinting in the birth of a new day. In the darkness before dawn though, nearly half of them had succumbed to their wounds and the elements. They were now a band of just twenty and three.

When the Comandante awoke, he led them to the high tide mark on the white strand for Matins. Genuflecting, he read from a small, worn leather-bound *Book of Hours*, given to him personally by His Excellency Diego de Deza, Archbishop of Seville, Inquisitor General of Spain. After reading the Hours for the Virgin, the Cross, and the Holy Spirit, he began the Office of the Dead. After each Psalm, the entire party quietly responded.

"*Requiem aeternam dona eis Domine.* Eternal rest give unto them O Lord and let perpetual light shine unto them."

Once they were finally able to survey the wreckage of the *Mano del Rey*, it was clear to all that the ship's bulkheads were cracked and beyond repair. Like the broken ribs of a beached whale, the vessel's superstructure had been twisted and warped during the storm. Now completely on its side, the *frigata* showed its cavernous belly to be half submerged. Comandante Gregorio had no intention of leaving his fortune and his future in the carcass of a ship lying in such shallow water. The first order of the day was to have a party of the most-fit *marineros* swim out to the wreck to assess the best way to recover the nine oak chests of gold and silver. Once that was done, they could commence stripping the wreck of anything salvageable. It could be many months before another ship might pass. They would have to establish some kind of fortification to shelter and defend themselves in the meantime.

Since the bodies of the *indios* had not been seen on the beach, the survivors assumed they had drowned when the *frigata* capsized. Only Claudio knew they had a chance to survive as well, and he cringed inside any time the topic was discussed.

The expedition's journal had come through the storm intact and without significant damage. Claudio made a crude ink of crushed berries and spittle in order to inventory all that was brought ashore during the day.

> *On the first trip, it was discovered that the longboat was still lashed to the hatch cover. Inasmuch as Providence had provided us a seaworthy vessel, much use of it was made to transfer nine, large sea chests laden with gold and silver. Other useful items were retrieved as well, including a señal cañón, that we might signal any ship that sailed within earshot. A small keg of powder, slightly dampened, was brought back to be dried for use in the thunder mug. The Comandante's sword and scabbard were collected from his cabin along with the ship's flag, the royal banner of Spain. Six pikes, two halberds, an armload of various swords, and a small coffer full of dirks and shorter daggers were saved from the armory. The arquebuses, rendered useless by the salt water and sand, were left behind. Even if they had been in good condition, we have no fuses or shot. Likewise, the crossbows were located on the bottom, where their waterlogged mechanisms would soon rust on shore, their bowstrings rot and on the whole, make them unreliable. Furthermore, the bolts had disappeared within the wreckage.*
>
> *One of our remaining company is the ship's carpenter, who made a point to rescue his tools in anticipation of the construction of a fort and possibly even a raft. Our crew now consists of two soldados, who*

46

will be lightly armed, the carpenter, several gunner's mates, and fifteen marineros. Our only officer is Comandante Gregorio, and I am the only midshipman, to whom command would be given should anything befall the Comandante, may God preserve him. Once the weapons and treasures were made secure, our attention turned to victuals. Among all else I have enumerated, we have been left with a small barrel of sea biscuits, a larger barrel of parched corn, and another the same size, containing dried beans, rehydrated and made salty from immersion in the sea. Two small barrels were also ferried ashore, one of wine and one of sherry. Even a tarro of olive oil was found intact and brought in. All together we have been blessed by God for these things to shelter, feed, and protect us. In the afternoon, we collected all the corpses left in the tide and those from among our midst who had passed away the previous night. The Comandante set a detail to bury them all in a long trench-like grave dug at the foot of the dunes to our north. The carpenter fashioned a large wooden cross from salvaged planks and erected it in the center of the dead. At sunset, our company knelt before them to say our vespers. God grant them peace.

8
~~Dead Man Bay, Florida~~
June 15, 1959

After the commotion in camp during the afternoon, the team had a quiet dinner. Lucky disappeared into the command tent early. With the blackout flaps in place, it was hard to tell if a light was on in there or not. Lonnie had gone back to the boat just before dark and appeared to have called lights out early. Jimbo lay on his cot, reading a book by lantern light. Only the three friends sat cross-legged by a small campfire in front of their own tent, talking in hushed tones, working on their third beer of the evening. Bill chain-smoked his Pall Malls, flicking the butts into the coals periodically. Ben started his last cigar of the night, trying to ration his supply. Dan was the odd man out, never having taken up the habit.

"So how did it go on the water today?" Dan asked, staring into the flames as if hypnotized.

"I think the magnetometer ought to work okay," Bill opined. "We didn't pick up any stray hits but it found the two targets we threw overboard."

"How big were they?" Ben was curious.

Bill gestured with his hands. "An old steel car wheel about sixteen inches across and a scrap outboard prop."

Ben nodded in approval.

"We were only in about ten feet of water though and this stuff was lying right on top of the mud," Bill continued. "It's not goin' to be any cake walk."

"It never is," Dan observed. "See any sharks?"

Nah." Bill brushed off the question.

"We still don't know if gold will register." Ben glanced at Bill.

"No, but I can tell you that right after we hooked it up, I put a silver dollar on it, and it measured it."

"Good ol' Dollar Bill." Dan yawned.

***

Work began in earnest the next morning after chow call. Jimbo was up a tall pine, rigging a shortwave radio antenna, with Lucky down near the command tent supervising. Dan, Bill, and Ben waded out to the boat with their snorkeling gear.

"Ahoy, skipper! Permission to come aboard?" Bill called as they got close.

Lonnie stepped out of the cabin and grinned.

"C'mon, y'all."

With the magnetometer cradled in a rack at the rear of the launch, it reminded Ben of the PT boats he had seen in the war with their stern torpedo tubes. There was a spacious cabin forward and it seemed well suited for work in the Gulf. As they hauled up the anchor, Ben stood next to Lonnie at the wheel.

"What kind of boat is this?" he asked over the rumble of the warming engine.

"Some guy on Long Island built it as a sailboat back in the thirties. I bought it and put in a thirty-five-horsepower gasoline engine with stern drive. It's forty-five feet long with a fifteen-foot beam and a four-foot draft."

It was clear Lonnie knew boats and loved this one. *Dreamboat*, he called her. The man was lean and wiry to the point of being scrawny. Older than anyone else on board, he was in his mid-forties with sandy blond hair that had already thinned to a pronounced widow's peak high on his perpetually sunburned forehead. He wore steel-rimmed glasses that made him look like he could be an accountant on vacation, but the three-day stubble indicated he spent a lot of time doing just this. Shirtless, his ruddy complexion and freckled arms bespoke time in the sun, his back always on the verge of turning lobster red. Dressed in khaki shorts and flip-flops, Lonnie steered the boat through smooth water at half-throttle.

"So what did you do during the war?" Ben asked him, mildly curious.

"Navy liaison, coast watcher," Lonnie explained without taking his eyes off their course. "I patrolled inshore, between Pascagoula and Pensacola, Mobile Bay. Worked out of Biloxi."

"In this boat?"

"Yep. That's where the radio equipment came from."

Until Lonnie pointed up, Ben hadn't realized that an omnidirectional antenna was on the cabin roof, capable of determining the direction, frequency, and range of any radio signal for nearly fifty miles.

"The Navy let you keep a Huff-Duff?"

"They never mentioned it and neither did I." Lonnie smiled.

"Did you not mention anything else, like a machine gun or depth charge?" Ben asked, only partially joking.

"I never had anything like that. If I was ever to get into trouble, I would just have to run like hell for the shallows. I think once I might have heard a U-boat, but nothin' ever came of it." Lonnie glanced at Ben with a wide grin. "I do still have my service forty-five." He patted a locked compartment next to the wheel.

"That counts," smiled Ben. He ducked into the companionway to join the rest of the team.

Below was a surprisingly large galley equipped with a full-size gas stove and propane-powered refrigerator. Bill hunched over a Formica counter checking all the connections for the magnetometer. "Okay, guys, this is how it's gonna go."

"Where's Dan?" Ben looked around.

"Over here," Dan called, tossing a *Mad Magazine* on the rack where he had been lying.

"Listen up," Bill repeated. "When I get the signal for a solid hit, I'm going to call the mark to Lonnie then he's going to holler to you. On my mark, I want you to take one of those inflatable buoys and heave the lead right towards the tail of the magnetometer. It's got a couple of long red and white floats trailing from the nose and tail. You'll be able to see it. The buoys have fifteen feet of line on 'em. I don't think we're goin' to be much deeper than that. Once we make a few runs in the grid, we'll go down and check out the hits."

Both divers nodded.

"Okay then, let's get this fish in the water. Lonnie!" Bill called toward the bridge.

"Yeah," Lonnie stuck his head in the door.

"We close?"

"Very."

A few minutes later, the engine died down to a slow trolling speed.

"All hands to your duty stations." It sounded like an order when Bill said it. He was used to giving them, and they were used to taking them. It seemed like ten years had never elapsed.

As Lonnie held the course, Ben and Dan put up a removable davit, hooking it to the center eyebolt on the magnetometer. Once it was cranked up about a foot, it was easy enough to swing it over the side and lower it into the water. The cable line paid out slowly as the machine sank like a giant fishing lure. Once it pulled taut, Lonnie picked up speed a bit until he could see the red and white floats skimming just under the surface, making a submarine bow wave.

"Fish in the water," Ben called to the cabin.

Bill sat hypnotized by the meter on the control panel that showed deflection. Black and white graph paper slowly unrolled from a small printer, the stylus recording only background noise. Ben lit a cigar and waited. This was so much like the Navy he knew. Hurry up and wait. Days of sheer boredom for a few hours of action. He wondered if it was like that for the guys at sea—weeks of drudgery replaced instantaneously by an hour of horror, fighting for their lives. He had never seen combat, just the results of it on ships and sailors coming in from a tour on the Atlantic. Those guys always seemed to be anxious, even paranoid when they left, at least in the beginning when the U-boats were everywhere. It was a crap shoot. A lot of them had good luck charms and superstitious rituals that made them less nervous.

Ben had never had to reach deep to face an enemy and not back off when his shipmates got cut in half by flying shrapnel. It used to keep him up at nights wondering if he had the guts for it. Never knowing the score was something he still carried with him. Courage under fire... The closest he had ever come was when he and Dan "borrowed" a motorcycle from the pool. When the MPs caught up with them, they threatened to shoot unless the guys pulled over. It was probably a bluff. Bill had managed to get their asses out of that sling after a night in the drunk tank.

As the day wore on, the tedium was exacerbated by the growing heat of the sun. Dan and Ben switched spots every hour, each taking their turn to stand with the puddle-shaped weight in one hand and the rope-wound, basketball-sized, white buoy in the other palm. Lonnie worked the waters about two miles offshore until they were off Bull Cove. Reversing course there, they sailed north again to the middle of Deadman Bay, just three miles from camp. They broke for a sandwich and soda while Bill radioed Lucky.

"Twelve miles this morning and not a single peep," Ben complained as he threw the crusts of his sandwich overboard for the gulls.

"Yeah, I wonder if this thing is working right," Dan muttered while draining his grape Nehi.

The early afternoon sun glinting off the water was giving Ben a headache, even with his sunglasses. He went below to get a BC Powder from his bag just as Bill signed off the radio.

"Well, Lucky wants us to make a couple more passes this afternoon a little further south." Bill slipped a chart on to the table and traced their assignment.

"We're to troll from the bay to Bull Cove in deeper water, about another half mile out. Then we need to head east to Bowlegs Point and see if we can scan the inside channel between Pepperfish Key and the shore. It'll be pretty shallow there. I don't know if we'll do anything but stir up the bottom."

"This is pointless," Ben complained.

"It all pays the same," Bill murmured as he lit a cigarette. "I'm going to relay this to Lonnie and make sure we can even get in that channel."

Dan came down the hatchway just as Bill gathered up his charts.

"Hamster Dan." He smiled. "Always a day late and a dollar short."

Dan raised his eyebrows.

"You missed the briefing," explained Ben.

"The story of my life. My wife says I'm gonna be late to my own funeral. So what's the poop?"

"Same song, second verse." Ben sighed and swallowed the powder with the last of his soda.

"How long you think this is gonna last?" Dan mused, already missing his cushy life back in Key Largo.

"Till the money runs out, I guess."

Money was the one thing Dan didn't have a lot of—new boat, a house, new truck, and his wife announced last month that she was pregnant again. Business was pretty good, except during the late summer when hurricane season peaked. It just hadn't been as profitable as he hoped it would be. He had toyed with the idea of opening a small restaurant, but couldn't see past the startup money. He had to be back home by August. Surely they'd be done by then.

The *Dreamboat*'s engines sputtered to life, and the two headed back on deck. Ben took the line and buoy station first. Dan leaned against the opposite gunwale in an uncharacteristically pensive mood. Bill sequestered himself below again. No one spoke.

Lonnie broke into a sea chanty.

"What shall we do with a drunken sailor? What shall we do with a drunken sailor? What shall we do with a drunken sailor, ear-lye in the morning?"

Ben and Dan joined in on the chorus.

"Way, hay, there she rises, way, hay, there she rises, way, hay, there she rises, ear-lye in the morning."

9
~~La Costa del Oeste de la Florida~~
30 Septiembre 1523

In the stillness of another early morning, Claudio sat on the top of the dunes, scanning the sea. Seeing nothing but their slowly disintegrating ship less than half a league away on the shallows, he picked up the leather tube and retrieved the folio containing their travels so far. He continued his entries, praying they might all survive this reversal. The journal would surely be published now and his fortune would be secured. Besides, it gave him hope. In writing, he felt less alone.

Having scouted the coast to our south, Comandante Gregorio took five experienced men with him on an expedition to the north. Leaving at first light on Septiembre twenty-eight, they searched for some passage into the interior where we might construct a proper fortificación to await rescue. There was, he said when he returned the following afternoon, nothing but vast reaches of marsh, still flooded from the recent storm. A small river mouth prevented the group from proceeding any further north. We would march south to bring us closer to the trade route from Havana, but such a course would undoubtedly bring us into conflict with the local indios in those parts, the Tocobago and the Calusa. The former have been known to loot treasure from wrecked ships such as ours and would certainly attempt to take what we have. The Calusa are a large tribe and as formidable as any standing army.

So it appears that we are castaways, marooned, in an isolated place not generally visited by the inhabitants thereof. In three days, we have constructed a small, low palisade between the dunes, partially blocking the entrance to our camp. A short distance behind it is a pit dug into the firm sand. As deep as a man is tall and two arms-breadth square, it is covered by twigs and palm leaves and disguised with a thin layer of light sand. With a framework of small trees, our canvas has been raised to such a height that a man might stand upright while protected from the sun and rain.

Claudio waited for the deep purple ink to dry before replacing the journal into its leather case. He had made the dark stain from blackberries he found in abundance just a little way into the jungle. The plant was a briar, growing in long tendrils within the palmettos. While the harvest was made painful by the many sharp thorns, Claudio had been more concerned with how he placed his feet. This new world seemed to have poisonous serpents everywhere. Several times, he heard the chilling rattle of the huge, fat serpents the Anahuac called *coatl*.

A lot of the jungle around them was impenetrable by humans, a uniform, leafy-green wall of vegetation. By night, it was the black, shadowy complement to the inky blue sea, with the white strand of shoreline hemmed in between. Even at high noon, the forest remained in twilight, with intertwining branches supporting a riot of vines and mats of gray-black mosses. Living with their backs to this untamed world was sometimes unnerving, but still preferable to the arid, brown and muddy land of the Azteca.

When Claudio first arrived in Cuba, he was amazed by the perfect beauty of the island. The colors seemed brighter, more vivid than anywhere he had ever been. Lush forests and rugged mountains were alive with the cry of birds that looked like they had been painted a shimmering green or iridescent blue. Never had he seen a more vibrant red than in the huge flowers that bloomed in profusion everywhere. His curiosity was piqued by horrifically large insects, his mind inspired by a land full of strange creatures. His dreams were permeated with the fresh, sweet smell of the air, the languor of the warm yet temperate climate, and the aquamarine seas. Yet this Eden was flawed. It could generate terrible fevers that left one shivering in delirium. In certain seasons, hurricanes of awesome power swept across the land, wiping clean whole islands.

However, it was the people he encountered which intrigued Claudio the most. For many centuries, they lived as innocents, naked and simple. Living on nature's bounty, they appeared to have no disease, no wants. That time had passed. The politics of power and subjugation had now arrived, fed by internal strife and the coming of those like himself. He had seen smallpox planted like a malignant seed. Men like Cortez and Gregorio manipulated the populace into new wars and cheated them of their independence, their industry, and finally their birthrights.

Hopping clumsily down the steep sand embankment, he approached several men engaged in cutting long, thick liana to weave back and forth between the trees, making a crude fence. Others found some native yucca, equipped with sharp spikes, to plant just on the outside of the perimeter to act as a deterrent. Complaining about the work, as is common among *marineros*, all tried to talk over the next man, not necessarily in response.

"¡*Ay me abraso*, I'm burning up!" called one, whom Claudio knew to be the leader of all the able-bodied seamen. "This place is hotter than Havana." Claudio tried to remember his name—Ricardo? Rafael? He wasn't sure.

"¡*Bastardo!*" interjected one of the younger men, a seaman apprentice, as he struggled to plant the spiny yuccas. Flapping his hand furiously, he flung drops of blood onto the sand.

"Careful," Claudio called to him, "you may need all you have."

The *carpintero* was sweating over a plow board, attempting to coax an ember to catch fire to a small pile of cotton lint and tar scrapings. Claudio offered to take a turn, knowing this was the only way they might get warm food and light at night. In the scramble to abandon ship, none had thought to put a piece of flint in their pocket. They had been more concerned with filling their purses with pilfered gold scrap and the odd pearl. When they scavenged the wreck, there were no tinder boxes to be found. Neither did they have a glass with which to magnify the sun's rays.

Finally, after nearly half an hour, the tinder began to smoke and the *carpintero* nursed it into a proper flame. Claudio quickly made a small nest of dead twigs to receive the rapidly burning cinders. Tending it with care, he carefully built it into a cook fire to the huzzahs of the company. At that moment, he became the *guardián del fuego* by popular consent, a trust he accepted gracefully. It would mean he would have to stay awake most of the night and rise early to harvest the smoldering embers, returning them to a living blaze again. If others were unable to bring in firewood, he would have to go out alone, even in the dark of night.

Gazing into the new coals, shimmering red and orange like the landscape of Hell, Claudio was reminded of the words to a dance tune he heard just before leaving Seville. It was called *El Fuego,* and he had wanted to learn it but never got the time. However, one line had gotten stuck in his head ever since that day—"*Que lo que da Dios no toma*; That which God gives, He does not take."

Several days passed with only Claudio counting. Time was no longer measured by the ship's hourglass or the number of knots counted on the hand line. The masts no longer acted as a sundial to indicate the length of their day. Now only the relative position of the sun and stars charted the length of their exile. More subtle signs confirmed the passage of days. Many of the crew had lost a frightening amount of weight. Their hair had become long and wild, their beards as shapeless as the dried sea grass that littered the beach. Claudio did not mind that his hair was now longer than it had been in many months, but he fretted over the stubble emerging on his chin. He normally obsessed to the point of vanity over his mustache, and the gritty feel of his cheeks made his face feel constantly dirty.

In the week following the storm, they made something of a home in the verge between the jungle and the sea. Ironically, the camp mirrored the division they had known on board the *Mano del Rey*. The Comandante slept and ate under the tarp, apart from the men. While the fire ring was democratic, admitting all, most of the men slept in the open, back against the dunes. As seasoned *soldados* and *marineros*, they were generally comfortable resting under the stars, and the sand beneath them held the heat from the day. Only the chilly, damp air at dawn enticed them to get up and move closer to the fire.

One morning, according to his reckoning, Sunday, the fourth of *Octubre* arrived and he went to notify Comandante Gregorio. He found his superior on the beach, quietly reading from the *Book of Hours*.

"*¿Señor?*"

"*Si.*"

"*Es Domingo*. The men should take their Sabbath." Claudio knew it would be a welcome respite from the incessant labor to secure the camp. Gregorio thought for a minute, then nodded and went back to his reading. That was the extent of his concern. He knew what day it was, but only his own soul was important.

That afternoon, the Comandante stood in the center of the compound and motioned for all to gather round. No one spoke. Only the light flapping of the flag planted on the crest of the dune kept the camp from being completely silent.

"By the will of God, we were brought to this place eight days ago. *Gracias a Dios*, we have survived. Since then, it has not rained. We have no fresh water, our drink and supply of food is running low." He paused as if still thinking through a plan.

"If we remain here, we will all likely die of thirst or starvation. I have decided to take a small force with me to explore the interior for fresh water and game. I will leave eight men here to defend the camp and watch for ships. We shall be gone a fortnight, perhaps more and carry only one day's ration."

There was some murmuring among the men, realizing that the expedition might be a death march. But as usual, the Comandante's grasp of the situation was both characteristically succinct and brutally accurate.

"Rafael, you will be in charge." It was the able-bodied seaman whose name Claudio had forgotten. "Diego." Gregorio looked toward the *carpintero*." You should remain."

"Of course, Comandante."

After calling off the other half-dozen who were to remain, Comandante Gregorio turned to Claudio and spoke in a lowered voice.

"Claudio, at sunrise tomorrow, take three men and go dig two more graves near the others. Choose from those who will go with us."

Claudio hesitated before nodding. He wondered what purpose this bizarre request might serve. There had been no natural deaths since that first night, no desertions. Did he mean to execute two of their dwindling band? What offense had occurred?

The burden of this command occupied him the rest of the day as he busied himself with small tasks—smoking fish and gathering driftwood and green palmetto fans. Trimming the thorny edges, he cut the branch short and chopped the ends of the leaf to form fans. From the pith, he deftly wove small crosses like the ones he had known back in Malaga. As a boy, the friars patiently taught him the craft and he had assisted in making many in preparation for Holy Week. Both constructions became instantly popular with everyone in camp, even the Comandante. Nevertheless, the anxiety of the next day gnawed at him. Perhaps it had been discovered that he had freed the slaves. He feared death, like any man, but he did not regret his actions. His conscience was clear before God.

He had little appetite for the fish, but drank his ration of wine. As darkness fell and the last sliver of moon rose in the eastern sky, he walked awkwardly over the dunes and stood on the beach with his back to the sea. That same slender crescent of light also rose over his home in Southern Spain and he was suddenly overtaken with melancholy. Had one of his family also gazed up and wondered where their brother or son was? Had he been forgotten, even thought dead? Did they long to gather him into their arms as he did them?

"*Padre, Madre,* I am alive. This your son, Claudio. Can you not hear me?" he whispered. He fell to his knees and recited the Lord's Prayer in full voice so the sea and the stars, the shore, and the forest, as well as all the creatures that lived therein, might hear his supplication to God.

Rising to his feet, his eyes swept the Gulf from horizon to horizon, vainly searching for the small light of a ship that might save them. Only the black sea, darker than the night, met his eyes. Then it occurred to him that, in two days, it would be the time of the new moon. They would be in the midst of a savage land then, in the belly of the beast. *May God preserve us*, he thought.

10
~~Bull Cove, Florida~~
June 16, 1959

Ben shaded his eyes as he checked the position of the late afternoon sun. Even though it wouldn't set until six-thirty or so, they were running out of light for diving, even if they found something. He was antsy to take a long break anyway. This had been one wasted day.

"Lonnie, what time have you got?"

Lonnie checked his wristwatch and called back. "Sixteen hundred, give or take a few minutes."

Since Dan had the buoy station, Ben moved closer to Lonnie so they could talk without raising their voices.

"So whattaya know about this whole thing?"

"Probably not much more than you do. Lucky keeps his cards close to his vest."

"I noticed. He's a piece of work."

"You know he used to be OSS."

"A spy guy?"

"Yeah. When I met him in forty-three, he was doing analysis of aerial reconnaissance."

"No kiddin'. That answers a lot."

Ben was beginning to wonder whose expedition this really was. Maybe this Noble Fischer guy didn't even exist.

Their conversation was cut short when Bill yelled from the cabin.

"All engines dead slow!"

Lonnie pushed the throttle almost to idle and Dan cocked his arm back to throw the lead. "Mark!"

Dan heaved the sinker out and let it snatch the buoy from his hand. It landed squarely in the wake of the magnetometer.

Bill stuck his head out of the hatchway.

"Lonnie, circle around and make another pass by that marker. I want to check the signal again."

"Pretty strong?" Ben asked.

"Strong enough."

"Maybe we got something, huh?" Dan was excited now.

"I wouldn't break out your flippers just yet," muttered Ben.

Going below, he watched the tape unreel over Bill's shoulder. Sure enough, on the second pass, he saw the spike rise and fall in a classic bell curve. Stepping over to the chart table, he checked their position. "About fifteen feet of water," he announced to no one in particular.

"Are you going to have enough light?" Bill asked.

Ben looked out the hatch toward the sky.

"I think so, but if we're going to do this, we'd better do it soon."

"Okay. Get your gear and I'll tell Lonnie to anchor close by."

"I'm going to free dive it." Ben opened his sea bag and pulled out his fins and a mask.

Once over the side, he was surprised that the water was cloudy. The slant of the sun didn't help. Following the line down on his first dive, he found nothing that would suggest a metal object. He poked the sand nearby with the sheath knife he had strapped to his calf. Nothing. Bobbing up for air, he immediately went back down the line and searched a couple of yards north of the marker. A dark round object in the sand suddenly caught his eye. Nature didn't create perfectly round symmetrical objects. It had to be man-made.

Surfacing one more time to fill his lungs, he swam back down, momentarily distracted by a large shimmer of light below the surface. A school of barracuda cruised by about fifteen yards away, heading for better hunting grounds. On the bottom, he cleared away the first layer of sand and debris to find what looked like a pot lid with a knob on top. Slightly crusted with barnacles, it was a dark green color and looked like it had been there a long time. It took one more trip topside to get enough air to allow him to dig around the edges of the object, first with his knife, then with his hands. Finally, he could see a cage-like structure hidden with a length of heavy iron rod attached. In all, it was about three and a half feet long and far too heavy for him to carry to the surface safely. Ben came back up and treading water, called to the boat.

"I think I got something. I need a net with some line."

Bill tossed out a net of heavy rope and watched the half-inch hemp line pay out. When it finally stopped, Bill and Dan took up the slack and waited. After what seemed like way too long, they felt two tugs on the rope and began to haul away. Ben reappeared and swam to the boat to keep the find from being damaged or lost again. Steadying the net as Bill and Dan lifted it with some effort, the object was finally on deck.

"What is it?" Dan wondered aloud.

Bill examined the object, turning it carefully to look for marks. Apparently made of bronze and iron, it showed a lot of time on the bottom.

"I think it's a ship's lantern. Old sailing ships used them to act as a stern light. They also needed light to help them see the compass at night."

"The end is bent," observed Ben. "It must have been knocked loose somehow."

"Lonnie, radio Duprez and tell him we're headed in with something. Guys, leave the buoy in the water. I got a feeling we'll be coming back. I gotta go mark the charts."

***

The blood red sun was just a few degrees above the horizon by the time the *Dreamboat* dropped anchor again in Deadman Bay. The four of them carried the lantern in its net to shore where Lucky waited. Showing the first signs of hopeful anticipation, he followed them to the mess tent.

The team gathered around the object laid out on the wooden table. Looking at it under the glare of a Coleman lantern, Lucky finally gave his opinion.

"I think you're right, Bill. Looks like a maritime lantern."

"How old you think it is?" Bill asked.

"Could be anywhere from two to four hundred years."

Ben gazed thoughtfully at their find. Now that it was drying out, the green patina of weathered bronze was evident. "It may have been two hundred years since this thing was lit."

Lucky nodded and did something he seldom allowed himself. He smiled. "Good work, men. I think we're on the right track."

Lucky disappeared back into the command tent as Jimbo fired up the grill. They would have steak tonight.

"Yep," sighed Bill, settling onto his cot to await chow call. "A good day's work."

"At least we found something he liked," grumbled Ben as he rubbed insect repellant on his arms and legs.

Dan sniffed the air. "What is that, eau de kerosene?"

"Bug off."

Dan didn't know if that was an explanation or a demand. Changing the subject, Ben looked toward Bill. "Lonnie told me that Duprez used to be OSS."

"Huh," was Bills only response. It was a comment, not a question.

"It doesn't seem odd to you that we've never seen or heard from the moneybags who supposedly paid for all this?" Ben continued.

"And?" Bill raised an eyebrow.

"I dunno. All of this is kind of like some cloak and dagger thing. I thought it was weird from the get-go."

"Maybe because of what we're looking for," Bill shrugged. "It's obviously something important, something valuable. If word got out, we'd have every Tom, Dick, and Harry looking over our shoulder. Wouldn't you want to keep that hush-hush?"

"I guess," Ben agreed after a moment.

***

At supper, they sat segregated again until Ben got up with his plate and moved over to sit with Jimbo. The man looked up at Ben for a long few seconds and then went back to eating. Ben was hoping to make some kind of gesture that might help make up for the things he said. It seemed to be lost on Jimbo. As far as the giant was concerned, Ben was just another cracker, the kind that smiled to your face, pretending to be your friend, then put on a bed sheet come Sunday night.

After they were done, Duprez stood up and cleared his throat.

"Men, since the focus of our search is shifting to Bull Cove, I've decided to move the camp to an area near Sink Creek, further south. Lonnie, you'll be able to run up the creek to the camp even at low tide, I think. The location is also more secure. We can't have peeping Toms at this next stage. Dan, Ben, I need one of you to stay behind tomorrow to help me and Jimbo break camp here and set up everything there."

"I'll stay," volunteered Ben. Anything was better than another long boring day on the boat. Immediately, he heard a small noise from Jimbo. When he looked, the big man was bobbing slightly in a silent chuckle.

"All right, Ben," Duprez replied. "We'll get started right after mess call in the morning. I need everybody to pack your gear tonight so you don't have anything left behind. In the morning, put your kit in the back of the truck. Any questions?"

No one said a word.

Duprez retreated, aloof and alone, behind the flaps of his tent. Leaving Jimbo and Lonnie in the mess tent, the rest of them slowly walked back to their bivouac.

"See? What did I tell you?" Bill asked as he broke up some small twigs to start a fire.

"Everything's been on the up and up as far as I can tell," Dan chimed in.

Ben was still not completely convinced.

"I'm still gonna watch him like a hawk." That was part of the reason he volunteered to stay behind.

"Let it go. There's nothing shady going on." Bill sounded irritated.

"Yeah, that's what you said when we got into that fake lottery on the base."

"How was I supposed to know that guy was going to skip town?"

"With our dough," added Dan.

"Whattaya mean our dough? I loaned you the ten bucks to get in on the action," Ben reminded him.

"You told me not to worry about it," pouted Dan. "Besides, Bill's the one who gave it away."

Bill smiled, thinking of the good times. They were all younger then, full of hope and ambition. Where had the years gone?

"Well," he said as he lit a cigarette, "you're gonna make more dough now than you ever did then."

"Here, here," his buddies responded. There was a soft clinking noise as they put their half-empty beer bottles together.

"I was sure I gave you back that ten-spot," Dan murmured.

***

The truck was loaded by midday, and Ben squeezed himself into a place on the bench between stacks of plywood and canvas. Duprez insisted on traveling with the flaps down so the rear end of the cargo bed was the only place to get some air. Ben was alone with his thoughts. As they slowly rumbled out of the woods, he lit a cigar and watched the world recede, thankful for the breeze. The place they were going didn't seem far on the map, but they would have to backtrack all the way to Highway 27 and cross over the Steinhatchee in order to pick up County Road 361.

When they stopped to get several bales of straw, Ben found himself following Jimbo to a small diner half a block away to get sandwiches. The minute they stepped inside, the place fell silent. Ben could feel every eye on him. Before he could order, a weaselly looking counterman pointed to a sign by the register.

"You see this sign?" the weasel demanded. "We reserve the right to refuse service to anyone. We don't serve your kind." His voice was grating, like a rusty hinge on an old screen door.

"All we want is some sandwiches to g—," Ben started to explain.

"We don't want no nigger-lovers in here either."

A weak round of laughter went around the room. Ben was starting to get worked up and was ready to argue. Jimbo grabbed his arm and pulled him outside. As they walked away, the big man took a deep breath, and then let it go in a rush of air.

"What an ass!" Ben repeated himself. "What an ass!"

Jimbo talked as they strode down the sidewalk, his voice lowered so no one else could hear. "Folks down here always pullin' that shit. Colored people got to go round back and beg."

"But why wouldn't he let me get somethin'?"

"If he had, I wouldn't eat what he gave you. Likely they'd spit on the bread, give us ol' moldy cheese, or throw the insides on the floor before they put it in the sandwich."

"What a jackass!" Ben repeated even more emphatically.

"Besides, you a nigger-lover now." Jimbo broke into a grin. "They gonna hate you almost as much as they hate me."

***

County Road 361 was a two-lane, gravel highway that seemed to lead to the edge of the world. Crossing a wooden bridge over the headwaters of Sink Creek, they could hear the timbers groan and crack under the weight of the deuce and a half. Somehow, Jimbo managed to navigate to the tiny dirt road Lucky said would take them to the island. It wasn't so much a real island as it was a sandy high spot surrounded by marsh grass and mud. If a really good rain came, it would become an actual island, cutting them off from anything beyond the green horizon.

Finally, they met the creek again on a sandbank bordering a small pocket of coastal forest. Shady and inviting, it was covered with red cedar, pine, water oaks, and sabal palms. The forest floor was fairly clean, layered with leaf debris, pine needles and the occasional gallberry bush or palmetto clump. Greenbriers, with their sharp thorns, climbed the pine tree trunks. Some of the older oaks were bearded with Spanish moss. On the west side, facing the Gulf, colonies of flat-leafed cactus had taken hold.

***

Jimbo and Ben were still organizing things in camp when the rest of the crew showed up. At least they had all the tents up. Duprez had successfully managed to buy groceries, ice, beer, and cigarettes at a little mom and pop store in Cross City despite Ben and Jimbo's experience a few blocks away. He had even found a pack of Ben's favorite cigars.

By now, Ben was sweating like a horse, hauling supplies to the mess tent.

"Catch anything?" he called as Lonnie tied the boat to a tree.

"Naw. They weren't biting today," Bill responded.

"We didn't have our good luck charm with us." Dan was in good spirits at least.

"I didn't even get a chance to take a swim."

"Hey, Lucky," Lonnie called.

"Yeah?"

"I think when low tide comes, there won't be enough water to turn the boat around. As a matter of fact, she might be sittin' on the bottom then or damn near it."

Duprez looked at his watch and thought a minute.

"Well, it's roughly high tide now."

"Looks like it may be starting to turn."

"I guess you fellas will have to shove off no later than 0500. Unfortunately, it'll still be dark. Daybreak will probably be another forty-five minutes or so if it's clear."

"I got a good searchlight on the boat." Lonnie jerked his thumb over his shoulder.

Supper was a paltry affair—every man for himself. Lonnie was on board the *Dreamboat* cooking something that might have been crab. Par for the course, Duprez was holed up in the command tent, and Jimbo seemed to be frying some fatback and potatoes at his own campfire. With a gibbous moon almost overhead reflecting off the sand, it was practically bright enough to see without lanterns.

Ben went over to the mess tent on a beer run and, coming back, noticed Jimbo was through eating and was draining the last swallow from his can. Dropping a couple of bottles at the communal campfire, he walked to where Jimbo sat.

"Need another brew?"

Jimbo looked up at him and waited a second or two before answering. "Yeah, sure."

"Mind if I sit down?"

"It's a free country." There was a tinge of irony in Jimbo's voice.

Ben handed the man a beer and collapsed into a crossed-legged sitting position. "Jimbo. Is that your real name?"

Jimbo looked at him sideways. "What kind of fool would name his kid that way?

"My name is James. I had a lieutenant in the Army, Ivy League man. He started calling me Jimbo 'cause he thought it was funny. He give it to me when I made sergeant, said I was gettin' uppity. Jimbo, Jim boy, boy—I knew what he was gettin' at."

Ben was going to say something to commiserate, but Jim's tone made him swallow the words.

"So." Ben tried to steer the topic in a different direction. "You were in the Army."

Suddenly, Jim stood up and saluted. "Carter, J., sergeant, serial number 1413059." He stood at attention for a few seconds then squatted down close to Ben. "Why you ask so many questions?"

Ben shrugged. "Just tryin' to be friendly."

Suddenly Jim's face looked like it was chiseled from granite. His words came out in a staccato clip. "We ain't friends, never gonna be friends, you unnerstand?"

"Sure," Ben rose to his feet and sidled away. It hadn't gone quite like he hoped. He liked the man, wanted at least to get along with him. Having him be alone, ostracized, just didn't sit right. One thing Ben did figure out was that all of them were ex-military, specialists in their field. How that played into what was going on was still a mystery.

11
~~ La Costa del Oeste de la Florida~~
5 Octubre 1523

Claudio awoke less than an hour after dawn, but waited quietly until he saw the men stir. As he made up the fire, he felt a presence behind him. It was Comandante Gregorio.

"Get the men to dig those graves. Come and tell me when it's done."

"Of course, Comandante."

Claudio watched his superior walk away. He was still uneasy about the order, but the Comandante had not specified which three he should choose other than they be members of the expedition. He hesitated a moment, then rousted the two remaining *soldados* and Miguel, a gunner's mate. He didn't know them, but if he was going to die, he didn't want an *amigo* to have to be the one to put him to the sword.

They filed silently out of the gate, carrying two wooden spades. It was already warm and humid. The morning sun hitting the white sand temporarily blinded them. Striding through the sugary soil, they approached the place where so many of their comrades lay. Finding a clear space, they set to work. Even though the men alternated their time in the holes, the spade's rough, crude handles quickly formed large blisters on Claudio's hands. The others were unfazed, having earned calluses from a lifetime of hard work.

After an hour and a half, they were done. Marching back to camp, Claudio went to find Comandante Gregorio.

"All is ready, *señor.*"

"There. Carry those."

The *carpintero* had made two crude wooden litters about five feet long and wide enough for a man to lie on. Stacked on top of them were the strongboxes, nine in all. Claudio motioned to the other three men to assist.

"Diego," the Comandante continued." Stand by the gate. No one leaves."

"*Si*, Comandante."

Struggling under the load, the men staggered out the gate, followed by their leader. Diego stood at the gate, glancing furtively down the beach at them.

Returning to the makeshift graveyard, Comandante Gregorio had them offload the boxes, placing them into the pits. He sighed deeply as they filled in the holes. Clearly, he was tired of the strain of watching over it all. Now it would be as secure as he could make it. When they were through, he simply waved his hand.

"Come," was all he said, and they walked back to camp.

The relief Claudio felt was immeasurable. The Comandante was only worried about his gold. Claudio would gladly give twice that fortune to be headed home to Spain. Now he knew why he had been instructed to choose men who were going inland with them. They would not be left behind with the knowledge of where the hoard was interred. If anything happened to it while they were away, the suspicion would fall on Diego, the only other man who saw them leave with the treasure, who saw where they went.

***

It took the company of fifteen only a short time to arm themselves and collect their meager belongings. Some were barefoot; some carried their shoes to save the leather. If the worst came, they could eat them.

Unlike the seamen and *soldados*, Claudio had never developed the thick soles of a deckhand. He had no stockings, but wore his shoes with moss as a cushion under his feet. Several of the men had no shirts, being unwilling to strip the corpses of their drowned comrades before burial. Claudio did have a long-sleeved shirt, even though it was becoming somewhat tattered. He had also made himself a head cloth, in the manner of the Arab traders he had seen in his youth. It covered his neck, shielding it from the tropical sun. In a small mesh net made from unwinding the strands of a halyard line, Claudio carried the journal in its *funda*, secreting his small dirk inside, arming himself with a longer stiletto. Slung over his shoulder with an extra piece of rope, it was no trouble to carry a few biscuits and a small pouch of gunpowder for starting a fire should they find a stone hard enough to strike sparks.

Showered with cries of *"Vaya con Dios"* and *"Que Dios te guarde,"* they marched out of camp with Comandante Gregorio at the head of their ragged column. He led them along the beach to a spot barely two hundred paces from their small fortification before heading into the trackless forest. The ground was firm here under the desiccated leaves of short palm trees and a carpet of needles from the twisted red cedars. It reminded Claudio greatly of the Mediterranean coast.

Trekking through the woodland was easy enough and they made steady progress. Here and there, tall oaks had colonized the sandy floor and made the shady canopy complete. There was little conversation. The entire group was both entranced by the place and vigilant on every side. To some, including Claudio, the mixture of light and shadow on stumps and in thickets became the silhouettes of *salvajes,* intent on murder, yet the utter stillness of the place remained intact. Only their footfalls and the strange cries of unseen fowl came back to them.

Just before breaking into a clearing, a loud series of thrashing noises made them freeze in their tracks. Claudio became aware of his heartbeat pounding in his temples. Momentarily, a startled peccary ripped from the underbrush, running away faster than any man in the company could follow.

"Run away, pig!" someone said in a loud voice. "Or you will become a *jamón ibérico!*"

Several others laughed, and it made their mouth water for the prized hams of the old country.

"I can smell it now," exclaimed another, licking his lips.

"Aye, what a *barbacoa* we could have made."

But they had no fire and no pig.

Comandante Gregorio waved them all forward to an opening in the trees, but the clearing turned out to be a vast marsh almost a quarter league across. Without hesitation, he plunged into the waist-deep reeds, hacking a path with his sword. Following in his wake, the company walked single file out onto the broad savannah. Buoyed by the thick roots of the coarse grass, their footing seemed somewhat easier than Claudio expected. The occasional patches of bare sandy muck were not deep, and the small pools of standing water were easily avoided. The worst misery by far was the clouds of blood-sucking insects that swarmed them mercilessly. Biting gnats and large horseflies joined countless mosquitoes in attacking every inch of exposed skin. The sound of buzzing in their ears was all but deafening. Some of the men stopped to smear themselves with the fetid mud in an effort to disguise their scent, but to no avail.

A commotion in the middle of the column, followed by a scream of pain brought them all to a halt again. Comandante Gregorio backtracked to where one of the men lay in agony on the ground.

"¿Qué es?" he demanded.

"Raoul has been bitten by an asp, señor," a shipmate spoke up. Several others helped the wounded marinero to his feet. He was favoring his right leg and was clearly shaken. Blood oozed from a double puncture mark on his calf.

"Where is the serpent?" Comandante Gregorio wanted to make sure it would not strike again.

"I killed it," another man answered, indicating the halberd he was carrying.

The Comandante inhaled deeply, then expelled the air forcefully, as if trying to rid himself of the tension they all felt.

"Come," he ordered, looking at the horizon. "We are nearly onto dry land. We will stop there and do what we can."

As they passed the body of the beheaded snake, each man seemed to step slightly faster. Perhaps he was not entirely dead. Claudio paused to examine the carcass, still slowly writhing. The creature was almost as long as a man's outstretched arms, thick bodied and colored a deep cocoa brown. It must be in the same lineage as the vipers that infested Andalusia. They had similar patterns on their body and a lethal bite. Offering up a silent prayer for the marinero, he made the sign of the cross and moved on.

Once on higher ground, Raoul was laid down in the sedge. The man was now shaking as if in a fit, his breath shallow and rapid. Using the sharpest blade they had, Comandante Gregorio slashed the wound to bleed him. Claudio softly murmured the words to an old folk song. His voice hinted at a melody, expressed such that it sounded like a distant memory.

"¡*Saltar y baylar con voces y grita*! We deny you damned snake! The Blessed Virgin will make you dance to the music."

Part of a traditional Spanish rite from centuries past meant to exorcise El Diablo, the practice was frequently adapted to ask for God's intercession for menacing serpents and snakebite victims. Claudio fervently hoped it would save Raoul.

"I need some cloth to make a bandage," Comandante Gregorio spoke with some urgency.

Claudio stepped forward, ripped the sleeves from his shirt, and handed them to him. Wrapping the wound snugly, the cloth was tied as tightly as the worn material would allow. It took just a few seconds for a spot the color of claret to appear, increasing in size with every heartbeat. The venom had already begun to break down muscle and blood vessels. The man gradually turned ghostly pale, a cold sweat glistening on his face. His skin seemed almost transparent.

"*In nomine Patris, et Filii, et Spiritus Sancti*," Claudio whispered.

A blank stare came into Raoul's eyes, followed by the death rattle. He was gone.

A *soldado* reached down and shut the dead man's eyes, making the sign of the cross on his own chest. The semicircle of men surrounding the body prayed without making a sound, only their lips betraying their act.

"Let us go," Comandante Gregorio ordered, breaking the spell. "Take from him his rations and weapon."

Raoul had been one of those *marineros* without shoes. The tiny store of food he carried was inconsequential. Not nearly enough to overcome the abhorrent thought of stealing from the dead.

"Can we not give him a Christian burial, *señor*?" Claudio was again appalled by his commanding officer's lack of sensitivity.

"We don't have the time," Comandante Gregorio responded. "We cannot stay here." He started to walk away, but realized no one else had moved. Turning to glare at them one by one, he finally relented.

"Do it quickly."

Digging a shallow repository in the muddy ground near the edge of the marsh became a group effort. They had no implements, so they clawed at the earth with their bare hands. They layered the gravesite, just deep enough to temporarily conceal the corpse, with driftwood in hopes of at least deterring smaller scavengers. Speaking his name aloud for the last time in their supplication to the Virgin Maria, the men slowly moved off, following their impatient leader.

They had not walked far before they encountered a small rivulet of tea-colored water. Frustratingly, it was both brackish and foul-smelling, unfit to drink. When they traced the tiny creek to its source, it appeared to be nothing more than a natural drainage at the foot of a hammock of pines. As they passed into the forest, Claudio made sure he collected bits of the loose bark that bore smears of pitch, useful in making fire when all else was wet.

Innumerable small waterways blocked their progress, and the Comandante was determined to avoid them, knowing that the murky streams often harbored alligators, larger and more aggressive than similar lizards in Cuba. Where these watersheds occurred, the forest disintegrated into vast oases of several types of palms. Tall and stately, a few resembled the coconut palms of Hispaniola with their relatively smooth gray boles and long fronds. More common were stocky types, shorter and possessing deeply notched trunks. They were greatly similar in form to date palms, which were also numerous. The group carefully scrutinized all that they came across, but the season for fruit had come and gone. All that remained were desiccated stalks.

By now, they were surely in the realm of the Timucuan Potanos, thought Claudio. Recent accounts had said that in this province alone the *indios* could muster an army of several thousand. Soon, he found that anxiety had begun to supplant his weariness. The further inland they trekked, the more he felt as if unseen eyes were watching them. He wondered if Yaotl was out there somewhere.

Where the ground was higher, they walked beneath scraggly short-limbed oaks, huge tracts of pine, and bay laurel. When traversing the low areas, the trees switched to sumacs, white maples, and a variety of cedars. Other than rodents and an ever-changing cast of birds, not another living thing showed itself.

After half an hour, the company came in sight of a pond, and they rushed to its grassy banks.

"¡Es fresco! ¡Agua dulce!" someone shouted. Every man pushed their way in, then drank like cattle at a waterhole.

Claudio knelt by the water's edge and lifted his hands to the sky.

"Gracias, Sante Madre."

As he filled his belly with water to the bursting point, he heard someone call alarm.

"Look out! Alligator!"

Claudio sat up and looked around to find it. An adolescent alligator some four feet long was cruising by, glaring at the intruders who trespassed in his territory. Some of the men threw rocks and sticks at it until it disdainfully submerged and swam away.

He had seen several kinds of these lizards in the new world. In Cuba, the crocodiles were short, fat, and heavy with a narrow snout. This one was more like the kind he had seen in New Spain, exhibiting a flat shovel-nose snout and greater length. Even a young animal could inflict severe wounds. Claudio had heard stories that adults could eat a man whole. If these creatures were lurking in the pond, it would not be a safe place to camp. Evidently, Comandante Gregorio came to the same conclusion. He ordered everyone on their feet, pushing further into the unknown.

12
~~Sink Creek, Florida~~
June 16, 1959

The *Dreamboat* left camp before sunrise, cruising quietly to the mouth of the small creek. At slack tide, the water ahead lay glassy and still under the glare of the searchlight. The gentle bow wake rolled over the muddy banks, scattering a host of fiddler crabs like a living echo of the wave. As the boat passed by, mullet jumped clear of the water, as if they were being pursued. Bill was in the galley making coffee, the rich scent teasing the rest of the crew huddled in the cockpit.

"Isn't that mud ready yet?" Ben called inside. He could hear Bill bitching below, but couldn't make out the words. Just as well.

"What's the game plan, Lonnie?"

"Lucky wants us to check out the west side of Pepperfish Key then move on towards Horseshoe Beach."

"Gettin' close to my home."

"Where's that?"

"Cedar Key. I could've saved everybody the trouble of coming to get me."

Exiting into the deeper waters of the Gulf, Lonnie kicked up the engine a bit. A false dawn brightened the sky slightly, enough to detect darker shapes and shadows from the blue twilight that surrounded them. Twenty minutes later, the first small sliver of golden sunlight emerged from the eastern horizon. They could already begin to feel the radiant heat.

"Gonna be a hot one," Bill opined as he handed up three porcelain cups of black coffee.

Dan shuddered as he sipped his. This was Navy coffee, strong enough to resurrect the dead.

By the time the magnetometer was in the water, Ben was bored already. While Dan was stuck with buoy duty, Ben slipped below and stood by Bill.

Engrossed in his monitoring, Bill spoke out of the side of his mouth. "Sit down, willya? You make me nervous looking over my shoulder like that."

Ben turned a dinette chair the wrong way round and plopped down. "Dollah."

"Yeah?"

"If we find something, I mean something big, you think we're gonna get cut out?"

"You on that kick again?"

Ben sat quietly for a minute, resting his chin on his crossed arms.

"This Noble Fischer guy, he's a real silent partner. What if we find something and Duprez doesn't tell him about it? It'd be a bigger cut for him. Maybe he's interested in taking all of it."

Bill glanced at him. "You're getting suspicious in your old age. Where's he gonna go? Somebody's bound to find out about it."

"He was in military intelligence. He's probably got contacts."

"You're forgetting about us."

"There are ways of making sure a man doesn't talk."

Bill looked at him sideways again. For the first time, Ben had gotten through to him.

Ben shrugged his shoulders and went back on deck to relieve Dan.

In the middle of the afternoon, Lonnie noticed a squall moving in from the west. Ben was so tired of doing nothing that anything was a welcome distraction. They were almost finished with the third and final pass off Bowlegs Point, so Bill had them leave the magnetometer in the water until the last minute. As they hauled it aboard, Ben watched the anvil-shaped thunderhead come closer and grow blacker. Long tendrils of rain were sweeping down and raking the Gulf not far away. He could smell the sweet scent of the storm. Cloud to cloud lightning played hide and seek in the boiling cumulus. Like an aerial Portuguese man-o-war, the thing moved toward them, ever more menacing. Finally, the first shotgun blast of droplets rattled the boat.

"I'm gonna see if I can run out from under this weather," Lonnie announced, pushing the throttle and the engine to full speed. The seas had become choppy with the rising wind, causing the boat to bounce as it cut through the water. Fifteen minutes at twenty-four knots got them out of the worst of it. Lonnie slacked off the throttle, relaxing a bit.

"That oughta do it."

Lonnie barely got a cigarette lit before he heard Dan curse.

"Ah shit! Waterspout!"

"Jesus, Joseph, and Mary," Lonnie invoked the Holy Family.

The waterspout seemed to have a mind of its own, traveling independently of the prevailing winds. It headed right for the *Dreamboat*. As Lonnie tried to shove the throttle back to full, the engine died in response.

"Gotta go, Lonnie." Ben watched the vortex of white water snaking after them, like the probing finger of a blind sea hag feeling for them.

"Gotta go now!"

Lonnie tried to crank the engine to life, taking several long and precious seconds to get it running again. They could hear the cyclone roar and sizzle it was so close.

"Thirty yards and closing." Ben called, backing up toward the cabin hatch. Lonnie took a tight grip on the wheel, trying desperately to outmaneuver it. The engines were straining, but they didn't seem to be making headway. It felt like the waterspout was sucking them backwards into its grasp.

"Brace for impact!"

Just before the whirlwind threatened to rip the stern from the boat, it abruptly dissipated. A heavy deluge of water dropped on them, no longer held aloft by the tornadic force. It was as if several fire hoses had been trained on them momentarily. Free of any restraints, the *Dreamboat* immediately shot forward until Lonnie shifted into neutral.

Not knowing what else to do, Dan broke into a nervous laugh.

"Well, kiss my foot," Ben responded, wiping the water from his face.

"Yeah, we came within a cat's ass of buyin' the farm this time," Lonnie drawled, still shaken.

Bill stuck his head out of the companionway. "Everybody all right? Any damage?"

"Everything's okay, I think." Ben nodded. "I might have wet my pants."

Bill smiled. "How 'bout some fresh coffee?"

Behind his back, Dan mumbled, "Haven't we been through enough this afternoon?"

"Mafungadoo, Hamster. Just for that, you make it."

Lonnie was on the radio with Duprez, explaining to him what had just happened.

"There may be some damage to the engine. I'm going to put in to Horseshoe Beach and have it checked out. Over."

"You can bring it back here. Jimbo's a pretty good mechanic. Over."

Duprez was clearly not comfortable with the idea of having the boat at a public marina.

"Negative. We may need parts. I say again, we're putting in at Horseshoe Beach. Over."

This time there was a minute or two of empty air. "Understood. Keep me advised. Over."

"Roger. Over and out."

Lonnie turned to Ben. "He didn't like that at all, did he?"

"It's a good call, though. We can pick up some supplies while we're there."

"Just so we can say we did, let's throw a tarp over that thing." Lonnie pointed to the magnetometer. "We don't need any sightseers."

It only took about three-quarters of an hour to reach the harbor at Horseshoe Beach. Lonnie went immediately to the harbormaster in search of a mechanic. Bill stayed behind to watch the boat while Ben and Dan went ashore.

"Ah, liberty call," sighed Dan, grinning from ear to ear in his best hamster smile.

Ben was intimately familiar with the town since it was only twenty-five miles from his home in Cedar Key.

"And this liberty calls for a cold beer," he responded. "Or two."

The town of Horseshoe Beach was really a hamlet, smaller than Cedar Key if that was possible. Home to about a hundred people, you could run Sixth Avenue from end to end and not be short of breath. Often, the middle of town didn't have any traffic beyond the occasional truck delivering ice. The place had always been a fishing village and was another place time had forgotten. It hadn't changed since the 1930s. The crab shacks and the fish markets near the marina looked like they would fall apart with the first high wind, but there they stood.

Ben picked a beer joint named Sal's Place, and they wandered through the screen door. It was a thoroughly disreputable joint, inside and out, in short, the kind of place the three of them used to haunt back in their Navy days. There were no glasses or jukebox, just bottled beer and a busted radio behind the counter.

A rather large, swarthy man brought them two brews.

"Hey, where's Sally?" Dan asked cheerfully.

Ben winced.

"That's me," the big man replied without a trace of humor. "I'm Salvadore."

Dan nodded his head. "Sally." Quiet now, he waited for the man to move off.

Ben punched his buddy in the arm, and Dan mugged a, "How was I supposed to know," face.

"So whattaya think about all this?"

"The job? I can handle it okay. Just as long as the paymaster's window is open when I get there, it's all right with me."

"I heard you were doing pretty good. Bill said you had it made now."

Dan made a buzzing sound with his lips.

"Got a great family. I own my own business, but it's not always that good."

"Yeah, how's married life treating ya? Your wife..., what's her name?"

"Cindy. Got a sweet little two-year-old we named Katie."

Dan decided to spill the beans about the pregnancy since it was just the two of them.

"I got another one on the way."

Ben's beer bottle stopped halfway to his mouth.

"No kiddin'! Congratulations, buddy!"

"Yeah, I'll have the whole nine yards then—a wife, two kids, a dog, and a house with a white picket fence around it."

"You make it sound like it's a bad thing."

"Nah. Sometimes I wonder where the years go. Cindy and I used to have some great times when we first got married."

"You'll grow into it, Pops." Ben clapped his friend on the back. Dan just closed his eyes and shook his head.

"This calls for another round." Ben tapped his empty bottle on the bar. "Beerkeeper, two more! My friend is having a baby!"

"Don't mention this to Bill or anybody else. They'll wear me out with the Daddy jokes."

"Who me?" Ben fluttered his eyes innocently.

"Don't make me poke you in the nose."

***

It was twilight when the two headed back to the boat. Ben noticed a familiar figure coming toward them.

"Oh, shit. Here comes Bill. He's going to put us on report for being AWOL."

"Where in sam hell have you two been?" demanded Bill in his Petty Officer tone of voice.

Shifting the boxes they carried under one arm, the pair saluted.

Dan was a bit wobbly. "How'd you find us?" His words came out thick and slurred.

"It wasn't hard to follow your wake." Bill looked closely at Dan. "Are you drunk?"

"Almost, sir. We ran outta money." Dan exploded into giggles.

Bill sighed. "You were supposed to be getting supplies."

"We did," Ben protested. "We got coffee and cigarettes, some pogey bait for Dan, some Vienna sausages and crackers."

"Yeah," Dan added. "And I got summa this for ev'rybody." He held up a grease-stained sack with the unmistakable smell of something deep-fried.

Bill opened the sack. "What? Hushpuppies?"

Dan snatched the bag back. "You dope. They're *bollos*."

"Oh. Cuban hushpuppies."

Dan tried to make a raspberry sound, but his lips wouldn't cooperate.

"Aaaand, I got this to go with 'em." He waved a packet wrapped in white butcher paper.

"Boiled shrimp." Bill sniffed the package without any prompting. "What else you got in there?"

Dan hugged the box closer to his chest and smiled another classic Hamster Dan grin. "Beer," he said in a stage whisper, breaking into a fit of giggles again.

***

The *Dreamboat* cast off in the dark and Lonnie slowly guided her out to sea. Bill radioed Duprez to update him on the condition of the boat and their intention to anchor just offshore to escape prying eyes. The cruiser's engines had checked out okay, apparently unaffected by their encounter with the waterspout. Finally, about a mile south of Horseshoe Beach, they dropped anchor and settled in for the night.

Dan had gotten nearly as boiled as the shrimp and collapsed into his bunk early. While Bill and Lonnie planned the search area for the next day, Ben went up on deck for a look around.

The lights of the small town they had just left were still visible on the horizon. He couldn't see the beacons further south marking several shoals near Cedar Key, but he knew they were there. It was funny that he had traveled all this way, only to come back to where he started. Lighting a cigar, he searched the sky for the constellations he recognized, but only the brightest stars shone through a light haze. Remnants of rain clouds drifted by overhead further obscuring the view.

In the Navy, he had never had to stand watch. There were a lot of things he never had to do. As salvage divers, they seldom ventured out of dry dock. The damaged tankers and Liberty ships they worked on had generally been towed in by tugs or had managed to limp home under their own power. Ben knew he had been lucky in his assignment, but a small sense of regret gnawed at him. Over the years, his sense of remorse worsened while he remained safe on land as others went to sea, fought, and died. He had no death wish, only a case of survivor's guilt.

***

It was hours later as he rolled in his bunk, chasing a comfortable position and the sleep it would bring, when he heard the first small sounds indicating they might not be alone. Holding his breath, he listened again. From his quarters under the bow of the boat, it almost sounded like bare feet moving around slowly, cautiously across the deck above. He exhaled and waited. When the noise began again, it seemed to come from the wheelhouse. Quietly, he slipped from his rack and eased into the main cabin. Glancing over at Dan, he briefly studied his friend's face, contorted into a mask of confusion. Clearly, he was in deep sleep, wrestling with a dream.

The noise stopped. Ben crept up the companionway onto the back deck, half-expecting someone to be standing there. There was nothing, no one. He peered into the black water starboard and port, looking for a floating log, a rogue wave pattern, a wake, anything that might explain what he had heard. The Gulf was calm, almost glassy. The haze around them had lowered and thickened, presaging fog by morning. His curiosity temporarily satisfied, Ben went below to resume his search for sleep.

***

At daybreak, the crew stirred, making ready for the work ahead. A moderate fog bank had indeed settled around the *Dreamboat*, turning the usual golden hues of sunrise into a drab palette consisting mostly of gray tones and indistinct outlines. Dan, looking like he had been dropped from a high place onto rough pavement, stumbled toward the galley to claim a cup of coffee.

"What a weird dream." No one responded, and more importantly, no one stopped him, so he continued.

"There was this face that came out of the darkness, looked like an Indian. He had kind of a big nose and long hair, all piled on top of his head. He had more tattoos on his face than a barracks fulla bosun's mates."

"Sounds like my ex-wife's mother," Lonnie drawled, stirring sugar into his coffee with loud clinking noises.

"He had the darkest eyes, all black." Dan was not about to stop now until he finished his story.

"He starts talking to me, but I can't understand him at first. Finally, I can make out a couple of words. He's saying go. Leave this place."

"Now what are we supposed to do with that?" Bill asked.

"I dunno. It was just a dream."

"Sounds like you got hold of some bad shrimp, Danny boy."

Ben kept quiet about the noises he heard during the night. It would either encourage Dan's imagination or draw Bill's sarcasm or both. Blowing away the steam rising from his coffee mug, he sipped the brew gingerly, trying to avoid burning the roof of his mouth.

It took more than an hour for the haze around them to burn off. When they were ready to get underway, Ben climbed out onto the foredeck to pull up the anchor. His heart jumped into his throat for a minute or two as he spotted a trail of damp, muddy prints leading from the bow to the cabin. They were in fact footprints. Whoever left this trail was not wearing shoes. Questions flooded his mind as he continued to pull on the anchor rope. How did they get there? How did they find the boat? Where did they go? The footprints stopped at the wheelhouse. Did they get into the cabin? As his brain tried to find answers, he wondered if Dan had not been dreaming, but actually saw someone.

13
~~En el Interior de la Florida~~
5 Octubre 1523

Every hour the sun dropped lower on the horizon increased Claudio's anxiety. The forest was no place to stop for the night, there was too much cover. The chance of an ambush by the Potanos or an attack by wild animals seemed far more likely within the tangled palmetto thickets than if they could find a place in the open to rest. Without any means to make a fire, they would be blind and vulnerable under a new moon. With luck, they might still be able to detect shadows, things darker than the night, moving across a clearing.

A few hundred paces from the waterhole, they came to a spot where the woods were bounded on either side by barren areas of rust-colored sand. Claudio's worry was finally allayed when Comandante Gregorio signaled a halt. The leafy canopy of this sparse strip of oaks would shelter them from unexpected rain while leaving an approach on either flank conspicuous. Claudio claimed a spot between two large exposed roots of a tree, and with the last orange light of sunset, he backtracked to the edge of the forest to gather an armload of fragrant pine needles. Having made himself a crude nest like the bedding of some caprine animal in a stable, he lay down to watch the soft blues and grays of twilight reveal themselves. He would much rather be sleeping in a goat shed than out here subject to nature's whims.

Self-absorbed in his despondence, Claudio hardly acknowledged a *marinero* who decided to sleep close by. It was not until he spoke that Claudio's eyes fluttered.

"*¿Como se llama?*" the man asked.

"I am Claudio, Claudio Hernandez."

"Ah, the midshipman.... They call me Eduardo. I was an able seaman. Now I am probably a dead man."

"It does you no good to think that way," Claudio admonished him. "God will deliver us."

"*La Santa Madre* has turned her back on me, on all of us. I pray hourly to Santo Jude that he will intercede." The man was interrupted by a rheumy cough.

Claudio seized the moment to change the subject.

"How long have you been at sea?"

Eduardo snorted.

"I was born a *marinero*. I was a fisherman at ten and sailed on caravels to África and the Canary Islands when I was but fifteen."

"You must have made a great deal of money."

"Aha!" the man laughed. "I have made *mucho dinero*, but sadly, I spent it all. That's it. You have it, then you spend it, and it's gone. I tell you, I was not meant to be a wealthy *hombre*."

"Don't you miss your *familia*?"

"My father drowned in a gale off Sicily many years ago." Eduardo's voice dropped several decibels. "My mother died of grief soon after."

"I am sorry for your loss."

There was an interlude of quiet long enough that Claudio thought the man had gone to sleep before he spoke again.

"What of you, *señor*? Do you still have *familia*?"

Claudio smiled in the darkness.

"*Si*. My *madre* and *padre* wait for me in Andalusia. I have not seen them in many months."

"Tell me about them, *por favor*."

"My *padre* is a professor at the university in Madrid. He is very smart and very patient. I learned everything from him. My *madre* always stayed home to look after us when we were *niños*. Now she has a garden to care for. I'm sure it is an easier task than raising us."

"And your sisters and brothers?"

"I have a sister, *muy bonita*. She is a musician, plays the lute, and sings. She has even played in the court of Carlos Rey."

"No *hermanos*?"

"I am the only son."

Another silence followed.

"You have had a very good life so far, *señor*. I pray it does not end here in this wretched place."

Claudio tried for hours to sleep, but eventually resigned himself to just watching the stars wheel around overhead. Between the whine of mosquitoes and Eduardo's snoring, any meaningful rest was impossible. Intermittently, he was startled by a sound in the forest. Every snapping twig in the dark could mean imminent murder. After a time, he began to recognize the noises of meandering raccoons, the creature the *indios* called *aracun*. Their soft chittering was punctuated by the scratching of claws and the thrashing of branches as they sought acorns in the oaks. Not far off, the calls of owls and other night raptors seemed by turns mournful and frightening. The night was endless, with time protracted as if in a bad dream.

***

The return of the light was celebrated almost as joyously as Easter morning. Survival was a double-edged sword, though. It was another chance to renew the hope they would be rescued. It would also be another day of privation and tension. Claudio had noticed his urine turning darker from dehydration and unintentional fasting. The entire company was suffering from the effects of exposure. Lesions had begun to erupt due to malnourishment. To make matters worse, some of the men were showing signs of dysentery. No doubt, this would soon lead to cholera, which might afflict them all. The specter of ague was ever-present, especially inland, away from the coastal breezes. To many, death was not the worst that a man might face, but rather the continuous slow torture of this green, living hell. Torquemada himself could not invent a device that so completely removed a man's will to endure.

Allowing a stale, hardened biscuit to dissolve in his mouth, Claudio painfully got to his feet and leaned against the tree for support. With no food and no fire, it was not long before the Comandante called for them to move on. Emptying the sand and twigs from his disintegrating shoes, he noticed the blisters on the sides of his feet had broken, blistered again, and then dried to a scaly white covering of dead skin. His stomach burned with hunger as if he had swallowed a live coal. Gradually, he realized that he too was losing the resolve to continue. As the column filed off into the forest, he reluctantly retrieved his stiletto and joined them.

As they advanced further, the marsh was replaced by thick jungle. Hourly, the trees thinned and the ground grew firmer until the jungle became woodlands. The smell of salt air was gone, replaced by the sweet spices of black earth and pine. Comandante Gregorio was leading them north by east, guided by the sun and a design only he and God were privy to. Driven by determination, his command was still not to be challenged, even now. They followed because he led, without question, as they had been trained to do. Even so, men collapsed as they walked, exhausted by privation and exertion only to be lifted to their feet once more.

By noon, they had made but two leagues and with the sun directly overhead, it was almost impossible to determine in which direction they were heading. Stopping in a small pine hammock, the company collapsed into the soft, sweet-scented needles, with many gasping for breath as if they had run the entire distance. A few crawled on all fours, eating the winged seeds embedded in open cones on the ground. Most fell into the sleep that only exhaustion brings. His hair plastered into ringlets with sweat, Claudio settled down beside Comandante Gregorio who was trying to comb his unkempt beard with his fingers.

"How much farther, *señor*?"

"As far as we must."

***

Comandante Gregorio remained undisturbed by the fact that he had no idea where they were and only a vague notion of how far they had actually marched. Accustomed to having native guides, he knew just the general direction from which they had come. Coupled with the fact that he knew next to nothing about the country, the company had been fortunate so far that it had not stumbled onto hostile *indios*. Having heard accounts from Ponce de Leon of a Potano pueblo that was called

Puturiba somewhere in the region, Gregorio had originally thought to raid the fields and stores of the inhabitants.

Sensing a bit of the Comandante's indecision, Claudio dared press him again. "If we encounter *salvajes* now, the men are too weak to fight."

"*Si, es verdad.*" The Comandante responded as if it were the first time he had considered it.

Claudio struggled wearily to his feet. "With your permission," he excused himself. If pushed, Comandante Gregorio would simply become more obstinate. If they were to turn around now, he needed to think it was not only a good strategic decision, but also his own idea.

Stretching out on the ground near Eduardo, Claudio sighed deeply.

"He will not go back." Eduardo seemed to be able to read his thoughts.

"Not yet," agreed Claudio.

"Ah, if we were still on the beach, we might have fish and cool breezes."

"But they have no water."

"Neither do we at the moment. And they have a better chance of being rescued. No one will find us here."

Claudio had no response. The logic was harsh, but it was the truth. "*Bueno,* we are where we are," he said finally.

14
~~Horseshoe Cove, Florida~~
June 17, 1959

The early morning haze cleared to reveal another postcard-perfect day. Carefully trolling the shallow waters of Horseshoe Cove, the *Dreamboat* seemed to move in slow motion. Ben fought off drowsiness as he worked on the second half of a cigar. He began to think that Dan was right. Even if the money was good, this was boring as hell. There was more action on a tugboat.

Lonnie put the helm over, making a wide circle to starboard to avoid a sandbar in the way that lay barely submerged. As the magnetometer trailed them in the slough of the bar, Bill called from below.

"Mark!"

Dan tossed the buoy, watching to see how far it drifted from the splash of the weight. A longer drift meant shallow water.

"Only about ten feet there," he called to Ben.

"Mark." Bill's voice was louder this time. Another weight and another buoy went out. It was still shallow water.

"Mark!" Bill's voice was becoming intense. Twenty yards later, he yelled again.

"Mark! Lonnie, shut it down and drop anchor." Coming up on deck, he was grinning as if he had just won big in a crap game.

"Boys, I think we hit the jackpot. Get over the side and see what's down there."

***

The visibility underwater was good, maybe thirty feet. Ben and Dan followed the markers in snorkel gear, scanning the white sandy bottom for anything that didn't belong there. It didn't take but a few minutes to spot a large, iron-colored projection. The large fluke of an old style anchor protruded from its shroud of barnacles. The rest lay buried deep in the sand. The next buoy had landed just two yards from the unmistakable shape of a small bore cannon, possibly an eighteenth-century deck gun.

"Ya think this is what we've been looking for?" spluttered Dan when he came up for a good lung-full of air.

Ben pulled his mask up onto his forehead.

"Looks like it could be. I'm no expert, but guns like that weren't used after the seventeen hundreds."

Hamster Dan was back again.

"Arrr, matey." He grinned. "Let's go see what else we got."

Slipping under the surface again, the two kicked toward the final spot Bill had gotten so excited about. It turned out to be a pile of ten-or-twelve-pound, cast-iron shot and a pair of larger guns, one lying across the other. The swimmers surfaced again.

"X marks the spot, me hearty!"

"Maybe." Ben wanted to err on the side of caution. "I can see why Bill was so excited. This must have shown up as a hell of a blip."

Whatever it was down there had been big for its time. No doubt there was more buried on the bottom, maybe something that might tell them what and when. Guns like that were never jettisoned. They had to come from a sunken vessel and a long time ago. This was no cargo schooner or island hopper. It was also not from this century.

Back on board the *Dreamboat*, Bill was having an animated discussion over the radio with Lucky.

"I say again, believe objective located. Waiting for identification to be confirmed. Over."

"Understood. Do you have the coordinates?" Duprez's voice sounded scratchy through the speaker.

"Will transmit by secure channel frequency. Unable to recover multiple targets without assistance. Over"

"Roger. Will expedite assistance."

"Changing frequencies. Over and out."

***

Ben and Dan took advantage of the rest of the day to scavenge the site, looking for clues as to exactly what they had stumbled across. Slowly, their trove on deck grew until it included a small gold crucifix without a chain, a fifty-five caliber musket ball, a small pewter tankard, and the top half of a handmade pottery crock. Conspicuously missing were gold coins and silver bars or anything like the treasure they had hoped to find. Whatever secret this wreck had kept for centuries was still on the bottom.

About an hour before sunset, Lonnie spotted a small launch approaching. He recognized one of the two men aboard. "Bill, Duprez is coming alongside."

Every member of the crew gathered on the back deck, curious to hear what Lucky had to say.

Lonnie murmured, "That man has never once set foot on board this boat since the beginning. It must be a big deal."

Ben surveyed the other man with him. Portly and pale, the baby-faced man wore a pin-striped suit, including a vest. The heat had made him remove his coat, which lay carefully folded over his knees. The Homburg on his head seemed to be glued on. As they helped him up the ladder on the *Dreamboat's* stern, Ben wondered how it had stayed put during the boat ride. Duprez ushered the visitor below where the artifacts had been spread out on the table next to a nautical chart of the area.

After everyone found a spot in the cabin, the stranger finally removed his hat.

"Good afternoon, gentlemen. My name is Noble Fischer."

Bill shot Ben a glance that could have meant anything.

"I understood you found something," the man in the suit went on, settling himself into a chair. "Tell me what we have."

Bill cleared his throat and pointed out the cabin window.

"What we think we have is a warship that sank sometime before eighteen hundred. Once we get the cannon up, we might be able to determine the country of origin and the era."

"Mr. Duprez assured me he will have a barge out here in the morning with a crane and dredging equipment. I have an expert in maritime history waiting in Tampa to examine those guns."

Fischer casually looked over the other finds displayed. Rolling the small piece of lead shot, he took a long deep breath.

"If we can establish with reasonable certainty that the wreck is a sixteenth-century Spanish frigate, then I believe we have located the *Mano del Rey*. As you probably already know, the *Mano del Rey* left New Spain in August of 1523 bound for Havana. She never made it."

Fischer stroked a fine, wispy mustache, obviously savoring the moment.

"Apparently, the ship went down in a hurricane. One of the survivors kept a journal. You probably also know by now that I have an authenticated, first edition copy. Claudio Hernandez relates that while shipwrecked on the shore about a hundred yards from the ship, they established a small garrison and buried most of the treasure they had carried. Now you understand why we need to verify that this is the site where the *Mano del Rey* foundered. Good work, gentlemen. I appreciate your diligence and persistence." Fischer mopped his brow and replaced his hat. "Mr. Duprez, if you please."

The mismatched pair exited the cabin, spending several awkward minutes trying to get the man in the suit back onto the smaller boat without one of them falling overboard.

Dan was the first to break the rapt silence with a long whistle, expressing his amazement.

Lonnie watched the launch as it returned to shore. "That's a queer duck," he observed as Bill came up.

"As long as his check doesn't bounce, it's all the same to me," Bill muttered.

"You think he was on the level?" Ben's voice came from the companionway.

"Maybe. Duprez wouldn't go to all the trouble to make up a dog and pony show for a fifteen-minute debriefing."

"I guess."

"I can't help but get the feeling we still don't have the whole story," Bill mused.

"I told you!" Ben gestured with his finger.
"Yeah, you were right. Something's missing."

***

The barge showed up the next morning, a rusted hulk with hoses for dredging and a squatty crane. It wasn't pretty, but it ought to work. Everything was rigged by noon when the diver-down pennant was planted on the *Dreamboat*'s bow. Using tanks on this dive, Ben and Dan carefully worked a web sling under and around the smaller cannon. About six and a half feet long, it was totally crusted over with barnacles. It would take a while to get it clean enough to see any kind of markings.

The larger guns were more problematic. Their center of gravity was hard to gauge. As they worked the sling under the topmost cannon, they startled a large green moray from its home in the barrel. Fortunately, it decided to leave rather than defend its territory. It took almost an hour to get both pieces onto the barge. Ben was happy Duprez had told them to leave the anchor and the iron shot on the bottom. The silt was already beginning to cloud the site, making an underwater haze around them.

By mid-afternoon, the work changed from recovery to exploration. Dan coupled up the dredging hose with the venturi set so that the intake of sand and water from the bottom would be slow and gentle. Ben worked the bottom in grids, a habit from Navy recovery jobs when they had to locate unexploded ordinance. Gradually, more bits and pieces of detritus revealed themselves. A pewter spoon, bits of block and stays, a decaying dagger, and an empty green bottle all spoke silently about life aboard the ship.

The minutes ticked away too quickly and soon Dan swam into view. With hand gestures made familiar by dozens of dives together, he indicated Ben's air would run out soon. Ben passed the hose to his partner and checked his tank indicator. As he turned to surface, he noticed the current was pushing the sand cloud from the dredge directly toward them, dropping visibility to about ten feet. As he turned to let his partner know what was happening, an ominous shadowy outline emerged from the murk. A big, male bull shark cruised by in a pass that was too close for comfort. Ben tapped Dan's forearm to alert him the neighborhood had just gone to hell. Even with two sets of eyes peering through the cloudy water, they saw nothing, as if a phantom had just appeared and then dissipated.

Dan made the okay sign and went back to work. Suddenly, the predator was back, barreling in so fast his nose knocked Ben aside. Terrified, Ben watched as the shark grabbed the back of Dan's leg and shook him violently. Blood immediately blossomed out into the water. As Dan flailed in the shark's grip, Ben tried to stab it anywhere he could. After a minute that seemed like hours, the shark let go and moved off. Dan's body drifted to the bottom. Grabbing his friend's tank harness, Ben cut him free and pulled his body to the surface.

"Gimme a hand!" he shouted to the deck crew on the barge. They had already seen the tell-tale dorsal fin and were lining the rails, anxious to get them both out of the water. As Dan was laid out on the deck, his leg continued to spurt blood like a water fountain.

"Jesus," one of the deck hands muttered.

The shark left a ragged tear in Dan's left leg, ripping out most of his calf muscle.

"Get a tourniquet on him! Move!" Ben was frantic. They weren't reacting fast enough. His partner was going to bleed out if they couldn't stop it.

"Dan, Dan, stay with me!" he said, leaning in close to his buddy's face.

By now, someone had flagged the *Dreamboat* and Lonnie got it alongside while Ben struggled to stop the current of crimson gathering into sickeningly large puddles on the deck. Dropping his gear, Ben cradled Dan's near lifeless body as they passed him over to the cruiser. He hopped over to the *Dreamboat*, kneeling down again to make sure his friend was still breathing. Lonnie shoved the throttle in as far as it would go, making for Horseshoe Beach.

"What the hell happened?" Bill asked, trying to make himself heard over the engine's rumble.

"Bull shark. Bastard came out of nowhere. It was like he only wanted to get Dan."

Bill looked at Dan's pale, expressionless face. He was almost waxy and turning gray.

"I don't think he's gonna make it, bud."

"He's going to make it!" Ben snapped. "He's going to make it."

It took an eternity to race those few miles. This was what he had been spared during the war. He thought about all the men maimed and killed during all the battles he had heard about in anguished tones by the survivors. Guadalcanal, Iwo Jima, Leyte Gulf—now he knew why they weren't boastful of their courage and took little pride in their successes. This was the cost. He could now comprehend the terror, the horror the men of the *Indianapolis* endured as they watched their shipmates and friends eaten alive, one by one. It changed them, made them haunted, full of guilt. Now he understood. It had already changed him, too.

***

The town of Horseshoe Beach had no hospital, no medics. The one doctor in town was an elderly general practitioner who had no surgical training. Someone had the foresight to call the fire department, which sent a ten-year-old Ford ambulance, to the docks. Once they got Dan loaded up, the two attendants got back in the cab, while the doctor balanced himself on the jump seat in back. Ben didn't want to leave Dan's side, but there was no place for him to squeeze into the rear of the ambulance. They left with the whine of the siren trailing behind them. It would be a long ride to Gainesville.

It was then he noticed Bill watching from about ten feet away. Bill dropped his head and walked slowly over, as if he was going to say something.

"Don't even open your mouth," Ben glowered. "He's going to make it."

"I—"

"Shut up. He's going to live. Ya know why? Because he's got something to live for. Not like you and me, we got nothin'."

After a minute or two of thoughtful silence, Bill finally picked up his head. "Come on, let's go back to the boat."

"Oh no, I quit!" There was no fear in Ben's voice, only anger.

"You don't mean that."

96

"Dammit, I quit! I don't care about the money. I don't give a damn about any of it anymore."

"You think you're the only one that feels bad because there was nothing you could do to stop your friend from getting hurt?" Bill's voice gained volume as Ben started to walk away. "You think you're the only man who saw his buddies go down and wondered why me? Why am I still here? Go ahead and walk away, ya coward!"

Ben spun on his heels.

Bill still hammered at him. "Come on. You haven't got what it takes to fight. You don't have the guts for it. You don't want to go on because you think this is all about you. It isn't. It never was. You can't understand it; you can't reason it away. You just have to go on."

Ben's clinched fists slowly relaxed. Finally, he looked over his shoulder at Sally's Place.

"C'mon," he said. "Let's go close this place down."

Bill nodded. "Just like the old days."

"Just like the old days."

15
~~Utina Provincia de Florida~~
6 Octubre 1523

In the heat of the afternoon, an oppressive stillness settled over the glade. The exhausted men snored lightly. Insects droned incessantly all around them. A sudden movement in the waist-high, golden flax at the edge of the clearing put every man on alert. Even those napping were suddenly wide awake, but it was not an *indio* that stepped out but a black bear, a sow. Comandante Gregorio stood slowly, silently drawing his sword. He motioned for the closest man to make his pike ready. The bear seemed unconcerned with their presence, except to cast a few baleful stares in their direction. She moved away slowly.

"Why doesn't he strike?" whispered Claudio, mostly to himself. "She will escape."

Then a half-grown cub appeared, following the female. Seconds later, another appeared. The young were more skittish, nervously grunting as they sniffed and pawed at the soft ground. Gregorio eased closer then charged the cubs, who began to bawl loudly as they ran for cover. Without hesitation, the sow raced back to defend her litter. Gregorio stood his ground, shouting, inciting her to attack. When she did, the Comandante executed a graceful pass and delivered the death cut, driving his sword deep into the animal's body.

For a moment, astonishment lay on them like a spell.

"¡*Ole!*" Claudio finally roused them. "I have never seen better in any bull ring!"

For the first time in nearly two years, he finally witnessed a smile on Comandante Gregorio's face. The men shouted "Huzzah!" in earnest. One man ran to the beast and cut off both ears with his long knife, offering them to the Comandante, who accepted them with grace. With confidence in his leadership restored, he again retired to the shade.

As they butchered the carcass, Claudio overheard one of the men saying it was a shame they had no fire. A sudden flash of inspiration struck him—the gunpowder in his bag. He had been single-mindedly searching for a piece of quartz, chert, or flint to make a fire as he had always done, but if he put the powder on a flat steel surface, and hit it hard enough with the butt of a short sword or knife, the percussion should ignite it.

"Excuse me, friend," he said, picking up one man's halberd. Laying it down in an open space, he carefully poured out half the black powder into a nest of dried leaves and the pine bark he collected. Already his behavior was drawing a small crowd of onlookers. Retrieving his stiletto, Claudio said a silent prayer and hit the flat of the hachet blade with the tang of the long knife. Nothing happened.

"Maybe the powder is wet," murmured one of the *marineros*, a gunner.

Claudio struck again with the same results.

"Saint Jude, guide my hand," Claudio prayed. Several of the men around him crossed themselves. Claudio hammered the blade with as much force as he had left in him. Immediately, a flower of flame erupted, accompanied by a good deal of smoke. The smell of brimstone never smelled so sweet. Quickly, he pushed the tinder together and felt the warmth of a steady flame radiating onto his face.

"It is a miracle," his companion Eduardo spoke. "¡*Es un milagro!* Everyone look at what Claudio did!"

"It was not my miracle, but God's," protested Claudio.

Gregorio watched from a distance. The group's admiration, and possibly their loyalty, seemed to have suddenly shifted. He, Bernardo Gregorio, Comandante of all the armies in the north of La Nueva España, *adelantado* by the King of Spain, had just demonstrated his courage and worthiness to lead, but even he could not compete with a miracle.

Once the bear carcass was divided, the company crowded around the flames, impatient to grill their portion. Claudio tended the fire as he had done at the beach camp, alternately building and spreading the coals. The smoke swirling around them became as myrrh, and the delicious smell of seared meat more piquant than frankincense. Both were a salve for the pain of their exhaustion, the misery of abandonment. Their souls were as starved as their innards, clamoring for sustenance. When they had sated their first hunger, they turned to feasting the rest of their senses.

In a rich baritone voice, Eduardo began to sing.

> "What happens in the tavern where the money's lost, you may well ask and hear what I say. Here no one fears Death, but throw the dice in Bacchus' name."

Claudio recognized the words as the opening of an old drinking song—a round about the perils of gambling and drunkenness. The men clapped in unison, keeping time as Claudio and Eduardo traded lines. Their tankards were empty of wine, but the cup of solace was passed around and all drank deeply of it.

Pushed back by a warm fire that lit the perimeters of their camp, this night held no terrors. Bolstered by a meal, nearly all slept as well as they had on board ship. Exchanging watches every few hours, the men gradually returned from the brink, reasserting their will, regaining their civility. From a starving band of lost souls, more animal than human, they were coalescing back into a company of trained *soldados* and *marineros*, slightly more capable of dealing with being cast away in a verdant purgatory.

***

When daylight slowly returned, the smoldering fire sent long tendrils of smoke into the forest, mingling with a light fog. When Claudio stirred, he looked for more firewood to stoke their miracle anew. Gathering whatever small twigs he could scoop up, he almost missed the small figure standing at the edge of camp—a young *indio*, maybe twelve, with a serious look and intense, dark eyes. For a moment, neither of them moved.

"Wake up," Claudio announced. "We are not alone."

100

The boy did not flinch. His eyes held no fear, not even inquisitiveness.

Claudio spoke louder, "Comandante, look here. ¡*Rápidamente!*"

Only when Gregorio stood up did the boy dart back into the woods, disappearing into the mist. Sword in hand, the Comandante gestured to Claudio and several others.

"Catch him!"

Even as he gave chase, Claudio wondered if it was a trap, a lure meant to draw them into ambush. He lost the boy's track almost immediately. Expecting an arrow or spear at any second, Claudio dodged from tree to tree, searching for the young *indio*. In the distance, he heard the clumsy footsteps of his *companeros* crashing about, heading in his general direction. The noise covered whatever faint sign he might have gleaned about any danger lying in wait. For an instant, he thought he saw the boy cross a small clearing ahead. Cautiously, he worked his way toward the spot and waited for reinforcements. The men behind him called his name several times. Then he heard one shout "Over here!"

Claudio paused to catch his breath. As the pounding of his heart slowed, he heard a quiet buzzing noise, like that of many insects. Easing into the small clearing, he saw it came from flies, dozens of them, all competing for the flesh of a severed head on a pike. It was the head of the *carpintero*. The skin had become loose and rubbery, while divesting itself of all natural color until it was as pale as a winter moon on an icy pond. The pallor only accentuated the many bruises around his head, the result of many heavy blows taken while he still clung to life. The eyes had been burned out, and the sockets filled with gold coins. The slack jaw and gaping mouth were stuffed with pearls and gems looted from the *Mano del Rey's* buried spoils. A missing tongue offered all the more space to push gold nuggets into the back of the man's throat. It looked like he was vomiting riches.

By now, the whole troop had arrived, with Comandante Gregorio slowly nudging his way through the tightly packed ring of men. The *carpintero* had been well-liked and was most respected. His skills had made him invaluable. Now his courage had bought them time. It was all too clear that there was no reason to ever return to the beach. No one would be left alive. The treasure was gone.

Gregorio felt the entire crushing weight of the enormity of his failure. He had lost his ship, his crew, his army, all the gold and silver, the jewels, the slaves—everything. Even the respect of the small group of survivors he commanded was waning.

They waited for him, for Claudio, for someone to tell them what to do next. Gregorio staggered to the edge of the clearing and sat with his back against a tree, facing back toward the west, toward the coast. His eyes developed a glassy, unblinking stare. He said nothing.

Finally, Claudio knelt and murmured prayers. One by one, the rest echoed him, until the sound of their prayers obliterated the obscene buzzing of the flies. In the end, they left the *carpintero* as they had found him, the wealth untouched, adding only a large, woven palmetto crucifix to the pike with a piece of vine.

16
~~Horseshoe Beach, Florida~~
June 18, 1959

It was just like the old days. Just as he used to do, Ben slowly worked his way through a six-pack of Schlitz, nursing a foul mood to a near-breaking point. Just like always, Bill hovered around him, keeping him out of fights and away from the cops. The ultimate flashback was that, just like the old days, Ben awakened with a corker of a headache.

Piece by piece, he surveyed his surroundings as best he could without taking his head from the pillow. His clothes from last night lay on a black and white linoleum floor. The checkerboard pattern was in stark relief to the white walls and ceiling, giving the whole space an almost institutional look. It also made him dizzy. He stretched cautiously under the sheets, gauging the firmness of the mattress and his body's willingness to respond without pain. He was stiff, but not hurt. The bed was too comfortable to be a hospital bed. Closing his eyes again for a few seconds, he recognized the rumble of a window air-conditioner near his head.

Steeling himself for the move, he slowly swung his legs over the side of the bed and sat up. The pounding in his head immediately increased. Someone had left a pack of Goody's headache powder on the nightstand with a glass of water next to it. *Must have been Bill, good old Dollar Bill.* His duffel bag from the boat sat on a small stand at the end of the bed, but his gear wasn't with it. At least he had fresh clothes and his shaving kit. Dosing himself with a double powder, he stood up. A sign on the door told him he was in the Checkerboard Motor Court and check-out time was eleven a.m. He had no idea what time it was.

Wandering into the bathroom, he squinted in preparation for switching on the light. Sure enough, the glare of the fixture over the sink nearly blinded him. The black and white ceramic tile came halfway up the wall in here, making the pattern even more intense. Pausing to look into the mirror, it seemed like a stranger was looking back. His inspection was interrupted by a knock on the door. Ben stumbled to pull on his trousers and opened the door a crack.

"Well, you did survive," Bill said as he stepped inside. A brief glance past the wooden portico beyond the threshold showed a drizzling rain.

"Not by much."

"If you can manage to shave and get dressed, Lucky is buying us breakfast at the place across the street."

The conversation continued across the threshold as Ben worked to make himself presentable. "Hear anything about Dan?"

A pause that was too long made Ben walk back to the sitting room, his face a mask of shaving cream. Bill stared at the floor, finally looking up at him.

"He's in critical condition, but they say he'll make it." Another pause. "He lost his leg. Had to take it off at the knee."

Ben turned as pale as the soap he wore, then went back into the bathroom. The conversation stopped for a while. There was nothing else to say. Nothing would change the way things were now, and Ben was beginning to comprehend what Bill had tried to tell him last night. You can't understand it, you can't reason it away. You just have to go on, but no one said he had to make peace with it.

***

A diminished and solemn crew of four sat in a corner booth at the Howard Johnson, sipping coffee and poking at their meal. Jimbo had taken the truck to get resupplied and to find a spot to camp somewhere south of Horseshoe Cove. Lucky said something about it being in the middle of nowhere, just north of where the Suwannee River met the Gulf. It was Lonnie's last meal with them. He was shipping out, headed back to Biloxi. There was no more use for the boat, and he had no intention of being a landlubber.

Lonnie had been shaken by the accident, too. Bloodshot eyes betrayed a sleepless night and too many nightcaps. He looked rough. Nobody mentioned Dan. He was the ghostly fifth at the table. In the room, Bill had said that Fischer was picking up the hospital tab and giving him a fifty thousand dollar bonus. *Guess that's all a leg is worth,* Ben thought.

When Duprez got up to pay the check, Ben finally forced the subject.

"I wonder how Cindy is handling this."

"Who?" Lonnie asked.

"Dan's wife," Bill explained. "I don't know. I'm sure somebody at the hospital told her."

"You didn't call her?" The intensity in Ben's voice ratcheted up a notch.

"Not yet." Bill averted his eyes.

An awkward five-second silence ensued before Ben spoke again. "You know, I don't get it. Why Dan and not me? I mean that shark knocked me out of the way to get to him."

"Just be glad it wasn't you," Lonnie said to his coffee cup.

"I guess that's it, isn't it? You feel guilty somebody else took the hit because deep inside you're glad it wasn't you. It could have been, maybe should have been, but it didn't happen that way." Ben stared at the table top as if it held the answer to such cosmic conundrums.

Bill nodded in agreement.

"I wonder why it's like that—life—I mean. A lean to the left or right, two seconds early or two seconds late, it all has to add up to something." Ben shifted in his seat, suddenly uncomfortable.

***

The ride to the docks in Duprez's Jeep was short. Ben stood morosely in the light rain as Bill and Lucky helped Lonnie get ready to cast off.

"Good luck, guys." Lonnie shook hands all around. "If ya get to Biloxi, look me up, and we'll go fishing."

As the engine rumbled to life, he turned to wave then slowly moved out into the harbor. He never saw Ben standing with his hand

105

suspended in midair in frozen farewell. They heard the motor pick up rpms and watched as the *Dreamboat* receded into the mists.

"Let's get to camp," Duprez said finally.

***

Camp was the same cluster of tents set close together on a sandy spit of land the locals called Shired Island. A high patch of ground deep in the Gulf Hammock, it was a short walk to a white sand beach and the Gulf. Ben noticed the mess tent was still rolled up in the truck with their gear. Before they could get moved in, Duprez motioned for them to gather in the command tent. Folding wooden chairs were arranged on either side of the entrance. A worn leather satchel sat on a long rectangular folding table.

"Have a seat, gentlemen." Lucky fumbled in the satchel for some papers before he started talking again. "Okay, here's the situation. Markings on the cannon that was recovered match those the *Mano del Rey* would have had, so we can say with confidence you found the first target. Good work."

Ben shifted in his chair, making the wood creak.

"The next task is to locate the exact location of the survivor's camp," Duprez continued. "The easiest way to do that is to cut a trench along the beach over there, between the high tide mark and the dunes. We should hit several unmarked burials. Using the Hernandez journal, that should allow us to pinpoint the camp."

"So we're gonna dig up some dead Spaniards just to find an old settlement?" Ben asked incredulously. "That's what Dan lost a leg for?"

"I'm guessing there must be buried treasure there, right?" asked Bill.

"Almost. There was buried treasure there. A lot of it. According to Hernandez, it was stolen, moved."

"Moved? Where? Why don't we just go where it was moved and look for it?"

"That's the question. To find where it wound up, we need to start from the site of the old camp."

"Oh, God," moaned Ben. "This gets crazier all the time."

"Now here's the bad news." Lucky ignored him. "The state is

fighting us about the wreck. They want to stop salvage and claim it as state property. They would probably shut us down if they knew we were excavating on the beach, too. We're going to have to do this quick and quiet. Maybe the wreck site will preoccupy them until we can find what we need. Tomorrow, we're going to put up the mess tent on the beach to give us cover while we dig."

Bill thought it over. "It still won't take them too long to get suspicious."

"Exactly. Everybody in?"

One by one, they silently nodded.

***

Outside, Jim waited for Ben to emerge.

"Mr. Wheeler," he called. "I'm really sorry about your friend. He didn't deserve what happened. He is a good man, has a good heart." The giant's face was softer than Ben had ever seen. His usual stoic scowl was completely missing.

"Thanks, Jim. That means a lot."

The man nodded awkwardly, then turned around and walked away. Ben did the same, wondering if maybe some good might come out of everything that had happened.

It was a quiet night in camp. Everything had changed. There was no horseplay, no joking around. That warm feeling of good friends together was gone. Everyone spoke in subdued voices, as if at a wake. A new sense of vulnerability had set in, feeding Ben's growing paranoia. Ironically, the feeling also seemed to draw them closer in. Even the tents in camp were now closer together, like wagons circled by pioneers.

After lights out, Ben glanced over at Bill's form stretched out on the adjacent cot. He knew he was still awake because he could see the bright red glow of a lit cigarette.

"Hey, Bill." Ben spoke in a low voice so their conversation wouldn't carry any further than the confines of the tent.

"Hmm?"

"Is it just me or do you all of a sudden feel like our asses are hangin' in the wind?"

Bill ground out his cigarette butt on the plywood floor.

"Yeah, a little bit. I'd like to know what we're really after, and what's going to happen when we find whatever it is we're looking for."

"This cloak and dagger crap is wearin' me out," Ben agreed. "I don't know what to think any more."

"I think I've got to know where this dog and pony show is gonna end before I set one foot on that beach in the morning."

***

In his own tent, Duprez sat at a folding table studying a half-dozen survey maps, plotting first one direction then another. The glare of the Coleman lamp was not doing his eyes any good. Somewhere out there on the beach lay a missing point he needed to complete his calculations. It irritated the hell out of him that he didn't know where it was. He knew just about everything else—the course the survivors had taken, descriptions of the landscape, even a few landmarks; but until he knew exactly where to start, the rest was almost useless. The weather and human encroachment over the last four hundred years had altered the area significantly. He could quickly get off track without that mark.

Laying everything else aside, he picked up a worn book that was dog-eared at the spot where a 1569 Spanish map of Florida was printed. Somewhere on here was the end of the rainbow, the pot of gold, so to speak. He began to muse about that ragged group of lost men. What did they feel as they wandered? How did they get so far? The accounts in Hernandez's journal were sketchy, but he had other contemporary stories of the century. Still, it had to be hell. Sighing, he turned out the lamp and stretched. It would be easier if he could just talk to them. But the only voice he had was Claudio Hernandez. It would have to be enough.

***

Jim woke suddenly after midnight, as if startled by something. He lay on his cot and listened intently for a few minutes, then heard the noise again that had come to him in a light sleep. It came from the beach, sent over the dunes by the sea breeze. It sounded like a group of people yelling or arguing. The voices were faint, but distinct, yet not clear enough to make out what was being said.

He quickly pulled on his dungarees and slipped on his brogans. Easing out of the tent, he heard Ben and Bill snoring in their bunks. There was no sign of anyone else in camp, no cars nearby to indicate unwanted visitors. Following the voices, Jim walked carefully to the top of a nearby dune and scanned the beach. A half moon traveled the clear night sky, reflecting brightly off the white sand. He could hear words now, snatches of heated discussion, punctuated with what seemed to be battle cries. Some of it was in Spanish, some of it in a language he had never heard, but the phantom noises came from an empty shoreline. Now and again, he thought he saw flickering blue lights, like torches burning with azure flames, moving among the dunes in the distance.

He listened and watched for a few more minutes. Then everything fell quiet. The only light he could discern now was the flicker of moon glow on the gentle waves of the tide as they met the shore. Despite the mild temperature, Jim felt goosebumps creep up his arms. This was a bad place to be in. The voices were an omen—a warning. Now he knew why everyone, including himself, was so edgy. Whatever they were looking for was never meant to be disturbed.

***

Daylight reversed the palette of sky and earth. Under the glare of an early morning tropical sunup, the whole area appeared as normal as yesterday's newspaper. Even Bill's bitching around the coffeepot seemed so right.

"I'm tellin' ya, I'm not stepping one foot in any direction—on that beach or anywhere else until I hear the whole story."

Duprez seemed bemused at first. Then surprisingly, he nodded in acquiescence.

"All right. Here's what you know. After the *Mano del Rey* went down in September of 1523, twenty-three survivors built a small defensive enclave close to where we are now. They rescued a huge treasury of gold coin, silver bars along with emeralds, sapphires, turquoise, and pearls from the ship and buried it along with the bodies they recovered. Nine days later, Commander Bernardo Gregorio took fifteen men out to look for a source of fresh water and food. While he was gone, local hostiles over-ran the camp, murdering the rest of the crew. Apparently, before they were massacred, those men were tortured until the location of the treasure was revealed. The locals reclaimed the loot and carried it off. The next time the treasure was seen all in one spot was after the search party was captured and killed. Supposedly, it's now in the bottom of a sinkhole. For all we know, that sinkhole may be full of water. That's why we still need you guys."

"Why don't we just go to the sink, then?" Ben pressed.

"Do you know how many sinkholes there are in Florida? And that's just the ones we know about. The Hernandez journal gives some rough distances and dead-reckoning bearings, and there are a few landmarks we might be able to find—creeks, lakes, and swamps—that kind of thing. But without the search party's point of origin, we could be all over the map. A small miscalculation in the beginning could lead to a huge miss at the end."

"We won't find it sittin' here drinkin' coffee," Bill said.

***

The big mess tent was set up on the north end of the beach within an hour. They set a line parallel to the tide mark with twine. Bill insisted on starting the trench himself. After that, Ben, Jim, and Bill took thirty-minute turns with the shovel as they wormed their way down the beach. By midmorning, they had nearly fifteen yards. It was time to backfill half of it and move the tent.

"These poor sons-a-bitches we're looking for would have traded that whole stash of gold for one of these, I bet," Bill muttered as he wiped his brow with a cold beer can.

"No doubt," Ben agreed. "I can't imagine lyin' here day after day with nothing to drink but rainwater, if that."

"Sounds like basic training, "Jim observed.

That brought a good laugh, especially from Ben, who was as startled by the fact that Jim was participating in the conversation as he was by the man's wry humor.

"Are we gonna drink or dig?" Lucky interjected as he arrived with another bag of ice for the cooler.

"Both," answered Bill, jumping back down into the trench, shovel in hand. As he did, the shovel handle hit the opposite trench wall, causing some of it to cave in.

"Careful there." Lucky was suddenly serious. "We don't need that thing collapsing on anybody."

Bill saluted and started shoveling the damp sand over the edge.

In two hours, they had another ten yards dug. Ben was on the shovel when Lucky came back with lunch.

"Chow time," Bill called.

His announcement went unheeded as the tip of the shovel hit something with a solid clunking sound. The others gathered around, peering down as Ben teased sand from around whatever he had hit.

"A big shell?" Bill asked.

"Nope. It's thicker than that. It's not a rock either. Give me a stick or something."

Jim tossed him one of the tent pegs and Ben dropped to one knee to try to clear enough sand away and see what it was.

"It's bone," he finally said. "Looks like a skull."

An electric charge seemed to jump from one man to the next. Ben continued to dig cautiously, exposing more and more of the burial. The jaw was wide open, showing a mouthful of sturdy, worn teeth. No shroud or trace of care had been taken when the body was buried. It looked as though the body had been unceremoniously dumped in the hole.

"Jesus," Ben muttered. "I think this guy was alive when they threw the dirt in on him."

"How do you know?"

"For one thing, there's somebody on top of him. I think there's another one below him."

Without warning, the entire trench around Ben collapsed as if the ground wanted to swallow him and bury him with the others. Everyone fell to their knees, digging furiously like wild dogs. Seconds ticked off, almost a minute and a half before they reached his upthrust hand. Jim straddled the spot and singlehandedly pulled his head and shoulder above the sand. An explosion of soil erupted from Ben's nose and mouth. He was alive. The three men helped as he crawled weakly to one side of his premature burial site. Bill sat with Ben's head in his lap, carefully washing away the sand from his face with melt water from the cooler.

When Ben could see again, he noticed Jim hovering close by.

"That's the second time you saved my life."

Jim's face curled up on one side, "You makin' it a habit."

17
~~Utina Provincia de Florida~~
8 Octubre 1523

The company lay paralyzed for an entire day and another night, some from fear, many from exhaustion. Mainly, they stayed in the same place, waiting for death or murder because no one said rise and walk. Comandante Gregorio withdrew into a shell of unreality, denying any responsibility for their situation, the loss of the ship, or the failure of the conquest. He had clearly abdicated his command, allowing it to settle on Claudio, either by design or negligence. The men still believed in the *ayudante's* courage and inner strength even if they had no more themselves.

When Claudio awoke after daylight, he went to every man, looking for signs of life or worse, illness. During the night two more died, one of starvation and one of dysentery. Another two had all the symptoms of cholera. He had no doubt they would die before the next sunrise. That left ten men still strong enough to move. The Comandante had to give the order to march. They needed to leave this place *de la muerte*.

As Claudio looked around, it was obvious the Comandante was missing. He must have left camp early. For a fleeting moment, Claudio wondered if Gregorio had deserted them, an act which he knew the man was certainly capable of committing. Had he gone out to piss or explore and become ill or injured? Claudio wandered the perimeter of camp, searching for him. A faint voice seemed to be coming from the forest, a mumbling, indistinct sound, and Claudio followed it. Quietly slipping through the trees, it grew louder as he approached the clearing where the head of the *carpintero* stood. As he approached, he could clearly make out Gregorio's voice as he muttered "Mine, mine."

Removing the gold and jewels from the cadaverous skull infested with maggots had made Gregorio's hands greasy with bits of decomposed flesh. He had not even bothered to brush the worms from his own skin.

"Comandante!" It was as much a reproach as a call for attention. He looked up and saw the horror and disdain in Claudio's face.

"¡*Imbécil!* These will probably save your life!"

"That is not nearly enough to bribe the saints for admittance to Heaven, nor even enough to buy you redemption from Hell," Claudio answered curtly.

"You and your piety," Gregorio spat. "You are nothing but a weak *niño*. You are ignorant of the true realities of life. I have survived more than you will ever know."

"At what cost? Your soul?"

"A soul is for priests and those with the *dinero* to afford them." With those words, Gregorio piled his treasure on a piece of cloth then gathered it into a pouch. Stuffing the makeshift purse in his waistband he hissed, "Go on. Save yourself. Save the others if you think you can. I will save Bernardo Gregorio de Seville."

He turned to storm off toward the camp.

"As you always have," Claudio yelled after him.

***

Back among the men, Claudio nearly shouted at the miserable group, exhorting them to gather all their strength.

"¡*Levántate!* On your feet. We have to move now!"

"*Señor*, I...I cannot go on," one of the most sickly stammered.

"Then you will die here." Claudio was surprised at how cold he himself now sounded. Kneeling beside the man, he grabbed him by the shoulder and helped him to his feet.

"This place is cursed," he whispered. "We must try to move on."

"*Sí*, the Devil is all around us," the man murmured. His eyes were glassy, and his skin burned with fever. He was not going to make the full day's march.

114

Across the way, Gregorio seemed amused as if he watched a scene at the theater.

"Go on, *mi teniente*. See if you can make them follow you."

Claudio ignored him, outraged and desperate to gain control.

"Men! ¡*Mis amigos*!" he called out, "We will travel by twos. Two columns. Help each other. One of you must have some kind of weapon. Let the stronger man carry it."

Finally they formed up, a small rank of broken men against the dark wild forest.

"Stay close!" Claudio warned. "We will walk slowly. Do not fall behind."

Staggering as much as marching, they moved off toward the northeast at the pace of a funeral procession. Claudio had no idea what his former superior had been planning, but it seemed logical to him that they must now make for the east coast of the peninsula. There, they might have a chance to signal a passing ship on its way back across the Atlantic to Spain. It was a grueling two hours before they emerged from the coastal hammocks onto permanently higher ground. Here, the earth was firmer, sandier, and deeply covered with the needles of towering pines. The air was sweeter, perfumed with the stringent pitch of their trunks. The breeze moved freely, unobstructed by the massive thickets they had left behind. Travel across this landscape would at least be easier. Scattered around them were open patches of forest carpeted with green ferns interrupted by clumps of bushes covered with red berries. The berries, they quickly learned, were extremely bitter and inedible.

"Sit. Rest awhile," he finally announced. He could not let them rest too long. The local *indios* were no doubt shadowing them.

His new *amigo*, Eduardo, settled down nearby.

"We are one less, *señor*," he said without much emotion. "Diego died after the first hour."

He was one of those sick with cholera.

"I carried him a way, but he was dead." The man crossed himself.

"May he rest in peace," Claudio responded. They would probably all die that way if they weren't murdered first.

"Have you seen Comandante Gregorio?" Eduardo asked.

Claudio's head snapped up and he scanned the group. Gregorio was gone again. *Bastardo*.

"*Señor* Gregorio is no longer leading this *expedición*."

Eduardo shrugged, "Then we will follow you, *mi amigo*."

Claudio glanced at him and saw the trust in his weathered face.

"If it is God's will, we will make it home," Claudio murmured. Divine intervention was all they had now. *God give them the strength to keep going*, he prayed silently.

As the sun reached the high point in its arc, no shadows fell to indicate their way. Weakened by the season and mitigated by a high overcast, the light of day seemed to hesitate, diffuse, and become untrue. It was as if they had strayed into some surreal world between heaven and hell where everything familiar had been cast out, made irrelevant. Some of them hallucinated with fever, hearing the hiss of unseen serpents or smelling fire in the absence of flame and smoke. Each face was a mask of pain and hopelessness, with skin now cracked and burnt by the pitiless weather.

Their utter poverty, both in spirit and in fact, was plain. The group stumbled forward half-naked, their clothes having long since disintegrated into rags. With filthy hair and matted beards, the entire troop resembled the mendicants that traveled the roads during the Black Death. Their souls were shattered. Every man's mind was focused solely on the next step, the next horizon, the next league. Many had even stopped praying. They were dead, eternally walking across the plains of Hades, cruelly trapped in limbo.

The ground underfoot had become sandier but was still firm with large brown oak leaves scattered in small piles. The scene was kept from being a complete desert by infinite acres of tufted, long-stem grasses. Tendrils of briars no longer tripped them. Instead, large burrows in the soil left gaping holes that might break ankles or legs made fragile by malnutrition. At one entrance, they tried to dig out the inhabitant, hoping it would be a tortoise. The short tunnel lead only to a perturbed rattlesnake. Nothing larger showed any sign of itself in the prairie-like terrain. Salvation was a mirage.

Claudio looked back only once during the afternoon. He counted eight men behind him. Somewhere in that featureless expanse, another had fallen. It seemed odd to recognize he felt relief instead of remorse.

116

Already learning to be a leader, he had compassion enough to share, but not a drop of regret. The missing man had been touched by the hand of Death before they ever left camp. God had taken pity on him and ended his suffering. Claudio almost felt envious.

Finally, an hour before sunset, they approached a clump of oaks surrounding a small depression. Hidden within was a shallow pond, half-covered in lily pads. Below them, the tea-colored water was fresh and sweet. They all fell to their stomachs and drank noisily, belching as they swallowed nearly as much air as liquid.

"*Gracias a Dios*," murmured Claudio.

Nearby, Eduardo called to him.

"*Gracias, Teniente.* Come, drink again. It tastes like the finest wine in all of Spain."

Claudio shook his head and smiled. "My belly is bursting now. *Hombres*, do not forget what God has done for you this day."

"God may have shown mercy on us, *Señor*," grinned Eduardo. "But it is you we will sing songs of in years to come. ¡*Saludos!*"

At twilight, they lay along the pool's sandy banks, the pain in their empty stomachs temporarily eased by all the water they could hold. Claudio stood watch as some had already fallen into the sleep of exhaustion. As he wondered how much further they could go, he saw a figure emerge from the wood on the far side of the little lake. At first, he thought he imagined the creatures walking softly along the bank, but then another and several more appeared.

"¡*Alarma! ¡A las armas!*" he shouted. The men were slow to rise, unsure of what danger might be at hand. They had but two halberds, three pikes, and three short swords. Claudio drew his stiletto and watched with apprehension as the figures approached. They were *indios*, but not warriors. Several carried wicker baskets and clay pots. None were heavily armed. They finally stopped some twenty paces away and set down their burden. With little hesitation, they abruptly turned and walked away briskly, melting back into the tree line.

Cautiously, Claudio walked out to where the small collection of gifts lay, followed by Eduardo. To their astonishment, the *indios* had brought food—parched corn, smoked fish, and a stew of meat and vegetables, still warm from the cooking fire.

Eduardo was uncharacteristically speechless, but fell to his knees, driven not by gratitude but by rabid hunger. Immediately, the company surrounded him, ravenous, with every trace of civility erased by desire.

As they jostled for a place at the feast, Claudio noticed a small deerskin pouch in the bottom of one of the baskets. As he bent to retrieve it, a single polished sapphire fell onto the sand. He knew then that it was not God, nor even the *salvajes* who had provided for them, but Comandante Gregorio.

Long before night completely blotted out the world around them, the men slept like innocents, snoring lustily. Only Claudio tossed and turned, rising occasionally to listen to the owls calling to each other in the darkness. It was not the *indios* he feared, but his own Comandante. Gregorio was treacherous and teetering on madness. Nothing, not even an apparent act of kindness could be taken at face value. He was out there somewhere, plotting and scheming to have it all, no matter what the cost. He would willingly sacrifice each and every one of them to get his hands on the wealth he had already murdered so many to amass. Gregorio would not allow these *salvajes* to steal back his hard-won plunder. Of that much, Claudio was sure.

He had only to wait until morning to get an idea of what *el Comandante* had planned.

***

About an hour after daylight, a lone *indio* walked onto the shore and approached them.

"*Buenas dias, señores.*" He addressed them in perfect Spanish. "I am Chulusi Eyolehecote, but my Christian name is Juan."

Claudio had so many questions. The first one that tumbled out was simply from curiosity.

"You are baptized?"

"*Si,*" the *indio* explained. "I was captured by a Spanish *expedición* five years ago. They took me to Cuba, where I lived with many fathers."

"You mean a monastery," Claudio deduced. "How is it that you are here now?"

The *indio* smiled broadly, showing his perfect teeth.

"I stole a boat!"

It was not the answer Claudio had hoped to elicit, but the response was succinct enough. He had to laugh.

"*Por favor, Señor,*" Juan continued. "My master—I think you know him. His *Excelencia* Bernardo Gregorio wishes the pleasure of your company. All of you must come now. He says not to wait for the main *compañía de soldados*."

It didn't take much for Claudio to grasp that somehow, Gregorio had convinced this group of locals that a large column of Spanish soldiers were on the way and that Claudio's meager band were but a small patrol.

"*Vamos,*" he nodded. Calling over his shoulder to the perplexed group, he shouted, "Follow me!"

Without question, they shouldered their weapons and grabbed the last small mouthfuls of food, then fell in behind him. Claudio wondered how long the ruse would last.

As they followed what appeared to be a faint game trail eastward, Juan kept up a stream of questions.

"You are Christians also? You drink blood and eat body of Christ?"

"Yes, we are all Christians, "Claudio assured him.

"It must be a great honor. I ate the heart of my enemy once. He was very courageous, but I killed him at last."

Claudio suppressed a shiver. It would be too difficult to explain to this half-heathen the difference between *Comunión* and cannibalism. Besides, if he could keep the idea afloat among the *indios* that they too might be eaten, it could help keep his small band alive.

Chulusi Eyolehecote or Blue Jay, was shorter than most of the Timucua and Potano they had seen. While his features were decidedly Anahuac, he was almost European in stature. Since he had been living in Anhaica when he first saw Spanish soldiers, he was probably an Apalachee. His abbreviated height did not prevent him from being quite muscular and agile. Only a slight recurve at the base of his spine and the awkward angle of his hips hinted at a possible genetic defect. Like every other *indio* Claudio had ever seen, Blue Jay went about barefooted constantly but wore cotton knee breeches and a flaxen blouse. He also wore his coarse black hair in European fashion, cut evenly around his head. His age was indeterminate. More than twenty but less than forty, he was still a young man.

"How much farther, Juan?"

"There." The man pointed.

About a hundred yards away, almost hidden in a grove of oak trees, stood a round palisade of stout-looking timbers. At their approach, a small cordon of warriors emerged from the barricade, painted in red ochre, with their long hair drawn up into top knots. These were definitely Potanos.

"What is this place called?" Claudio asked. He wanted to be sure to write it in the journal.

"Puturiba," Blue Jay responded.

"And your *patrón Señor* Gregorio is here?"

"Oh, yes. He holds the daughter of the *cacique* Caliquen hostage."

Claudio was not surprised but uneasy at the slender thread of deceit and treachery he was now being drawn into. The balance of power was precarious. No doubt it would grow untenable within a few days. They had to be well clear of this place by then.

The gate to Puturiba was designed as a narrow corridor that followed the spiral of the outer wall like a nautilus shell, channeling all who entered and exited within a claustrophobic set of fences made from mature pine trees lashed together. From the slits between the trunks, Claudio could feel many eyes on them. Inside the barrier, some twenty or twenty-five huts made of saplings covered with palmetto fronds stood clustered around a larger central structure constructed in the same way but without walls. Cooking fires smoldered everywhere, but barely a soul showed themselves. Naked children peered apprehensively from within the dark, cramped family shelters. When the ragged band had assembled in front of the council house, a familiar figure slowly arose from a hammock inside.

"*Buenas dias*," Gregorio called to them. "God is good."

18
~~Horseshoe Cove, Florida~~
June 19, 1959

Ben wallowed in the gentle Gulf surf, trying to rinse the sand from his ears and face, letting the salt water occasionally go up his nose. It stung badly, but he felt like he had snorted so much beach it was packed in his sinuses.

"Whaddya trying to do, drown yourself?" Bill called from shore.

"No, "Ben coughed. "Tryin' to get this sandbox outa my throat."

Secretly, Ben would be glad to get away from the seaside for a while. He had had enough of the sticky salt air, the sand in his clothes and the glare of the sun. Already two shades darker than when he left home, the only part of him that wasn't red or dark brown was his ass. He was pretty sure that was still the original deathly pale white he had been born with.

***

Up near the dunes, Lucky and Jim worked with a theodolite, trying to measure distances south of the trench. According to the Hernandez journal, the burial ground had been only thirty yards or so from the camp. After staking out what he estimated to be the site of the massacre, Lucky measured out another two hundred feet. *Now the real search begins*, he thought.

Unwittingly, they had set up camp right on top of what must have been the survivor's trail. Climbing on top of the deuce and a half, Lucky surveyed the eastern horizon with his field glasses. Those men had obviously been desperate. There was nothing out there but saw grass and mud. They had marched on hope and willpower alone. He knew there was no fresh water for miles. Without muskets or crossbows, they would have had little hope of getting fresh meat. They probably didn't know how to forage. Even if they had, the only thing around them would have been swamp cabbage and coontie. They had to avoid quicksand and dozens of gator holes without a trail or guides. Despite the fact it had been in the middle of fall when they set out, there would have been clouds of mosquitoes and deer flies. His admiration for their toughness and tenacity grew with every discovery.

He was as curious as Hernandez had been about why Bernardo Gregorio struck out almost due north. Was he relying on Ponce de Leon's descriptions of Florida's east coast, written ten years earlier? If so, was he headed for the St. Johns River?

Duprez thought back to the operations he had led during the war. In the OSS, everything was on a need-to-know basis, but he could always rely on his troops' deeply ingrained sense of duty and their unswerving faith in the chain of command that governed their lives. How had Gregorio managed to lead this pathetic group so far? Intimidation? Charisma? They might have revolted at any time. The order of things could have collapsed on so many occasions. Were they afraid of him, or were they just too exhausted to care? Some men needed structure in order to feel secure. They were satisfied to be a grunt, part of a unit, a faceless, blameless cog. If things went well, they got rewarded like everybody else, regardless of their contribution. If things went badly, well, it wasn't their fault. They were only obeying orders, following the rules. Share the glory, spread the blame.

By the time the others returned to camp, Lucky had a topographic map of the area spread out on the hood of the Jeep. They all gathered around to see what he had figured out.

"We know from the book," he began. "The first day's walk was just over five miles north by northeast. That would put them somewhere near here." He pointed with a long, articulate finger. "Near Amason Creek, just west of County Road 357."

"At least we can ride there," Ben observed.

"Shouldn't be a problem," agreed Lucky. "There's a fire road that cuts over into the area we need to check out. If we can find a fresh water source located about two hundred feet from a field of clay or hard pan, it would be pretty strong evidence we're on the right track. Let's break camp and get after it."

***

The abbreviated convoy rumbled down the macadam highway—Lucky and Bill up front in the Jeep with Ben and Jim following in the truck.

"So other than the muscle and the company," Bill shouted over the noise of the wind through the open cab, "what is it that you need us for? You could have cut us loose a couple days ago and saved yourself some dough."

Lucky glanced at him.

"We might still need your special skills."

"As divers? On land? Whattaya gonna do, have us swim to the bottom of the pool in some motel?"

"Close." Duprez checked the rearview mirror before continuing. It was as if he was stalling.

"I understand you and especially Ben did a lot of underwater salvage and repair."

"Yeah, sure we did."

"Ever dive inside a sunken ship?"

"A lot of 'em."

"Dropping to the bottom of a spring or an underground river can't be much different."

Underwater cave diving was a lot like swimming into a torpedo hole below the waterline of a ship, but without the occasional body floating by.

"Nope. No difference at all."

***

"When we get to a lake, the first thing I'm gonna do is go skinny-dippin'," Ben announced to Jim over the roar of the deuce and a half's exhaust pipes.

"Thanks for the warning," Jim said. "I'm gonna get a cane pole an' a cup of worms, set on the bank, and watch that cork dance. I don't even care if I don't get a bite."

"My momma used to take the little fish I'd catch with bread balls, dip 'em in pancake batter, and cook 'em on the griddle for breakfast." Ben gestured as he spoke.

Jim shot him a look that was equal parts amazement and disgust. White folks would eat anything.

"No." He shook his head. "Fish gotta be dipped in buttermilk and dredged in corn flour, then fried. What the hell is wrong with you people?"

Ben laughed easily.

"I just hope I sleep better than I did last night. All I did was flip and flop."

"You, too? Did you hear all that racket on the beach?"

"Naw. What was it?"

Abruptly, Jim stopped talking, as if he'd thought better about it. "Nothin'," he said finally. "Must've been the wind blowin' the noise from some beach party toward us."

It took less than ten minutes to cover the same distance the beleaguered Spaniards struggled to make in a day's hike. Parking the vehicles on the side of the road, Ben and Jim went with Lucky down a shady dirt road to look for anything that resembled the place Hernandez had described more than four hundred years earlier. A tree farm, full of knee-high, yellow pine saplings covered at least fifty acres, each of them rooted in a heavy clay soil. The road turned from sand to crushed lime rock as they trudged west.

"I don't see any sign of a lake or pond," Ben said, clearly disappointed.

"Mebbe it dried up," Jim offered.

Lucky gestured toward a line of mature trees that seemed to form a wall or island.

"We've got another quarter mile or so to go. The water mentioned in the journal would be a little south of that treeline."

The fire road ended on a thickly wooded island, meeting another just like it going north and south. About seventy-five feet later, they found themselves on a natural causeway barely wider than the track they were walking. Covered in moss-draped oaks, it split the clay fields, with more of the sandy orange hard pan stretching off another two hundred yards on the opposite side.

"This looks promising," Lucky said. "Now let's find the water. Amason Creek is only a hundred yards from here."

"A creek? I thought we were looking for a small lake," Ben wondered aloud.

"When the water is high, like after a lot of rain, I bet this creek spreads out," Lucky surmised.

But it hadn't rained lately and the creek was a muddy trickle running through a culvert under the dirt road. Lucky walked carefully down to the bank, watching for cottonmouths, and scooped up a handful of water. Sniffing it, he smiled.

"It's fresh, not brackish."

"I wouldn't drink it." Jim shook his head.

"You're not a dehydrated Spanish sailor," Lucky pointed out. "Those guys would have been happy to find anything that wasn't salt water."

Looking around, they could see several depressions in the swampy bottoms among the trees. It could be the spot.

"No lake here now," Ben belabored the obvious. "No swimmin'."

"No fish, either," Jim murmured forlornly.

Lucky smiled. "A lot of things change in four centuries." Unfolding his map, he spread it out on the ground, aligning it to the compass points. "So, if this is the first camp, then the next one should be about six miles to the northeast." Measuring the course and distance at least twice, he finally stood up and folded the map. "Let's go see what we can find. We have only about three hours of daylight left."

What he didn't say is that he was not at all sure this had been the way the castaways had come. There was nothing to make concrete his assumptions. At best, it was a by-guess and by-God proposition. Still, it felt right. He could almost see their emaciated forms lying along the road, wracked with fever, thirst, and hunger. The longer he studied the journal, the thinner the veil of time seemed to get.

They drove on under the late afternoon sun, feeling the temperature mellow slightly in the wind on their faces. Lucky let Bill drive the Jeep as he studied two different maps and the roadside. This next spot was going to be harder to discover. No roads actually went within a hundred yards of where he thought it might be. There wasn't much light left to them, despite the fact that the longest day of the year—the summer solstice—was just three days away.

***

Lucky's memories of another June came back to him unbidden—June 6th, 1944, the invasion of Normandy. That day had truly seemed to be never-ending. It was fifteen years ago now, but in his mind it was fresh and raw. He had just been promoted to captain and was attached to an Army Intelligence team charged with helping organize the French resistance on D-Day. He had only set foot in France once, bringing contraband radios to the main cells along the coast, instructing them on the codes. The Army brought him back to London on the eve of invasion, leaving those he had trained to wait for the signal. He would have given anything to have been with the partisans that long night before the invasion, despite knowing the worst that could happen.

In the dimly lit war rooms beneath the streets of London, the stench of stale cigarette smoke hung everywhere, mixed with the pungent aroma of too many bodies packed too tightly together. The smell of sweat had already begun to build with the growing sense of anxiety and near-desperation. The upper command, the generals and their staff, they talked about everything in abstracts like "acceptable losses" and "collateral damage," as if it were not men's lives they were committing. It was at that moment he understood that command without leadership was meaningless.

***

The county road they followed merged with the main road between Cross City and Horseshoe Beach, and his reverie nearly caused him to miss a turn onto yet another unnamed dirt road to the southeast. Half a mile later, it degenerated into a much smaller, narrower, and rougher track. Even this stopped abruptly after a few minutes. All that was left was a wide trail leading into a ravine. Once they shut off the vehicles, the silence was deafening. There were no birdcalls, no crickets, no

126

cicadas, nothing.

"Better grab a couple of flashlights in case it gets dark before we get back," Lucky suggested.

Ben strapped on his .45. "Just in case things get weird," he said.

"If we're anywhere close to the right place," Lucky said, "this ravine should lead to a wide low spot lying between a clearing in the woods to the west of us and a little rise to the southeast. Hernandez called it a 'swale bewixt our encampment and the knoll where we found the *cabeza de el carpintero*'."

"*Cabeza de el carpintero*?" Jim asked.

"The head of the carpenter," offered Bill.

Ben looked at Bill with a bemused look.

"What?" Bill asked. "You think I didn't learn any Spanish on those fishing trips to Cuba?"

"Why didn't you tell me you could speak Spanish?" Ben grumbled.

"You never asked."

"So why does he call the rise, that little hill, the head of the carpenter?" Jim was more interested in the story than the argument.

"Because." Lucky smiled knowingly. "That's where they discovered the severed head of their shipmate impaled on a pike, his mouth stuffed with jewels. The natives had gouged his eyes out and replaced them with gold coins."

"Damn," Bill mumbled after a short but intense silence.

Much to Lucky's relief, the wide flat-bottomed ravine did end in a low dry wash at the foot of a sandy mound. It looked right.

"Ben, why don't you come with me and let's check out that hammock over there. Bill, you and Jim see what's up on that hill."

Ben and Lucky wove their way through the underbrush, calling back and forth as they moved through the thickets.

"How far you think we need to go?" Ben asked.

"Maybe forty or fifty yards. Hopefully, there's a clearing still out here somewhere. Should be a grove of oak trees close by."

As if on cue, Ben stumbled into an opening shaded by dozens of black-jack oaks. Momentarily, Lucky emerged as well.

"I'll be a son of a bitch," he swore softly. It had to be the camp of the dying.

Back on the high ground, Jim and Bill stood on a bald patch of earth, open to the sky. Dusk was rapidly approaching, and both men were keen to start back. Nothing marked the spot as being special or significant except for a vaguely ominous feeling that seemed to intensify with the gathering twilight. It was nearly twenty minutes before they heard Lucky and Ben approach through the forest below. Invisible among the trees, only their familiar voices gave them away.

"Whatcha got up there?" Lucky called.

"Nothin', really," Bill answered. "Just a hill."

"No *cabeza*?" Ben teased.

"Shut up."

"Maybe we should come back in the morning and do a little digging. Maybe there's still some of that gold around," Ben persisted.

"No," Lucky responded. "There won't be any. The journal says the Spanish commander took all the treasure off the corpse and took it with him."

"Jesus. That's a hard-ass."

The ravine was already in darkness and the trees along its rim were now silhouettes against the fading light. Blacker than the early evening sky, the trees took on grotesque shapes, twisted and malefic. Somewhere an owl hooted, adding to the general creepiness of the place. Suddenly, Bill stopped and shined his flashlight toward a spot just above them.

"What?" Lucky demanded.

"I thought I saw someone."

"Where?" Duprez waved his flashlight in the same general area.

"Right there, where I got my light."

"There's nobody up there," Lucky said after a second or two.

"That looks like somebody standing right up there." Jim pointed to an opening in the tree line they had just walked past.

The flashlights weren't quite strong enough to pierce the murky shadows. The ravine felt uncharacteristically cool, even cold. *This isn't right*, thought Lucky, *this is the middle of summer, a Florida summer.* His skin crawled.

"Shit, that does look like a person." Ben unsnapped the cover on his holster.

"Come on, let's keep moving," Lucky suggested.

After a minute and a few more yards, Jim halted.

"Hang on! Listen!"

As they all stood completely still, they heard the soft rustle of leaves and the occasional sharp crack of a dead branch. There was definitely movement. It was coming from everywhere.

"There's another one," Jim whispered.

"Where?" Ben drew the heavy .45 and put his thumb on the safety.

Jim pointed. The unmistakable outline of a human figure watched them from the top of the ravine ahead.

"Oh, my God. They're all over the place," Bill said. He tried focusing his flashlight on the closest shape, but the light flickered and then quit. He slapped the barrel of the flashlight, trying to bring it back to life.

Barely visible, dozens of shadow people now lined the ravine on both sides. A few stood with their arms hanging by their sides. Others showed no features at all beyond a head and shoulders. Small details like eyes or even faces were indistinguishable in the gloom.

Ben flipped off the safety and jacked a shell in the chamber.

"Easy," Lucky ordered. "Let's just get the hell outta here. We're almost back at the truck."

The faint glow of the only other working flashlight reflected from several pairs of pale yellow eyes floating about five or six feet off the ground behind them. Whoever or whatever it was would follow but never quite approach them. Ben spent the next twenty or thirty yards walking backwards, occasionally bumping into Jim.

"Watch who you shoot," Jim muttered.

It was a relief to get back into the vehicles, get the motors running and some lights on. Lucky was sweating profusely with gooseflesh now up and down both arms. Fear lay like a fever on them all, and no one said a word until they got back out to the hard road.

It was only a few minutes more down Highway 27 to Cross City. Lucky picked out a small motel on the south end of town. When he came out of the office, he wore a very worried face.

"What's up?" Bill asked.

"When I called Fischer to check in, he asked me when Lonnie left Horseshoe Beach. Seems he's about twelve hours overdue in Biloxi."

129

Bill shrugged. "Maybe he's just taking the long way home. That big paycheck he got might be burnin' a hole in his pocket."

As Lucky passed out the bungalow keys, Jim was conspicuously missing.

"Jim has a friend that lives about four blocks from here. He's going to stay there and will meet us after breakfast tomorrow," Lucky explained. "When you guys get your gear squared away, I'm gonna give him the Jeep to use."

"What's for dinner?" Bill changed the subject.

"The desk clerk said the chop house across the street is pretty decent. Let's rendezvous there in about fifteen minutes."

***

Ben's room was a lot like the one he had woken up in the day before, except a big brown rug covered much of the cold linoleum floor. Pine paneling softened the contours of the space, and the warm yellow light shed by a cypress knee lamp helped make the whole place feel welcoming after what they had just come from. It was like stepping from one world into another, from primitive mysticism to the ultra-civilized. Ben could feel the tension fading, slipping from his shoulders as he unbuckled his belt and stowed his gun deep in his duffel bag. It had made him feel better to wear it, to have it in his hand, but he had begun to think it would have been useless out there. Whatever they had seen was not human, not natural. He wasn't ready to believe in ghosts or evil spirits yet, but he couldn't explain what had happened and he couldn't quit thinking about it.

19
~~Puturiba~~
9 Octubre 1523

"God has indeed been gracious unto you," Claudio responded. If Gregorio had thought he would shock anyone by his reappearance, he must be disappointed.

The Comandante gestured grandly for them all to enter the long house, striding back to his hammock slung across one end. A young *indio* woman sat forlornly nearby, her hands tied around one of the posts that supported the hut.

"This is my *esposa*. I bought her from the *cacique*. It is his daughter."

Claudio was again unimpressed and unfazed.

"Do you not think she was worth the price? I told you that handful of treasure would save our lives."

"So what will you do now?"

"You have so little imagination, *niño*. Look around you. We have food, water, and shelter."

Claudio dropped to one knee and stared into the girl's face. He had never seen such a mixture of misery, fear, and abject hatred contained in a single glance. "I see we are delivered into the hands of our enemy."

"They," Gregorio waved his hand toward the villagers, "believe otherwise. Caliquen has been given to understand that a massive army follows us and that by the token of my marriage to his child, they will be spared."

"And how long will that illusion last?"

"*Tiempo suficiente*, time enough."

Claudio cast a sidelong glance at Juan Blue Jay, squatting outside in the courtyard. He might be a Christian, but he was still an Apalachee, an *indio*. He also understood Spanish. What had he heard? If he told the Potanos, Gregorio would never know until it was too late.

"You trust him?" Claudio finally asked.

"Juan? He is simple-minded, an *esclavo*."

But what would he do to gain his freedom from both masters, Claudio wondered. He suddenly realized Gregorio was staring at him oddly.

"Go! Eat. Rest. They will give you what you need," Gregario told him.

Claudio re-entered the courtyard and stood next to Eduardo.

"Have the men find shelter. The *indios* will provide food and water. We should get as much rest as we can."

"Are we not staying here?" Eduardo asked.

"*Si*, for now. We are living a lie and only God knows how long it will protect us. Keep your weapons near. Be careful."

Eduardo nodded, leading the rest of the band toward a cooking fire where an animal of some sort hung on a spit.

Claudio wanted to see more of the village while the sun was still high. Walking toward the perimeter, he made notes and sketches in his journal. From time to time, several little boys approached him, close enough to watch. Claudio smiled thinking of the consternation it must cause them to see this stranger making peculiar marks on something that looked like bark. Surely they must be wondering what it all meant. When he turned to look, they ran away, but he could sense their presence when he faced forward again. At any rate, their giggling and whispering usually betrayed them.

Slowly, he realized there were too many huts for the number of people he was seeing. It took a while longer to recognize that the missing part of the population were female. Except for the *cacique's* daughter and a few old crones, no women were in the village. They must have been hidden in the forest somewhere. Every conversation became muted as he passed by; everyone spoke in hushed tones even though he could not comprehend one word of their language. Even those who were bold enough to speak aloud did so in brief phrases.

Like many of the *indios* he had seen, the women who remained in the village went bare-breasted and wore skirts of fresh palmetto leaves. Some had sashes around their waist made of black moss. In contrast to the men, they wore their hair down, allowing it to grow long without ever cutting it. A few decorated their faces with intricate lines of charcoal or ochre, imitating the fearsome tattoos etched into their men's faces, arms, and legs. He noticed all of the men had a musky smell, not from body odor since they seemed to bathe quite often, but from the animal grease they used as pomade. They wore their hair wound in a ring around their head then pulled up into a large knot on the top of the head. So carefully and skillfully was it done, it almost seemed they were wearing hats instead of hair.

As he walked, he came across communal gardens, simple patches of cultivated ground growing squash, gourds, beans, and wild corn. The faint but unmistakable stench of human feces lingered above the ragged plots, indicating that the *indios* were fertilizing with night soil. Inexplicably, clumps of holly also grew in some spots, along with herbs he couldn't identify. Occasionally, the acrid plume of a smoldering fire sought him out, carrying with it the sweet scent of smoked meat. In some ways, the village was much like any small *pueblo* in Cuba. The only thing he hadn't seen was a well.

Inside the abandoned huts, he saw wooden and clay fetishes, oyster shell scrapers, bone awls, but no iron tools. They were clearly expert weavers, making mats and baskets of reeds, palm leaves, and a grass that resembled flax. They had mastered the art of tanning hides to a buttery soft texture and preserving furs. Nowhere did he see a single scrap of gold or silver, no turquoise or emeralds. No wonder Gregorio's ostentatious show of wealth had made such a big impression.

Passing one hut, he noticed an older man fletching an arrow. It was not the activity, but rather the flint arrowhead that caught his attention. From experience, he knew that flint was not local. Another warrior passed by with an obsidian knife in his hand. That could only have come from New Spain. With some alarm, he realized it must mean that they were in contact with other native people hundreds, even thousands of miles away. A few of the *indios* wore pendants or necklaces of amethyst or blue jade, earrings of copper—all from distant places. Maybe he was just imagining the extent of their connections, but if they were trading goods, they were exchanging information. The Potanos had known they were coming. That's why the women were gone. Why were so few warriors in the village? Where had they gone? They must already know there was no army. What were they waiting for?

Eventually Claudio made the entire circuit of the enclosure, returning to where he had left the men. Only Juan sat cross-legged outside the long house as if awaiting a call from his master. Gregorio appeared to be napping in his hammock, so Claudio took the opportunity to borrow his interpreter. "Juan, where does the village get their water?"

The little man smiled and pointed to the southeast. "The Rio Aguacaleyquen. It is not far. Do you have thirst?"

"No, but I wish to see it."

Juan scrambled to his feet and led Claudio from the encampment. Following a well-worn trail, they had barely gone a few hundred paces before Claudio noticed a low mound of barren earth in the forest. It was almost as long as the deck of a caravelle and twice the height of a man.

"What is that place?"

The ready smile on Juan's face disappeared completely. "That is the burial mound, *señor*."

For a few moments, he said no more, until a peculiar birdcall evoked another grin.

"*Tinibo pira*." He laughed, imitating a pecking motion. "Woodpecker"

It was less than a quarter league to the banks of a fairly wide river where dark brown water flowed west. They startled a young man filling his clay water pot, and he wasted no time hurrying back to the village. For a second, Claudio thought he saw suspicious glances exchanged between his guide and the young *indio*, as if each mistrusted the other.

Claudio picked up a small flat stone and expertly skipped it out into the river. One, two, three hops...

"When did the women leave the village?" he asked.

"*¿Qué?*" Juan pretended not to hear the question.

Claudio selected a slightly larger stone and flung it. One, two, three, four, five hops.... "I asked, when did the women leave the village?"

Juan stepped a little closer. "Two days ago, Your Excellency," he said in a conspiratorial tone that was almost a whisper. "The morning after the general appeared."

Claudio reached into his waistband and retrieved the sapphire Gregorio had sent him. Letting the sunlight hit it, he asked one more question.

"Where are the rest of the warriors?"

Juan's eyes glazed in greed. "*No se*, I don't know, *señor*," he stuttered.

Claudio drew his arm back as if to fling the small stone out across the water.

"No!" Juan stepped in front of him. "I swear on the Virgin Mary! I am but a slave here. I am not allowed in council, but thirty men left the same morning. They had taken the black drink and were ready for battle."

"Which way did they go?"

Juan pointed to the far side of the river. "Across there."

Claudio dropped the precious stone into the *indio's* hand. Gregorio had been right about one thing. Wealth could buy almost anything. But a man who can be bought can only be trusted as far as the extent of his avarice. This *indio esclavo* might be groveling at his feet now, but if someone else offered a higher price, he would just as quickly murder every Spaniard in sight.

***

Well after twilight, the men in the village stoked the council fire. Gregorio stepped down from the long house and struck a commanding pose in front of the rising flames as if waiting for something or someone. Juan squatted beside him, like a faithful hound. Gregorio had the smirk of a man who was supremely confident, standing aloof from everyone else, white and *indio*.

As Claudio watched, the gathering parted like a disturbance in a small pool, allowing a tall, rather elderly man to enter the circle of light. He wore a crown of reeds and feathers, adorned with small shells and bear claws. This had to be the *cacique,* Caliquen.

Caliquen was old by any standard, in his fifties at least. He was blind in one eye. A layer of opaque white membrane covered his pupil.

His hair had not yet dissolved into a natural salt and pepper color, but carried unnatural streaks of platinum through it. His chest and arms showed half a dozen wicked battle scars that broke up the tattoos lining his breast. When he turned to one side, Claudio spied a pale white pattern of burns that spidered their way across his left shoulder and halfway down his back. He had seen that kind of mark before, etched onto a sailor who had been struck by lightning and survived.

The *cacique* spoke in a rich, clear voice. Juan translated each phrase for Gregorio.

"I am glad you are well, my new son."

Gregorio bowed in his best royal manner.

"You have said there are many soldiers who will come soon. My people do not believe you will be able to stop them from burning our village and sending us away as slaves."

"I have given you my sacred pledge." Gregorio gestured back to where the *cacique's* daughter sat in the shadows.

Caliquen hesitated. "Your army did not listen to the word of your god when Chulusi Eyolehecote was taken." He pointed at Juan.

Gregorio looked down at the *esclavo*, his countenance changing from feigned injury to something harder. Before he could reply, Caliquen spoke again.

"I know you seek gold. More than scalps, more than slaves, your people need it. It is what they live for, why you have come." He could see from the quickening in the Spaniard's breathing that this was true.

"We have no gold, but we have this." Caliquen tossed a small leather bag close to where Juan crouched. The diminutive *indio* retrieved it and offered it up to Gregorio.

Gregorio poured the contents of the *bolsa* in his hand and slowly smiled. Returning the items to their purse, he handed it to Claudio.

"What think you now, *niño*?"

Inside were more than two-dozen, steely black opalescent pearls, almost perfect.

"I will show you where you may gather all you wish, if you will lead your army away from here so the people may live in peace," Caliquen said.

"How far is this place?" Gregorio asked.

136

"No more than three days across the Aguacaleyquen. They grow in the spirit river, Ibi Unuchua Chucu."

"We leave when the sun rises." Gregorio spun on his heels and climbed back into the long hut.

Claudio thought he noticed the vaguest of smiles on the *cacique's* face. He himself tried to remain inscrutable to keep the *indios* guessing. Juan Blue Jay had been studying each man's reaction carefully, trying to decide who had the advantage. Maybe he was just eyeing the swag of pearls. It didn't matter. Claudio wouldn't be able to sleep tonight anyway.

20
~~Cross City, Florida~~
June 19, 1959

Jim drove slowly down Warren Street, a crumbling asphalt road, dodging the worst of the potholes. It was clear nothing had been spent on infrastructure in this part of town since the thirties. Reading the mailbox numbers carefully, he watched for 2843. He found it in front of a wood frame shotgun house on a weed-choked lot. The porch was cluttered with a bicycle frame, bits and pieces of what appeared to be a lawn mower, and a moldy couch. Maybe he was at the wrong house. The man he remembered had never been sloppy.

The front door was open. The living room lights were on, so Jim knocked on the frame of the screen door. A boy that looked to be about eight years old peered at him from across the room.

"Is your Daddy home?"

From another room, a familiar male voice shouted with some irritation.

"Who is it, Bobbie?"

"Jessie!" Jim called through the screen. A man stuck his head out from the kitchen in the back.

"Who you?"

"Jessie, it's Jimmy C."

"Well I'll be damned. C'mon in, come in!"

Jessie Leroy was a slight man, dark-skinned with "good" hair. Dressed in work trousers and a pit-stained undershirt, he seemed less than the man Jim recalled. Back in the day, Jessie had always dressed sharply, even when he wasn't in uniform. From the stubble on his face to his dusty brogans, he was anything but sharp looking at the moment. *Maybe I just caught him at a bad time*, Jim thought.

"God, it's good to see you," Jessie said, retrieving his work shirt from a chair back as he crossed the living room. "Mae! Mae! Come here! Jimmy's here!"

Mae was a couple of years younger than both of them. Jim had introduced her to Jessie when she was still waiting tables at a juke joint in Columbus, a little dive just half a block from the base. What was it called? Henrietta's House, that's right... A light-skinned girl from North Carolina with shoulder-length hair, Mae was the girl next door. Fresh-faced with almond-shaped brown eyes, her smile was infectious. As she came down the hallway, wiping her hands on her apron, Jim could see she hadn't changed much.

"Mae, you're still cute as a bug."

"You still tryin' to get her away from me, ainchu sport?" Jessie laughed. The shirt he put on had a patch on the sleeve that read "Compton's Septic Service."

Jim almost regretted introducing the two of them. Their life together could have been his.

"This is our boy, Bobbie." Mae gathered her son.

"Bobbie, this is your daddy's best friend from the Army. You can call him Uncle Jim."

Jim took the boy's tiny hand in his massive paw and shook it gently.

"How ya doin', little man?"

"C'mon, let's have a beer," Jessie said. "I got a sack of oysters ready to roast out back."

As they all walked down the hall, Jim paused to read a framed document on the wall, Jessie's honorable discharge from the Army. Jessie came back to stand next to him.

"The old Triple Nickel," he murmured.

"I was always jealous that you got to be a paratrooper."

"I was a glorified fireman," Jessie grunted. "Besides, they don't make parachutes big enough for your giant ass."

It was Jim's turn to laugh. "Motor pool was okay."

"Okay? You were in the Second Armored. One of Patton's glory boys..."

It took only seconds before they both had a good guffaw over it all. It never mattered where they put you or what outfit you were with. Even with a war on, you were just another nigger in fatigues. It was a white man's war, and acting like a white man stopped being important the minute you got your walking papers. Wearing your dress uniform in 1945 would still get you nothing but insult or assault. Whites were happy to see black men go into the military, but they were just "uppity niggers" when they came back out.

Jim took the beer his friend handed him. "So you got a pretty good job."

Jessie shrugged. "I drive a pump truck, a shit wagon. It pays the bills mostly. You don't look like you missed any meals."

An enigmatic smile worked across Jim's face.

"Once a grease monkey, always a grease monkey. Mechanic for hire, will travel."

"At least you get to use what Uncle Sam taught ya. Unless a septic tank in the middle of the woods catches fire, I won't be jumpin' out of a plane any time soon."

The laughs started to flow more easily, the missing time in their friendship eroding away.

Bobbie burst back into the kitchen and confronted his father.

"Why you burnin' charcoal in my wagon?"

Jessie glanced over the table at his friend before answering.

"'Cause we got nothing else big enough to roast oysters on." Seeing the look on his son's face, he added, "I'll get you another one."

"A new one?"

"Sure."

The boy looked cockeyed at Jim, suspicion in his eyes. Jim nodded in agreement.

"He's somethin'." Jim smiled after the boy went back outside.

"Jus' like me." Jessie grinned.

Out in the backyard, their conversation turned to happier things. It wasn't 1941 all over again, but better somehow. The bad parts could be left out, glossed over. Only the good stories seemed worth retelling anyway. Little adventures grew into tall tales for Bobbie's benefit.

Sitting in the dark, the two friends talked about Jim's first airplane ride as a stowaway in the back of a DC3 jump plane on a training run.

Jessie had once taken a turn as the unauthorized driver of an armored half-track Jim had signed out to test repairs on. During that joyride, they managed to sideswipe a field latrine and almost got the huge vehicle stuck in a creek.

All the guys they spent meals and quarters with eventually showed up in memory around the little wagon grill. They had lost touch with most of them—Pukin' Parsons, the airsick paratrooper they always had to push out of the plane and Slack Jones, the most laid-back farm boy Jim had ever met. He was a helluva transmission man, though.

After Bobbie went to bed, the recollections continued in words spoken more softly. Fueled by beer and tempered by two decades of experience back in the world, the talk turned serious, the mood cynical. Candid observations uttered in conspiratorial whispers started when Mae went inside, to be interrupted at her return with a wink and a smile. Mostly though, they talked about the glory days, a time when they thought they had a future. In sharing, each tried to make the other think those days might be coming round again.

***

Jim awoke to find that Bobbie had already left for school. By the time he showered and dressed, Jessie was getting ready to leave.

"Sorry I slept in," Jim apologized. "I was gonna have breakfast with you."

Jessie smiled as he pocketed his keys.

"Mae's got some coffee for ya. She still cooks as good as she looks."

The two men shook hands.

"It's been great seeing ya again," Jessie murmured. "Just like it used to be."

Jim nodded. "I'll come back when I can. Next time, dinner's on me."

He watched his friend leave with mixed feelings. Jessie seemed to be doing okay, but he had changed..., a lot. Maybe that's the way it was supposed to be. People get older, they become someone else. A soft voice behind him startled him back to the present.

"Want a cup of coffee?" Mae asked.

"Sure," Jim smiled.

"Black, right?" her voice trailed off as she walked toward the kitchen.

"Uh, yeah, right." He followed.

She took a mug from the dish drain and poured coffee from a tall electric percolator into it. Made of carnival glass, the mug made the dark, steaming brew look as if it had an oil sheen. "It's really nice seeing you again," she said.

Jim looked at her hands. She had slim, elegant fingers. Her nails, once cut brutally short for waitressing, were now long and carefully polished. She wore a simple gold band on her left hand. *"Guess they can't afford much jewelry,"* Jim thought.

"I enjoyed meeting Bobbie," he said. "He's a good kid."

Mae flashed that terrific smile as she sat across the table from him. They sat with an awkward silence between them for a minute before Mae started up the conversation again. "What are you doing now? You never did say."

Jim toyed with the coffee mug while he answered, studying the sunlight through the kitchen window as it reflected off the glass. "Not much, really. I'm working for a guy right now as a mechanic." *Who has the better life*, he wondered to himself.

"At least you're working. Ever get married?"

Jim pursed his lips and shook his head. He tried to make the gesture nonchalant.

"Oh." There was a lot unsaid behind that one word.

"Never seemed to find the right time or the right..." Jim left the sentence unfinished and took a sip of his coffee. Finally, he re-worded his response. "I just hadn't thought much about it."

"You were always a nice guy." She made it sound like admiration, not consolation.

Jim took a deep slug of coffee and stood up.

"Thanks, Mae. Thanks for everything."

She followed him to the front door. Just before he reached for his duffel bag, she gave him a hug. He hugged back. He could feel her whole body against him, and they held the embrace for a few seconds longer than they should have.

"Goodbye, Jim," she said finally, backing away.

"Goodbye, Mae. Jessie's a lucky man." It was the same thing he had said to her thirteen years ago, right after Jessie proposed to her. Jim pushed himself out the door and was careful not to look back.

***

When he reached the motel, Lucky, Bill, and Ben stood outside the office under the breezeway. Their faces were solemn. At first, Jim thought Lucky was going to bitch at him for being late. It turned out to be something a lot worse.

"I just talked to the Coast Guard," Lucky said as he and Jim swapped keys. "Lonnie and his boat are missing. They're doing a sweep now between St. Marks and Galveston. No one's heard from him. No radio contact, nothing."

"Maybe he wound up having engine trouble again," offered Jim.

"Maybe. Ben's going to ride with you again. Just follow me."

Jim nodded and walked over to warm up the big truck's motor. *Not a good sign*, he thought, *not good at all*. Coming close on the heels of two near-fatal accidents, Lonnie Baker's disappearance had to be more than a coincidence. This whole thing was jinxed.

"I'm beginning to think this enterprise is cursed," Ben muttered as he climbed into the cab.

Despite the fact that Ben had homed in on his very thought and said it out loud, Jim wished he would shut up. It was bad luck to talk about curses. It would only make them stronger, more potent. He knew a little about hoodoo tricks and bad mojo. That kind of stuff was bad enough. Whatever it was that was following them was much worse. He had felt it back in that ravine. It was straight out of hell.

21
~~Puturiba~~
10 Octubre 1523

Claudio finally fell into a light sleep just after the moon set. His eyes fluttered open again when he realized it was light enough outside to see. Even those few hours of rest seemed to recharge him. At any rate, they could not afford to be caught unaware. Just outside the hut, he picked up the acrid scent of a lone smoldering fire near the village entrance. The quiet was eerie. Not a single bird sang to the early morning or to the promise of warmth the rising sun would bring. A single *indio* lay by the dying embers. As Claudio approached, he realized it was Juan Blue Jay. Otherwise, the town looked deserted.

Quietly, Claudio moved from shelter to shelter, stirring the men. He could just make out Gregorio's silhouette in the long house, pulling on his boots. "Comandante," Claudio called softly.

"*Buenas dias,*" Gregorio returned. "Eat what you can now. Bring with you any food you can find. Have the men ready to leave by the time the sun is fully risen."

"Where are the rest of them, the *indios*? Did they leave last night, deserting us?"

"They're here somewhere. Caliquen would not leave his beloved daughter."

The *cacique's* daughter remained tied to the post behind Gregorio. She was almost catatonic.

The pale light continued to gather, making the tree line glow in soft pastels. Juan Blue Jay stumbled to his feet, splashing water on his face from a nearby pot. "Where is everyone? Claudio repeated his question. "*¿Qué donde es?*"

Juan pointed beyond the palisade. "They went to the shaman to pray for a safe journey."

"Where?"

"The Mound of the Sun. It's near the river."

"Comandante, we need to leave now!" Claudio called over his shoulder.

Gregorio strode toward him, his hostage in tow. "What is it?"

"The *indios* have already left. Juan says they went to the riverbank. They may already be waiting in ambush."

Gregorio tipped his head slightly. "Come!" he ordered. "Let's go!"

"*Señor*, they only go to pray. They wait for the sun to rise," Juan protested.

Gregorio pushed him aside as the men began to file out of the village.

"Hernandez! If this is a trap, make sure you kill him first."

The small procession made their way through the forest in silence, following a narrow track toward the Aguacaleyquen. A thin haze drifted just above the ground. As they passed the burial mound, the eerie cry of some unseen bird wafted through the woods, setting pulses racing.

Claudio took his cues from Juan Blue Jay. He watched to see if the man was glancing left or right, anticipating an attack, but the little *indio* kept his head down, watching where he placed his feet, completely oblivious to the tension everyone else felt. The *cacique's* daughter awakened into a panic, her head swiveling back and forth, looking frantically for any chance to break free and escape. Only the noose around her neck and the sisal rope leash Gregorio held tightly in his left hand prevented her from doing so.

At the riverbank, seven dugout canoes lay beached in preparation for the crossing. The sun was cresting over the far bank. It would soon dispel the fog that floated over the water. They stopped and waited, listening for any sign that the *cacique* approached.

He appeared out of the mists over the water. They heard the splash of the paddles, but could see no rowers. Caliquen stood majestically,

145

head and shoulders above the low cloud bank. He beckoned for them to follow with a slow wave. It was only then that Claudio and the others realized that several men from the village had approached from behind. Sorting themselves into the canoes, the group pushed off quietly from the shore, their guides following the sound of the *cacique's* raft. Ghostlike, the entire flotilla moved out into the river, as if into nothingness.

For several minutes, they paddled blindly. Claudio could feel the current beneath them, pulling on the canoe as if trying to claim it. The paddlers compensated by turning the craft against it. It seemed to take longer than he thought it should. What was happening? Then he caught sight of a forested shoreline through the haze.

"Stay alert!" he called to his shipmates." If they intend to attack us, it will be here." He gripped his stiletto tighter.

"Hernandez!" Gregorio's voice came out of the fog nearby. "Remember."

"*Si*, Comandante."

Juan Blue Jay glanced over his shoulder at Claudio. Claudio was in a grim mood and he suspected it showed on his face. He would follow his leader's command and Juan probably knew that.

A shallow sandbank came into view and Claudio counted the number of canoes as they grounded on the shore. They all made it across. Splashing ashore, the company regrouped at the tree line. Caliquen looked at them carefully, one by one, almost as if counting their number. Finally, he turned and led them down a well-worn game trail into one of the thickest forests Claudio had seen yet. Quickly swallowing them, the landscape was lush with pines growing so thickly a man could barely squeeze between them. Gnarled cedars blocked out the sunlight, and the understory was a wall of palmettos and briars. This was an old wood, unchanged since creation. The air was thick with the earthy smell of rotting trees, vegetal decay, and faint floral scents. Even the heaviest tread was nearly silenced by pine needles and cedar bark strips covering the moist black earth underfoot. Sabal palms filled in the gaps between other trees so that a solid living curtain sheltered anything more than fifty paces off either side of the trail.

Two hours walk led them to more open country, with tall grass meadows interspersed with oaks, walnuts, and wild cherry trees. The sun had risen well over the tree line now, but the air was still cool and sweet. Claudio began to daydream, thinking of a future for a change. He wanted to stop walking and lie out in the grass to stare up at the sky. After all he had been party to, would God allow him to become a simple peasant again? He wanted to be like the *indios*—wanting for nothing nature could provide. Living gently, listening to the soft voice of the Creator and rejoicing in His bounty, what else could be desired? But could a man who had witnessed so many evils be allowed back into the Garden of Eden? Could that be? He had transgressed many times, failed on numerous and many occasions; surely, God would test him first. Even if that was the case, it would be slight tribulation to be allowed to live as the *salvajes* did. Maybe they were wrong to try to convert them. Maybe they knew God by another name.

Before long, they approached a dark line in the distance, marking an arroyo. Sheltered by cedars and tall, thick sycamores, they had to draw close before they could hear the murmur of running water. Here and there, black gum trees guarded the reed-choked banks. The trail ran parallel to the watercourse, dipping into a low swale and then climbing a small rise.

"*Dios mio*," someone said. "The water runs uphill." In fact, it appeared to do just that, ignoring the laws of nature.

Abruptly, Caliquen stopped them.

"*Ibi Unuchua Chucu*," he announced. "The Spirit River."

"This is where you get the pearls?" Gregorio surveyed the area. The water could flow any direction it wanted as long as it yielded the promised treasure.

The *cacique* pointed over the hillock. Cresting the mound, they could see the river widened and slowed, then formed a large dark pool that swirled slowly, dragging bits of flotsam on its surface. When they finally got to the rim of the whirlpool, the river simply ended as if the earth was swallowing every bucketful of water the stream delivered.

"Here," Caliquen announced. Ceremoniously, he cupped his hands and dipped them in the cool, dark waters of the whirlpool. Letting the water spill out over his face, he stood for a few seconds with uplifted hands, as if in silent supplication. Then he turned to look at his daughter, still tethered to Gregorio. After a long pause, he motioned for the villagers to go into to the river. They waded in slowly, feeling the bottom with their bare feet. One by one, they reached under the surface to dredge up small, blackened mussels, prying them open with small stone chips, sharpened on one side. More than a few held glimmering steel gray pearls. These were handed over, still in the shell to the *cacique*, who offered them to Gregorio. As he took them, the Spaniard dropped the rope, allowing his hostage to run to her father.

"Comandante," Claudio shouted. She was probably the only reason they weren't all dead yet.

"Shut up." Gregorio was still inspecting the shells, scooping out the pearls like seeds from a pea pod.

The air suddenly whirred with noises. The *indios* dove underwater as a storm of arrows rained down on the men left standing. Juan Blue Jay lunged for the river. Claudio had no choice but to throw himself into the tall grass to avoid being a target. He could hear the screams of wounded men and Gregorio's shouts of "Treachery!" Someone ran past him, headed back the way they had come. Then all was quiet. He lay face down for several minutes before many hands pulled him to his feet and disarmed him. Caliquen still stood at a distance with his daughter close by. He was conversing with a tall *indio* who stood with his back to Claudio. Juan Blue Jay knelt on one knee next to them. Every member of the ship's company lay dead or dying, riddled with long, stout arrows. Their blood seeped into the sweet, green grass, their faces a uniform expression of surprise and horror.

Looking up, Claudio saw several *indios* marching Gregorio back over the hill toward him, struggling every step of the way. Juan passed by with a guilty glance, clutching two silver coins in his left hand. What should have been surreal and devastating was almost a relief to Claudio. It had been inevitable. The *indio* pinning his right arm stared at him for a moment, and Claudio caught sight of a brand on his cheek. He was stunned to realize it was one of the *esclavos* he had set free from the wreck, the one they had called Chorotega. Glancing back up at the tall warrior ending his talk with Caliquen, he shuddered to think what might come next. But why was he still alive? Why had they not murdered Gregorio? When the *indio* turned to face him, it all became clear. He was once again staring into the scowling face of their old enemy, Yaotl.

22
~~Old Town Hammock, Florida~~
June 20, 1959

"Don't look like much, does it?" Bill surveyed the expanse of land Lucky had brought them to.

"Before they took out all the trees and bush-hogged, it was pretty wild," Lucky defended his orienteering.

"Besides, that waitress at the restaurant said there was some crazy guy who lived out here who could take us right to the old Indian town site."

"Out here?" Ben was dubious.

The whole area had been thickly wooded at one time. Numerous stumps bore witness to the wholesale slaughter of the old growth forest. When developers decided they wanted to make a grand subdivision, they cut nearly everything flush with the ground, but when they ran out of dough, any other improvements were forgotten. Surveyor stakes rotted in the sandy ground on each lot. New street signs stood over unpaved dirt roads. Ditches ran where water and sewer lines had been planned. It was as if everyone broke for lunch three years ago and never came back. Now the native undergrowth was reclaiming the clearing, like a four-day-old beard. Gallberry bushes and palmettos jostled for space under the grasp of greenbriers and enormous patches of blackberry.

A small column of dust announced the approach of an unidentified vehicle. Soon an old, dark green pickup truck arrived and a spry little man hopped out of the cab.

"Who're you?" the man demanded.

Lucky ignored the question and countered with one of his own. "I'm looking for Clark Buchet. Know where I can find him?"

The little man with curly gray hair grinned widely. "Yer lookin' at him."

"Nancy said you could show us where the old Indian town is."

"I know where it is. Whattya want with it?"

"Just to see it. Look around."

Clark craned his head back and scratched his grizzled neck. "Nancy sent ya, huh?"

Lucky walked back to the Jeep and returned with a small cardboard box.

"She sent you some biscuits and a piece of pie."

Buchet's eyebrows narrowed. "What kind?"

"Sweet potato, I think."

The little man's face returned to a broad smile.

"She's a sweetheart." He took the box and jumped back in the old Plymouth, waving for them to follow as he turned the truck around.

"You didn't bring me no pie," Jim observed.

"I pay you," Lucky reminded him. "Buy your own damn pie."

They stopped again less than a half mile from where they had started. Buchet pulled the old truck onto a small lot that was shady and covered in a mat of pine needles. Obviously, this is where he camped, what he called home. A low-roofed hut made of loose cinder blocks topped with a single sheet of corrugated tin served as his house. Next to the hut stood a fifty-five-gallon drum full of rainwater. A fire pit built with broken pieces of asphalt and concrete sat not far away. In one corner of the lot stood a larger windowless shed that looked like it could have once been a garage, but the front end was enclosed with field fencing to form a kind of paddock. It clearly wasn't for hoofed stock though since the top was secured with chicken wire. Along the side, various traps were stacked, some meant for live capture and some old-fashioned jaw clamps.

Amidst it all, Clark Buchet stood with his hands on his hips, like a king surveying his domain.

"Not bad, eh?"

Bill was the first to speak. "Where ya go to use the bathroom?"

"If ya gotta pee, just find someplace over there." Clark waved his hand toward the empty part of the lot about ten yards away. "If ya gotta shit, there's a hole over yonder. Ain't got no tollet paper, though. Just be sure ya put a shovel of sand over it when yer done. Keeps the flies down."

Bill stayed where he was.

"It looks like a comfortable camp." Lucky glanced around admiringly.

Clark flashed another smile, now showing a number of missing teeth.

"Comfortable! Why, I'd rather be here than in some fancy place in town. Wanna see a wolf?"

"A wolf?" Ben couldn't help himself.

Clark marched over to the paddock and disappeared inside the shed. A half-second later, a large coyote bolted from the cover of the shed, looking anxiously at the fence, nervous at Clark's intrusion.

"That ain't no wolf," Jim muttered.

"Right," announced Clark, herding the animal back inside. "I didn't think you city boys would know the difference." The small man chuckled as he re-pinned the clasp on the door.

"Whattaya going to do with it?" Lucky asked.

"Sell it to the university so's they can study it. They'll eventually turn it loose again."

Lucky waited until Clark came back out of the enclosure before he continued.

"So the Indian town, you can show us where it was?"

Clark looked each one of them over, studying them, and they did the same in return.

Buchet was naturally dark-complexioned, but hours in the sun had deeply tanned every bit of exposed skin. Long grooves creased his weather-beaten face made old before its time. He wore a long-sleeved, khaki work shirt over khaki work pants, held up by thin suspenders. Where his pants legs met his brogans, the cuffs were tattered with wear. He was the last of a breed, a true Florida cracker.

"It'll cost ya," he said finally.

"How much?"

Clark shrugged. "A pound a coffee if ya got it."

Lucky jerked his head toward the truck and Ben ambled back to get the price of admission.

When the unopened can was in his hands, Clark smiled easily.

"Ya ready?"

"Yep."

"Let's go."

Fifty yards down a dirt road, Clark struck out through the underbrush along a game trail, weaving around briar thickets and muddy depressions full of fiddlehead ferns and deer moss. Only once did he pause to get his bearings.

After about fifteen minutes at a brisk hike, he stopped and pointed.

"That's where it was."

There was no indication anyone, much less a group of people, had ever lived on the patch of ground he indicated.

"If ya notice, there's no really big trees growin' out there," he said. "The brush is high now, but when the college folks came out to dig up the place, they chopped a lot of it back. You can still find broken pots and bowls, arrowheads and the like if ya know where ta look."

Lucky wasn't interested in the village so much as the burial mound he knew had to be close by.

"There's a mound near here, isn't there?"

Clark seemed surprised his visitors knew that. "Yeah," he said slowly.

"Can we get there from here?"

"Shore." The man seemed hesitant, but headed off toward deeper forest.

As they walked, a stray cloud hid the sun, cooling the air markedly. The light coming through the trees lost its contrast, softening and darkening the scene. Soon, Lucky could make out the long, low profile of a midden, disguised by cedar trees and thick, rope-like vines. Clark stopped to announce they had arrived, but Lucky led them on past until they reached the riverbank.

"The Suwannee River," Clark said to no one in particular.

Lucky stared across the tea-colored water for several minutes before he turned to the group.

"They crossed here."

Ben looked around the empty shoreline, then across the river to the

152

jungle on the other side. For the first time since they started this crazy scheme, he felt the reality of what had happened so many centuries before.

"The Black Mouth is out there somewhere," Lucky murmured.

"The Spirit River," Bill mumbled, as if sizing up the journey ahead.

"What?" Clark asked.

"Nothing," Lucky snapped out of his daydream. "Never mind." He shook hands with the short man, palming a ten-dollar bill.

"Thanks for showing us around, Mr. Buchet."

***

When they stopped for supplies in Trenton, Ben knew they were getting ready to be out in the boondocks for a couple of days. He had no idea exactly where, other than Lucky had mentioned some place called the Black Mouth. Bill called it the Spirit River. As they put cardboard boxes of groceries into the truck, it struck him that if Bill knew what the place was called, he must know more about things than he was telling. How did Bill know that name? Were he and Lucky in cahoots now? Was that why they always rode together while he and Jim were stuck off by themselves? The thought of it pissed him off. He and Dollar were supposed to be buddies. Bill had always looked out for his guys. Maybe now he was looking out for himself. Ben decided he had better do the same.

The highway out of town was as empty as any they had seen. Two miles from the store, they were in the middle of a saw grass savannah interspersed with thick forests of pine and oak. Twenty minutes later, Lucky signaled a left turn onto a narrow county road leading out into the woods. Somehow, he spotted a dirt road that meandered out into the middle of nowhere. Bouncing down the rough dirt track, swallowing dust thrown up from the Jeep out in front, Jim managed to keep up until they finally halted at a clearing. Lucky signaled them to back the truck up into the tree line. When the big engine growled to a halt, all they could hear was cicadas.

"This is it," Lucky said, looking satisfied.

Ben and Jim looked out the windshield and then at each other.

"Here we go again," Ben mumbled.

***

The tents were up and dinner was on the grill long before sunset. As it grew dark, Jim built a smoky fire from some rotten oak that did little to drive away the mosquitoes.

Lucky hunkered down upwind of the thick mantle of fumes coming from the fire.

"Men, we're here because we need one of the last pieces of the puzzle. After this, we may be able to locate the spot we've been trying to find all this time."

Like a good storyteller, he paused for effect as he lit a cigarette.

"We've been tracking down the loot from a Spanish ship—over a million dollars in gold, silver, gemstones, and pearls. When that ship went aground, the Spanish off-loaded all of it. They had it with them when the local hostiles attacked and took every scrap of it away. The Indians then hid it where they thought no one would ever find it again. But we're close. It's all in Hernandez's journal."

"So what are we looking for here? What's this Black Mouth River got to do with it?" Ben asked.

Lucky took another long draw on his cigarette.

"Somewhere out here is a river that was sacred to the aboriginals. They called it the Black Mouth, probably because it disappears underground in one spot."

"Bill, you said it was called the spirit river." Ben couldn't help himself, "How did you know what it was called?"

Bill never looked over at him. "You think Lucky's the only guy around here who reads? I saw it in a Ripley's Believe It or Not comic one time."

"It figures that the only part of the paper you might read would be the funnies," Ben said sarcastically. "I just wondered if you were starting to pick up sixteenth-century Spanish classics."

"Anyway," Lucky continued. "We need to find that sink. It'll tell us where to start and how far to go, even in what direction to head."

"One more thing." Lucky flipped the butt of his cigarette into the fire. "This river ought to be pretty easy to find. It runs uphill."

"What?" This time Jim spoke up. "Ain't no water that runs up against a grade."

"This one does." Lucky sighed slightly as he rose to his feet. "I'm turning in. We need to get at it early in the morning."

"Me, too," Bill said, leaving the circle of light abruptly.

Ben added a few pine cones and some sprigs of green needles to the fire, trying to coax a bit more illumination from the fitful flames. In the distance, an owl called, his interrogative refrain echoing softly through the forest.

"Ya damn right, who?" Ben muttered. He wasn't sure now who he could believe, who he should trust, or what the hell was going on.

"What?" Jim asked from the opposite side of the fire.

"Nothin'." At least he was pretty sure of Jim's motives. In fact, right this minute, Jim was the most stand-up guy of them all.

In a dark forest, it always felt later than what any clock might read. Ben's watch seemed frozen, barely moving beyond nine o'clock. He finally wandered off to bed, leaving Jim alone by the fire.

***

Jim had decided several days ago that things were slowly going from bad to worse. When they did find the gold, if they found it, he wasn't sure these white folks wouldn't all stab each other in the back for it. He was sure of one thing. When it came to dividing up any loot, his name was going to be on the bottom of the list. Ol' Nigger Jim, was goin' to be an afterthought. Still, that might be okay. The treasure they were after had already been steeped in hate and bought with blood. He was pretty sure he didn't want any part of it. The gold itself was cursed, he was sure of that. It would never bring anything but trouble to anyone who owned it. He would be content to just collect his paycheck and get the hell out of this waking nightmare. That cash could buy him a nice future.

He sat hypnotized by the coals for a long time, watching the shimmering flames dance in changing hues of red, blue, and gold. Even as the fire crumbled into angry red embers and the light all but disappeared, he sat immobile. He thought to get up and add a log, but never moved. Paralyzed, he imagined he saw fantastic shapes in the glowing charcoal. Phantoms of smoke, tricks of light and shadow rose before him.

It had to be close to the witching hour when distant sounds stirred him from his waking dreams. Just like before, he heard shouts and screams, faint and indistinct. Cocking his head first one way and then another, he finally sensed it was coming from deep within the forest, maybe even beyond. After a few minutes, the noise faded, swallowed up again by the night. A different man might have gotten scared. Jim already knew he was dealing with demons. They had all made a bargain to steal a fortune from the devil, and it was not going to come cheap. He lifted a silent prayer for his soul's sake and went to go sleep in the cab of the truck.

***

When the light returned, it revealed a sky with many clouds. The morning air was still cool from the night before, thick with humidity as the team fanned out into the woods. The screech of blue jays followed them and occasionally the rasping of a mockingbird would make their passing obvious. No sound came from the forest floor, however. With pine needles layered over soft, moist black earth, it absorbed every footfall like a deep shag carpet.

They took less than an hour to work their way out of the woods and onto a broad grassy savannah full of low, rolling hills that looked like swells at sea on a breezy day. In the distance, a line of dark green marked the edge of some watercourse—a large stream or small river perhaps. The four men gathered before starting across the prairie.

"Think that's it?" Ben asked.

"I'd be willing to bet on it." Lucky glanced down at his field map. "If it is, all we have to do is follow it until we come to the sink. It's probably off that way." He pointed toward the northeast.

"The Santa Fe isn't far off, maybe five miles or so. We can't get too lost."

They advanced four abreast through the high grass, with Lucky taking the point. A brilliant shaft of sunlight burning momentarily through a gathering overcast washed away the uneasiness as they trudged onward. The air was sweet with the bouquet of green-growing things and laced with the smell of water. It was not the clean scent of rain on the wind, but rather the brackish aroma of water made to linger, gathered in pools. The green line soon revealed itself to be a corridor of sycamores, cedars, water oaks, and tupelos, cloaking the dark waters of a shallow stream. It was about twenty feet across, too wide to jump and the banks were steep.

They followed the river as it flowed north, walking single file now. Sheltered from the sun, the trail was easy until they encountered the rise and fall of many low hills, like furrows in a garden. The river never seemed to change course or elevation, ignoring the wrinkled earth. Eventually, they came to a hill larger than the rest that dropped quickly into a wide depression that might have once been a lake bed. On the far side was an equally tall bluff, one that did not deter the river.

"Willya lookit that!" Bill said incredulously. The black water seemed to be surging up and over the rise without hesitation.

"It's running uphill," Jim breathed.

"I'll be damned," Ben said, shaking his head.

"Helluva sight, ain't it?" a voice called from across the river. At first, they couldn't see anyone until a short figure stood up and stretched.

"It never ceases to amaze me," Buchet added.

"How did you get here?" Lucky said irritably.

"Hell. You ain't th' only one that knows somethin' about this place."

"Whattya mean?"

"I mean, I know about the treasure."

"What are you talkin' about, old man?" Bill joined in.

"When you showed up yestiddy, I figgered out pretty quick you weren't no perfessors and you damn sure weren't tourists. You must be huntin' the injun gold."

"There's no gold here," Lucky said finally.

"Ain't none ever been found," Clark agreed. "Used to be a lotta freshwater pearls in the river, but they disappeared a long time ago. My great-granddaddy used to tell stories about finding mussels when they went crawdad fishing. I ain't never seen one in here."

While the team tried to figure out what to do, Clark continued talking.

"You prolly wanna see the suck, where the river goes underground."

"Yeah, sure," Lucky admitted.

"C'mon. I'll show ya."

Leading the way from the opposite bank, Clark led them over the hill to a broad pond nearly hidden under massive cypress and cedar trees. At the bottom of a wide crater, the river flowed into a massive, slowly swirling eddy. Since there was little evidence that the pond rose or fell, as much water had to drain out as in. This was the Black Mouth.

"I bet this flows all the way to the Santa Fe," Lucky mused.

"I wouldn't be surprised," Clark agreed.

Several of the enormous bald cypress were big enough to have seen the Spanish refugees pass under their broad canopies four hundred years ago. These were trees who could count their lives in centuries, even millennia. *What had they witnessed?* Lucky wondered.

Making a few cryptic notes on his map, Lucky surveyed his bearings, looking for landmarks. It was obvious he wasn't going to be able to get rid of his sightseer, so he decided to try and make use of him.

"So what do you know about this Indian gold story?"

"I know what I heard from people use ta live out here."

Bill came up and stretched out in the grass, pulling a stem to chew on.

Clark was surprisingly forthcoming.

"The Spanish was runnin' for the east coast. Guess they thought they might find a ship there. This bunch had some balls. They were tryin' to make the local tribe help 'em."

Clark stopped to roll a cigarette. He refused Lucky's offer of a store-bought.

"Anyways," he continued after the ragged smoke was lit. "It didn't work out. Another tribe showed up and massacred the lot of 'em."

"What about the gold?" Ben asked, walking up from behind.

"Story goes that the Injuns buried it all somewhere hereabouts. Th' old timers use ta dig for it all the time. Some folks say they threw it in the suck." Clark indicated the whirlpool below them.

"Well if it's down there, it'll have to stay there," muttered Jim, bringing up the rear.

Clark turned to him with a knowing look. "That was the idee, buck."

Lucky was satisfied that unless this little redneck was smarter than he looked, the secret was still safe. He knew for a fact that the treasure was miles from here. Hernandez had said so. His problem was still how to get rid of this nosy son of a bitch.

"Thanks for the help and the story, Mr. Buchet."

"I don't mind, don't mind it at all." The man hitched up his pants and put out his cigarette underfoot. "I gotta git. It's a long way back to camp."

Lucky breathed silent thanks to the powers that be. "Good to see you," he lied.

"I'll catch up wit ya later," Clark called out over his shoulder.

Like hell, thought Lucky. He glanced down at Bill.

"Bill, get up," he said abruptly.

"Why? Are we in a hurry to go somewhere?"

"No, but your arms are covered in ticks."

Bill clambered to his feet, brushing off a dozen tiny seed ticks. He spotted more and more as he inspected himself. They crept around the back of his neck, as if running for cover in his hairline. Goosebumps pimpled his arms as he realized the bloodsuckers were swarming his body.

"Lucky, you got 'em all over your trouser legs."

Lucky dusted himself off, almost in a panic. He fought off an urge to drop his pants right there and check his legs. Somewhere, he and Bill had wandered through a nest of the tiny voracious insects.

"Dammit," he swore with intensity. His face became flushed.

"We gotta go de-louse ourselves. C'mon."

"Why don't ya just get in the water?" Ben asked.

"Good idea." Bill stripped down as he headed for the riverbank.

"I'm going back to camp and get my bug dope," Lucky announced.

159

He was not ready for a cold bath yet. Jim followed as Lucky headed back across the open field to the woods beyond.

***

"He's doing double-time now," Ben observed, watching the pair stride briskly out of view. A huge splash behind him redirected his attention. He grinned as he watched Bill bob up and down in the waist-deep water, scrubbing every place he could reach. Ben sat on the edge of the steep bank to wait for his friend. The shade had become deeper, darker as the clouds overhead massed into large thunderheads, blocking out the sun. Lighting up a cigar, he watched the smoke spiral away on a freshening breeze.

"Gonna rain soon. Looks like a storm coming in from the Gulf."

"Suits the hell outta me," Bill spluttered, rinsing his hair for the last time. "It was getting too hot anyway."

"I wonder how Dan's doing?" Ben mused as Bill washed his shirt.

"Still in the hospital, I'm sure."

Ben puffed on his cigar in silence.

"You don't still think any of that was your fault, do you?" Bill asked.

Ben was slow in answering. "No. I guess it just happened that way."

"Still think Duprez has something up his sleeve?"

"No." Ben was being truthful. With everything that had happened, the only person he was losing confidence in was standing in front of him.

A rumble of thunder in the distance interrupted their conversation. Bill climbed the steep bank and wrung out his wet shirt.

"Guess we'd better head back."

A louder clap of thunder spurred them on. They managed to make the tree line before the rain began to fall in huge drops. Wordlessly, they trudged through the ensuing downpour, dodging windblown debris coming from the treetops. Half-blinded by the rain, Ben caught glimpses of shadowy figures moving through the forest. Hesitating for a second, he watched as a flash of lightning lit up the scene.

"What's wrong?" Bill yelled over the roar of the storm.

Ben shook his head and moved on. The silhouettes and dark shapes continued to slip by them on either side, dissolving into the underbrush whenever he looked directly at them. *It's a trick of the light*, he thought. Nevertheless, it made him wish he had worn his pistol instead of leaving it in the truck.

Walking with their heads down, they were both startled to abruptly discover a huge hulking dark figure standing in front of them.

"I was afraid you might get lost," Jim called.

"Thanks. We weren't sure how much further it was," Ben yelled back. The rain fell as hard as ever. It was like standing under a high, cold waterfall.

The bright light of a Coleman lantern under the dining fly illuminated a big pot of chili bubbling on the grill. Ben thought it was the two best things he had ever seen. Lucky had already sequestered himself in his tent. In the premature twilight, only the dim glow of a candle lantern shone inside, occasionally revealing his movements. They huddled around the grill, trying to dry out, dipping hunks of bread into the pot. The communal meal was exactly what they needed, strengthening the bonds of respect. Little was spoken, but much was said. Their shared misery at being wet, cold, and tired was somehow mitigated. *Had there been a moment like this for that shipwrecked crew?* Ben wondered.

23
~~ Potano Provincia~~
10 Octubre 1523

The dead had no complaints, but the moans and cries of the dying escalated into shrieks of pain as the *indios* cut off ears as war trophies. Some took whole patches of scalp with hair attached, waving their grisly souvenirs with shouts of victory. Watching over all, Yaotl stood impassively, speaking only to prevent any mutilation of his two living captives. His apparent protection only chilled Claudio's blood further. Obviously, their fate would be much worse than simple murder. The sight of the *carpintero's* head was still vivid in his nightmares.

As the few weapons the Spaniards had carried were collected, two natives grabbed his arms and tied them tightly to his side with a coarse hemp rope. Claudio recognized it as being part of the ship's stores that were salvaged from the wreck. A few yards away, other *indios* held Gregorio down as they lashed his arms to a stout sapling cut from the riverbank. When they finally raised him to his feet, a length of rope was tied around his neck like the leash he had used on the *cacique's* daughter. As they dragged Gregorio forward, Claudio felt a shove in the back. Staggering a few steps, he turned to see Chorotega beside him, motioning for him to walk.

Half a league from the Ibi Unuchua Chucu, they cleared the low hammock surrounding the river and walked out onto the relative openness of a vast upland prairie. Broken by alternating patches of meadow and hardwood forest, the countryside was dotted with lakes, ponds, and sinkholes. Yaotl seemed to be navigating eastward using them as landmarks. Several times, Claudio was allowed to drink the cold, clear water of many small springs with the rest of the group, but he noticed that they were keeping Gregorio from it. Only once did he see an *indio* pour water over the Comandante's face, allowing a few drops to trickle down his throat. Exertion and dehydration were taking their toll on the man. His face was flushed a crimson red, while his hands had turned waxen from the lack of circulation. When they marched, he stumbled forward with eyes half closed, a grimace of pain on his brow. Whatever antagonism Claudio had had toward him rapidly evaporated as he watched him suffer.

He wrestled with his conscience as they crossed the wilderness. If he had not rescued Yaotl, they might not be in captivity now, but he could not have simply allowed the *indios* to drown, chained to a doomed ship. He did not have it in him to murder, even by neglect. Christ had compelled him to act, to free them to take their chances with everyone else. Now he would have to trust that Christ would deliver them. Yet there was the cruel irony that while he was not willing to kill another in the name of God, he must be prepared to die for that belief. It was God's will that they were as they were. It was not by the hand of man that Gregorio was now subject to the torture of bondage and thirst. This was the purification, a chance to return to a state of grace.

> *We covered nearly two more leagues by nightfall and, in the darkness, we found Utinamocharra. A modest town of sixty or so* indios, *it sat open-sided on a small plain, without any palisade or other defenses. A dozen small cook fires were immediately made to blaze up as Yaotl brought us in for the tribe's inspection. Paraded in our humiliation as trophies of war, they offered him great admiration. All the demons of hell could not have howled and screamed louder than those savage, violent, and horrifying shapes half-lit by raging flames. The whole village shared in our ignominy. Even the children threw sticks and clods of earth at us, participating in our capture by proxy.*

My bonds were cut so that I could eat in relative comfort. Chorotega gave me acorn bread, baked in the ashes and a stew of wild game. A large clay pot of fresh water was placed beside me. I saw Gregorio at a distance, still encumbered by his yoke, struggling on his hands and knees to reach the scraps of food they threw on the ground in front of him. He ate like a beaten dog, fearful and yet ravenous. Bolting raw pieces of offal, he choked and gagged to keep it down. Finally given a dipper full of water to slake his thirst, it foamed on his lips as he collapsed in exhaustion.

I hoped that Yaotl thought to offer me the same choice I had given him. Perhaps my Christian act of compassion might serve to spare me whatever horrible torture that they planned to visit on Gregorio. Yet, these were Potanos, not Christians, with their own brutal justice and savage code. If Yaotl intended to move us further east, we would soon be in Atimuca country. He might be inclined to sell me into slavery there. But whatever occurred, it seemed that Comandante Gregorio and the Anahuac cacique were destined to end their blood feud here. Gregorio would not, and could not live much longer.

- *El diario de* Claudio Hernandez

Amazed that the *indios* did not return to tie him up again, Claudio sprawled on his back in the leaves under a huge live oak and began to approach a degree of relaxation. The night became cooler as the hours went by. He watched the moon rise through eyes heavy with sleep, yet true rest eluded him. From time to time, he rose on one elbow and stared intently at the body of Gregorio, slumped in a heap, but still breathing. Occasionally, he could hear Gregorio's hacking cough, as if at any moment he would breathe his last.

In the center of the village, the tribe gathered around the coals of the council fire. Claudio could hear them murmuring in some deep discussion. He thought he saw Yaotl standing before the group. Clearly, their fate was being debated. Soon, the muffled sound of wood against wood resonated across the clearing. The beating of the medicine drum began—a gentle thumping noise like a heartbeat. Gradually, it grew more distinct as more drummers added their energy. It became alive, the pulse of the planet.

Clumsily gaining his feet, Claudio stealthily crept forward, hoping to hear or see something that might give him an idea of what to expect at sunrise. He caught a glimpse of the *cacique* squatting by the fire. When Yaotl stood, he had a double handful of red-hot coals. Blowing on them to make them glow, he walked to where a small pile of kindling lay. Carefully depositing the embers into the small twigs and short branches, he stood up and waited for the newly laid fire to erupt into flames. In the orange light, Claudio could see that neither of Yaotl's hands showed charring, nor any sign of burns. The *indio* then stepped onto the bed of coals left by the council fire and indicated that they should lay on more wood. Soon, he was surrounded by tall, angry, yellow flames. Claudio could see the heat shimmering up, making Yaotl an apparition that flickered and waved, but he did not catch fire. After a few minutes, the man walked serenely out of the conflagration and offered himself for inspection. The drumming abruptly stopped. Claudio found himself holding his breath. There was not a singed spot on his body, nor was his long hair touched. Truly, he was a *brujo*.

***

Not far away, an owl hooted under the sickle-shaped moon. The mournful moan echoed through the forest like the notes from a flute, low and sorrowful.

"Techlotl chants the death song," Chorotega murmured to no one in particular.

"It is the omen of death for the enemy," Yaotl agreed.

"Yaotl," Chorotega asked as they settled back down by the fire. "Why did they name you that? It means warrior, but also enemy."

Yaotl inhaled deeply before he answered. "Before I was born, our village was raided by many warriors from another tribe. My mother was raped in the attack. I was the result. She named me Necoc Yaotl, the 'enemy of both sides', so that I might never forget. I was born under the sign of Ceacatl, the mark of the witch and the sorcerer. I was

165

given great power and secret knowledge by Tezcatlipoca, but I have been cursed by him, too. I have seen my own death and with it, the end of this world."

"What did you see?"

"The world will be destroyed by great earthquakes. When the earth is shattered, Tezcatlipoca will steal the sun. Darkness will swallow everything and even the stars will fall from the night sky. Four demons will come to devour all human life. It will be the end of all things."

Chorotega shivered slightly. Somewhere out in the darkness beyond the village, a tzitzimine, that most horrific of demonic beings, might lurk. With long unkempt hair nearly covering their glowing eyes, dressed in a necklace of human hearts, they waited for the unwary. Their long bony fingers, like talons, could snatch a man without warning. With fangs sharper than a jaguar, they could render human flesh in seconds. To imagine a perpetual night in a broken landscape among the tzitzimitl was to glimpse the seven levels of Mictlan.

***

The sun returned in a clear blue sky, hanging as if reflected in a deep lake. Chorotega again bound Claudio's wrists together, but did not leash him. Claudio watched as they removed Gregorio's yoke and hobble, tying his arms to his sides instead. Pulling on his leash, as a man might coax a stubborn burro, they eventually got him to stand. Yaotl set a casual but steady pace out of the village, southeast through the forest. It was clear they were now traveling an Anahuac road, well-worn and headed directly toward the provincial capital of Potano.

They were being marched to certain death, yet even in his fear, Claudio recognized that he was seeing land no white man had ever laid eyes on. The air was sweet and clear, scented with the fresh aroma of green things growing in profusion. The oak canopy was full of the sounds of songbirds. Treading the leafy pathway, strewn with scattered patches of soft grass, he again thought he glimpsed a kind of Eden. It was the life, the land they should be seeking, not gold or silver. If he was to die, it should be here—not in battle or at sea—wracked with disease or frail with the infirmities of old age. If God took his life now, it would be on the doorstep of paradise.

We entered the city just before noon. Sequestered in a large clearing near a bog, it was marked by several earthen mounds twenty to thirty feet in height and a slightly taller mound in the center. I saw several hundred inhabitants of diverse age and sex.

Our previous humiliation was repeated, more vociferous than before, with demeaning gestures and what were, no doubt, vile epithets in their language. We were led to the base of the central mound where several racks held the numerous skulls of previous captives in various states of decay. At the top of a long flight of palm steps was a broad-shouldered, stocky man with a placid stare. It could only be the great cacique *Potano himself.*

We were dragged up the stairs unceremoniously so that he could inspect us further. When we were closer, I saw that he was a man in his mid-forties, bearing different tattooed markings than any of the others. In fact, he bore more resemblance to the Mexica than the native Potano or Timucua. He wore a wide chest piece of turquoise, amber, and mother of pearl that covered his shoulders. In his nose and ears were bangles of fine gold. His hair, worn in the local fashion, was bedecked with bright pink plumes and many jet black feathers. Carrying a large mace, studded with sharp slivers of flint, he had the bearing of a king, the giver of all law. In his presence, we had become the salvaje. *He gazed upon us as a man might consider livestock.*

His retinue contained many warriors, some of whom carried Spanish weapons—halberds that had been cut down to make battle axes. One of these stepped forward to force us into a prostrate position, at which time I noticed a large basket near the cacique's *feet. It took little effort to recognize its heaped contents as the silver and precious stones that had been part of the* Mano del Rey's *cargo. Even in his weakened and*

167

demoralized state, Comandante Gregorio's eyes widened
at the sight. Then just as abruptly as we were ushered up
the wide steps, we were dragged back down and forced
into a low, small hut.
     - *El diario de* Claudio Hernandez

As soon as they were alone in the darkness, Gregorio inched closer to Claudio.

"Hurry, *niño*," he hissed. "Untie my hands and we will escape."

"Where would we go?" Claudio asked incredulously. "There are fifty *indios* within a spears throw."

"Do you want to wait until they come to murder us?"

Claudio hesitated. Gregorio had been marked for execution. But there might be a possibility that he, himself, might yet be released. It was only a vague hope, a foolish notion, but it was better than following Gregorio to what would be a short run to freedom.

"You will get nothing but a shaft in the back, a war club to the head. Run now and you have no chance. If I untie you, they will discover it and separate us. Together, we might have a chance."

The whites of Gregorio's eyes glimmered as he stared in disbelief.

"So you will not help me?"

"No."

"Then may God have mercy on you. I knew from the beginning you were a weak-minded poltroon. Coward!" Gregorio spat the last word out as if it had a foul taste. He looked around in rapid desperate glances. Whether from fear or circumstance, the man had descended irrevocably into madness.

"Did you see that basket?" Gregorio seemed to be talking to the air, maybe to an unseen spirit.

"Booty from the *Mano del Rey*," Claudio murmured.

"Thieves!" Gregorio almost shouted. "It belongs to me. Mine. I will have it back. Then I will burn every last *bastardo* alive and feed their entrails to the pigs. You will die like the rest, traitor. Pray for your soul." Gregorio turned his wild-eyed gaze back upon Claudio.

24
~~Gilchrist County, Florida~~
June 22, 1959

Bill, Ben, and Jim stood around the Jeep while Lucky spread out a map and his papers on the hood for one more morning briefing. They were tired, tired from a soggy mosquito-ridden attempt at sleep the night before, and tired from the stress of the journey. They were not the same men who had gathered on the beach at Dead Man Bay a week ago. It seemed as though a month had gone by. With one friend in the hospital and one MIA, the seriousness of the expedition had intensified. It was no longer an adventure, but a quest. Work, real work lay ahead of them. The money had looked like a boon. It was going to be easy money, money for nothing. A hundred and twenty-five a week didn't feel like it was enough now. But they were well past the point of no return. They owed it to Dan to stick it out. Hell, they owed it to themselves.

"So from the Black Mouth," Lucky said, tapping his finger on the map. "They were marched fifteen miles east, first to a spot near High Springs, then to Alachua. The first Indian town he mentions was somewhere southwest of High Springs. The journal says it was just a half-day's walk to Potano, which was south of Alachua."

"Do we know where that was?" Bill asked.

"Not exactly. I'm going to charter a small plane at Gainesville to see if I can find the actual location."

Lucky scratched his chest vigorously. The rash of chigger bites covering both arms was plainly evident. Ben knew from childhood experience that the man was being eaten alive. Red bugs burrowed into your skin and made themselves at home. His dad had always used Parsons to kill the insects and relieve the itch. There wasn't enough ammonia in the state to kill all the parasites Lucky was carrying around. "Better get some calamine lotion while you're there."

"Yeah," Lucky grimaced. "Need a shot of antihistamine, too."

"Are you allergic?"

"Yeah, I think so."

If Lucky was truly starting to have a reaction to the bites, it wouldn't be long before he swelled up. Sometimes people got to where they couldn't breathe.

"Anyway, what I was saying is that when we can pinpoint the location of that last Indian town, we have a pretty good line on where the treasure was hidden. The village ought to be pretty easy to spot. Hernandez said there was a thirty-foot-high mound in the middle of it.

"Jimbo, we're gonna take State Road 236 over to High Springs, then 441 down to Alachua. We'll gas up when we get there. There's a VFW post about three blocks south down Main Street. You guys hole up there till I get back from Gainesville this evening. Any questions?"

No one had any, at least none that they wanted to ask in front of each other.

The road to High Springs was empty, lined only with farmsteads. The highway between High Springs and Alachua was more of the same, only the road was wider—four lanes instead of two. In fact, to the casual eye, there wasn't much difference in the two towns except that the core business district of High Springs hugged Highway 441 as it ran west to east. Alachua's Main Street and the downtown hub lay off the highway, having grown up along State Road 235, which ran north and south. Beyond that, the two places were much alike in nature and character. Ten years behind the times, like most small towns in Florida, they existed in cultural isolation. A sort of conservative miasma permeated them, as palpable as the humidity in summer. Both were stifling.

The VFW was a nondescript, white clapboard building that reminded them of the temporary barracks that used to be on Boca Chica during the war. It sat next to a softball diamond, and the dirt parking lot was shaded by several large live oaks. They had spent time in worse places while waiting for something to do. Bill went inside and brought back a round of beers, the bottles dripping with condensation. They sat on the running board of the truck, drinking and dreaming.

"So whatcha gonna do with the money you're getting, Jim?" Ben swilled the icy Blue Ribbon beer and belched.

Jim shook his head, "Ain't really thought about it much. I might go into business with one of my buddies back home. He's always wanted us to open a garage out in Selma. Been after me for years to work with him. He's got a contract for the city buses. Makes good money."

"What about you, Ben?" Bill asked.

"I dunno. Maybe since the accident, Dan might need somebody to help him run that business of his in Largo."

Bill raised his bottle in a toast. "You're a compassionate man, Ben Wheeler."

"Fuck you. So what are you gonna do?" Ben countered, just to move the conversation along.

"I am gonna get me a little sailboat and take it over to Eleuthera Island in the Bahamas. There's a little bitty town called Spanish Wells about fifty miles northeast of Nassau, a beautiful place right on the water. I'm gonna fish, sleep in my hammock, drink rum, and chase women for the next twenty or thirty years."

"And what are you going to do if you catch one? You oughta be settling down and having kids." Ben laughed.

"If I married every woman I swore I was in love with, I'd have six or seven ex-wives by now. What about you? Whatever happened with you and that captain's daughter?"

"Susan? I haven't thought about her in years."

Susan was a diminutive, redheaded tomboy who had gotten sweet on Ben when he first reported for duty in Key West. She was a redhead not just in complexion but in character, too.

"She had a bad temper," Ben explained. "I was always afraid she was gonna haul off and sock me."

"She would have, too if she'd ever caught you with anybody else. Jim, what about you? You got a gal stashed away somewhere?" Bill laughed.

Jim smiled sheepishly and shook his head. For the second time in as many days, he lied to himself and the others.

"Ain' no woman gonna have me."

***

Fifteen miles away and thirty-five-hundred feet above the deck, Lucky tried to make himself comfortable in the small plane as he scanned the ground intently. The Piper Cub floated like a bumblebee, barely making fifty-five knots, circling the sky in a wide search pattern. He felt feverish, but distracted by his study of vague shapes on the ground, Lucky managed to preoccupy himself. Alternating between wide scans of the horizon and watching the ground below through binoculars, he tried to ignore his growing physical distress. His skin was raw, covered in small, red bite marks that in some places merged to form wide purplish swaths of infestation.

Fortunately, it didn't take long to spot what he was looking for. Deep in the San Felasco Hammock, nestled between the mouth of Moonshine Creek and a large water-filled sink, was about four acres of forest that looked right. At some point in the past, it had been disturbed, the land manipulated. It could be Potano. It was in the right place and about the right size. Less than three miles to the east, he saw a sizable ravine—something the journal mentioned. Lucky was satisfied. Now he had to get down and find a medic.

***

It was well into twilight and the streetlights were blinking on by the time he got back to the VFW in Alachua. Lucky was so painted over with calamine lotion he looked like some kind of witch doctor.

"Jeez, Lucky. You look terrible," Ben observed with genuine concern.

"Believe me, I feel worse than I look." Lucky almost fell out from behind the steering wheel. "We're pulling out. Now. Bill, you drive the Jeep. It's blackout rules tonight. No fires, no lanterns. I don't want anyone to know we're in there."

Back in the Jeep, Lucky waved his arm in a "follow me" signal and they headed back out through the quiet neighborhoods. It was starting to feel real, like they were actually on to something.

Five miles south of town, they pulled onto the shoulder to black out the headlights. During the war, anyone driving at night had to have special covers for their headlamps that limited the beam to a narrow strip of light focused on the road ahead. This prevented enemy observers from spotting traffic on the highway. Tonight, black electrical tape over the tops and bottoms of the lenses would have to do.

Heading east now, they took just three minutes to reach a left turn onto a wide sandy road paved with centuries of pine needles, falling from tall, slender slash pines. Jim followed the glowering red taillights of the Jeep as it bounced along the track. In the quiet forest, the deuce and a half sounded like a locomotive, but soon the underbrush began to muffle the sound, diffusing it. Eventually, they stopped in a small clearing and Bill came back to tell him to shut it down. The next sound they heard was Lucky puking his guts out from his seat in the Jeep.

"Damn. He needs to be in a hospital." Jim voiced everyone's thought.

"No hospital," Lucky gasped.

"Get him in the back of the truck so he can lie down," Bill suggested.

They were all going to share the truck bed as barracks tonight. Jim made a pallet for Lucky inside the canopy near the cab. Bill stretched out on the tailgate in the open.

Slowly, the night noises picked up and descended on them. The frog songs and cricket rasps matched each other in volume and intensity until the resulting pulsating rattle sounded like the hum of a machine. High in a hazy sky, the full moon had risen, outshining most of the stars overhead. Branches filtered its pale, cold light, dozens of broken patches of moonshine and shadow hitting the ground.

***

Somewhere close by, a screech owl whinnied. Bill thought about the old superstition that an owl's call meant imminent death for someone. He glanced into the canopy of the truck, trying to pick out the sound of Lucky's breathing.

A slight sound in the underbrush distracted him and he rolled over on his elbow, better to hear. The soft snap of a small twig out in the darkness made his heart beat faster. Maybe it was just a hungry possum, looking for insects or even a gray fox, coaxed in by curiosity. Bill watched for a long time, listening intently, holding his breath every so often. Nothing moved. Only the dull sound of his pulse, pounding in his ears came back to him.

He waited for nearly twenty minutes before glimpsing movement through the edge of a gallberry thicket. A tall shadow momentarily blocked out the dappled moonlight. Grabbing a flashlight, Bill eased himself off the edge of the tailgate and he worked his way silently toward the bushes. Stepping cautiously through the darkness, when he was about twenty feet from the undergrowth, he aimed the flashlight and turned it on. The light illuminated a tall, dusky gray man, dressed only in a ragged loincloth and well-worn sandals. His skin looked like blubber, slick, as though it had begun to decompose underwater. Faint tattoos covered his body, and long, tangled silver hair lay matted against his back. The face made Bill jump back. Black, rotten teeth lined a mouth circled by blue lips. A silent snarl wrinkled the being's face, accentuated by two red eyes that flickered like coals in a fire.

"*Die!*" the creature hissed loudly.

The sheer force of the sound made Bill's hand shake. He dropped the flashlight. Staggering backwards, he retrieved it and pointed it again at the spot. The trembling halo of light wavered through the bushes. The thing had disappeared. *Die*, it had said. Bill snickered nervously. It had almost given him a heart attack.

He walked somewhat stiff-legged back to the truck and hopped back up on the tailgate, making sure not to leave his legs dangling.

"What's up?" Ben asked through a yawn.

"Nothing. Not a thing. I had to take a leak," Bill lied.

***

The false dawn just before daybreak, lightened the sky. They were awakened by the sound of Lucky coughing and wheezing. The moon had set, and a quick look at his watch with his lighter told Ben it was five a.m.

174

Jim was checked on the patient. "He ain' breathin' right."

"That does it." Bill sat up. "Jimbo, let's get him loaded into the Jeep, and you can drive him to the hospital in Gainesville. Take him to the emergency room, or otherwise he's gonna die. He's goin' into shock."

Jim turned the Jeep around while Ben and Bill carried Lucky to the tailgate. Even in the low light of predawn, Ben caught a good look at Duprez's face. Puffy and swollen, he was almost unrecognizable. His hands were like fat paws, double in size. His whole body felt doughy. They strapped the barely conscious man into the front seat of the Jeep and watched with a mixture of anxiety and relief as the vehicle disappeared into the deep shadows of the forest.

"I could use some coffee," Bill mumbled. Ben set about building a small fire with twigs and charcoal briquettes to heat up some water.

As light gathered on the eastern horizon, a haze gathered in the low places, hanging just above the bushes. It put the forest around them into soft focus, not obscuring anything wholly but blurring fine details. The two men sipped instant coffee in silence, waiting for the sun to rise above the tree line. Ben sensed a vague uneasiness in himself that he had not felt around Bill before. Bill was in charge now. That was clear, but that wasn't what he was picking up on. How did years of friendship dissolve into distrust? He felt it, he knew it, but it made no sense. It had to be the money, this thing they were after.

Soon the dark blues and deep greens of twilight gave way to the orange and gold of sunrise. Bill tossed out the dregs of his coffee and walked over to the truck to retrieve Lucky's satchel. Ben knew the book was in there. Bill slung the strap over his shoulder.

"Let's go."

The woods they walked into were sparse compared to other areas they had trekked through. The canopy was mostly yellow pines, blackjack oaks, and scrub hickory, widely dispersed. Often, the floor was covered only in leaf litter and pine needles, with patches of Indian grass and clumps of deer berry. Hiking with the new sun on their backs, it took only a few minutes to reach a low, sandy bluff that formed the east bank of Moonshine Creek. Across the narrow watercourse, the forest was thicker, darker, carpeted with lush grasses and hardwoods. Following the creek, they headed southeast, without discussion, without anything passing between them. In silence, they tramped along an invisible path dictated by whatever the book contained. Only Lucky and now Bill knew where they were to wander. Ben was beginning to think no one knew for sure. Then they intercepted a faint game trail. Bill studied it for a minute and then nodded almost imperceptibly. At least one of them thought they were on track. Eventually, the trace led down to the creek and across, into the woods beyond. Under twisted and mossy oaks, they walked single file, keeping to the path made by countless generations of deer and other animals. No doubt, they traveled it as a human would a highway, familiar with where it came from and where it went. They would know where to stop and eat or rest for a time. To the two men, it was just a nameless track in the earth, crossing through the middle of nowhere.

Abruptly, the underbrush thinned and dwindled, opening onto a small, secluded glen. As the men stepped into the sunlight, a dozen scrub jays shrieked in alarm. Following their flight, Bill's eyes fell on a grassy knob dead ahead. As he looked around, several smaller mounds began to reveal themselves among the trees.

"I think we found what we were looking for."

"Potano." Ben breathed.

Silence fell back over the glade like frost, chilling without blocking the sun. Standing in what would have been the main plaza, they surveyed the city. In his imagination, Bill thought the place would have been more impressive. Instead, it was a few nondescript dirt mounds in the woods.

Shivering in the morning air, he could feel the eyes, the stares of the long dead inhabitants on him. Invisible, they were still here. The echoes of the past were audible to both of them.

They slowly climbed the central mound, a hillock of about thirty feet. The top was the same height of the surrounding forest canopy, offering neither a compelling view nor even a sense of accomplishment. Bill hunkered down and pulled the Spanish diary from Lucky's satchel. They were less than a mile from the truck.

"If what this book says is true, then the end of the rainbow is just about a mile and a half that way." He gestured toward the southeast. "Pay day."

25
~~Potano~~
11 Octubre 1523

How long we lay in the darkened hut, I know not. We could hear a great commotion outside that must have been a gathering of the entire town. There was much music as the Anahuac make, mostly shrill clay flutes and the hypnotic rhythms of many drums. Occasionally, we could hear the braying of conch shell trumpets and the chilling rattle of stone-filled gourds. It was a chorus of diablos *wailing our death knell.*

About an hour before sunset, several warriors dragged us outside. Squinting against the sudden advent of daylight, we were made to kneel again. As if from the contents of a madman's nightmare, we were confronted by a figure draped in the skin of a puma. The pelt had been tanned in such a way that the creature's paws had been preserved intact and fit like gloves, exposing the claws. The demon wore a mask of leather covering the entire head. The mask was decorated with facets of obsidian and turquoise, drawn in alternating bands across the face, and the eyes were ornamented with large cowrie shell rings. Most horrifying of all were the rows of human and animal teeth fixed inside the mouth. Long ragged braids of what appeared to be human hair had been woven into the scalp.

The shape reached out and slowly dragged its claws across each side of Comandante Gregorio's face,

drawing blood with each swipe. The Comandante barely flinched. The horrible face turned to me and only stared deep into my eyes, as if examining my soul. Slowly, it backed away and melted into the crowd, disappearing like a phantom. We were pulled to our feet and walked to the edge of town. A procession of many warriors walked before and behind us as we were led down a well-trod path. I thought of our Lord as he carried his cross to Golgotha. I prayed he grant me courage and a swift death. The path descended into a wide ravine that opened onto the shore of a deep blue, crystal clear lake. Skirting the shore, we ascended a tall bluff where two large fires burned. My blood froze as I believed they meant to burn us alive. That would have been merciful compared to what actually happened on that hill. The memory of it haunts me constantly, the smell of smoke and seared flesh, the primal screams of pain, and most of all the brutality.
  - El diario de Claudio Hernandez

Cresting the top of the hill, Gregorio calmly surveyed the tableau before him. Convinced God had granted him invincibility, the scene held no terrors for him. Mad in his greed and full of zeal for revenge, he saw only the structures of a smelter. His twisted mind recognized the shape and function of a crude refinery. Like many he had overseen in New Spain, the beehive ovens and mounds of glowing charcoal were designed to melt raw gold into liquid, fiery lakes of gleaming metal. Now he would have what was rightfully his.

The second blaze was a bonfire of oak with flames reaching some twelve feet into the onset of twilight. In front of it stood Yaotl, his face blackened with soot and ochre. His raven hair hung loose about his shoulders. He wore bandoliers displaying the spoils of war—shriveled human fingers and ears smoked over a fire to preserve them. From a leather thong around his neck hung the bony lower jaw of another victim with teeth intact. His powerful legs were smeared in white clay and ash, giving them a skeletal look. It was as if he had just climbed out of the fiery abyss, an emissary from Satan.

178

The whole scene was laid out across a sandy clearing that ended in a precipitous drop-off to the lake below. On the far horizon, a blood red sun touched the treetops. It was horrifyingly surreal yet oddly beautiful.

Separating the prisoners, two men quickly hauled Claudio to a large pine and tied his hands behind it. With the soft crumbling bark at his back, Claudio was close enough to see the smoking metal within the ovens and feel the heat of the fires on his cheeks.

A man with a wooden war club knocked Gregorio to the ground. Cries of approval erupted from the Potano that had gathered. As he lay face down in the sand, a warrior approached him with one of the shortened halberks and violently hacked at his ankles. Gregorio tried to rise, but immediately, another Potano leaped on his back, sitting on the Spaniard's shoulders. Claudio could make out the gleam of the blade as it crudely cut through sinew and bone.

The muffled grunts and visceral moans of pain Gregorio uttered with every blow were involuntary outbursts. Hardened by battle, he would not give the Potanos the satisfaction of hearing him plead for mercy or weep in fear, but his captors seemed uninterested in capitulation or even humiliation. The punishment in New Spain for trying to escape the slavery of the Spanish mines had been amputation of the feet. For stealing food, they would cut off the hands. This was about justice.

One by one, the Comandante's bloody feet were cast into the bonfire accompanied by a round of whooping and derisive laughter. Then dragging him by the stumps of his legs, the Potanos rolled him onto his back by the furnaces. An old man carefully placed a wide, shallow clay bowl under his head. Two other men sat on his chest and legs to prevent Gregorio from moving anything but his head.

Claudio felt his heartbeat in his throat, but was paralyzed in horror. He could not seem to close his eyes or even blink. Stuttering in fear, he murmured prayers for the soul of his companion.

Slowly, menacingly, Yaotl lifted a small cauldron of molten gold from the furnace and brought it to the spot where Gregorio lay. Speaking in broken Spanish, he recited words he had obviously rehearsed.

"*¿Oro quieres?* Here is your gold."

Slowly, he poured the white hot metal into the clay bowl.

Instantaneously, Gregorio's hair erupted in flame, and he screamed like a woman in labor. His eyes glazed over as the heat coddled the part of his brain that gave him sight. His body twitched in violent spasms as his ears sizzled like fried pork. When the stream was directed onto his forehead, Gregorio's eyes immediately melted. The screaming continued until the last of the gold was poured into his mouth. Even from a distance, Claudio could hear the teeth snapping in two from the enormous temperature. After one last cough and spasm, Gregorio lay still.

Taking a bloody halberd, Yaotl took just two blows to cut off his enemy's head. Preserved forever in lustrous gold was Gregorio's pain and suffering. The sunken eyes still gleamed deep in their sockets. Faint whispers of hairs from his beard and eyebrows clung to the soft metal on his face. His teeth and the stump of his scorched tongue now shone in a permanent plating of the gold he had so long coveted. Ramming a pike up the remains of the dead man's neck, Yaotl lifted the head high for all to see. The gathering fell silent, mesmerized by the spectacle.

Finally, he turned and walked to the edge of the bluff, hurling the spear with the golden head out into the dark waters below. Claudio could hear the splash and sizzle as it struck the surface and sank out of sight. Yaotl waved his arm and all the smelters were emptied of gold. Several heavy clay cauldrons were poured out at the brink of the hill, cascading in long red tongues of fire. The lake boiled as it received the offering.

Striding back to where Claudio was bound, Yaotl stared at the young Spaniard for many minutes. Producing the very hatchet Claudio had used to cut Yaotl's chains, Yaotl carefully chopped the bonds holding the young man to the tree. Claudio sank to his knees in exhaustion. Slowly looking up, he saw that the *cacique* was now offering him the weapon, as Claudio had done in the belly of the ship. With shaking hands, Claudio took it. Yaotl walked away and watched as Gregorio's mutilated body was thrown in a heap on the large bonfire. Claudio rose on weak legs and lurched toward the lip of the bluff. He tossed the hatchet over and waited until he heard it smack the water. He could feel the heat of the fire on his back and turned to see the men raking the discharge of the smelters into the funeral pyre. Charcoal

180

smoke and the smell of burning human flesh nearly choked him. He managed to lumber a few feet away before collapsing and losing consciousness.

* * *

When Claudio opened his eyes again and became aware of his surroundings, he found himself back in the small hut in Potano. He was unfettered and crawled to the doorway to look out. The sun had risen, but a heavy fog obscured much of the town. The dew was refreshing. An old woman approached and he shrank backwards, but she brought a clay pot of clear water, a wooden bowl of corn mush, and several dried plums. The mush was bland, but the water was cool and sweet. He ate with his fingers, as the *indios* did. He glanced around the dim interior of his thatched prison, thinking he might see Gregorio, hoping that all he had witnessed had been but a nightmare. He was completely alone.

Suddenly, a voice outside called to him. It sounded vaguely familiar.

"*Señor.* Show yourself!"

Claudio stood up, crouching to walk beyond the threshold.

It was Juan, Chulusi Eyolehecote, the runt. He looked even more disfigured standing next to Yaotl. The sorcerer said not a word, but thrust Gregorio's sword and scabbard into Claudio's hands. Juan smiled briefly then handed over a bundle wrapped in rags. It turned out to be Claudio's journal and the Comandante's copy of the Book of Hours.

"The great *cacique* Potano has decided you should be set free. It is on the condition that you leave, return to your people. Tell them all what you have seen. Tell them what will happen if they return. Go and do not come back."

"But I am alone and lost. I have nowhere to go."

"I will take you to the far shore where the sun rises from the sea. Spanish ships pass by there often. You may be able to signal one."

Juan flashed that wide deceptive smile. He spoke almost patronizingly.

"No harm will come to you. I have the *brujo's* talisman to protect us both."

181

Claudio hesitated, but Yaotl's icy stare stopped his tongue. He nodded.

"*Bueno.* We leave now. *Vamos, señor,*" Juan beckoned.

No one watched them walk out of town except Yaotl. Claudio could feel the man's eyes boring into the back of his head. He would not be back. If he ever stepped on the shore of Spain, nothing on earth could make him return, but he knew others would not listen. Others would return with more ships, more *soldados*, and bigger armies. The Old World's greed was unquenchable and now their hatred would be inexhaustible. He had seen Paradise. He could not share it, but neither would he watch it be despoiled by the conquistadores. No, he would not come back.

It was many leagues to the east coast of La Florida, but Juan Blue Jay was true to his charge. We traveled easily through the territory of the Timucua people, the Utina, and Saturiwa. Chief Potano had sent an emissary ahead to provide provenance of our status, and his word was respected. It was the end of October before we arrived at a small village called Motoa, situated at the mouth of a large river, surely the same mentioned in reports by Juan Ponce de Leon some seven years ago.

I languished in Motoa for six months until a Spanish ship appeared offshore and sent men to land for fresh water and food. They were amazed to see a kinsman and marveled at the story of my survival. The ship took me to Havana where I was able to beg passage back to Spain from the Adelantado Diego Velasquez de Cunlar. So it was that on June 23rd, 1524, I set foot once again on the stone quay at Malaga. I had been gone two years, eight months, and sixteen days.

- El diario de Claudio Hernandez

26
~~San Felasco Hammock, Florida~~
June 23, 1959

The morning was more than half gone when Jim returned alone in the Jeep, definitely a bad sign.

"So what did the doc say?" Bill was the first to ask what Ben wanted to know.

"He said Lucky was named right."

"What?"

"He said that if the man had waited a few more hours, he'd be dead."

"Damn."

"Yeah. Said somethin' about some kind of shock. He's allergic to bug bites. His throat was all swoll up. They had to put a tube in so he could breathe."

No one said anything for a few minutes.

"How long we gotta wait for Lucky to get out of the hospital?" Ben asked.

Jim shook his head, "I don't know. He was in pretty bad shape. There's one other thing you oughta know. When I called Mister Fischer to let him know what was goin' on with Duprez, he told me they found Lonnie's boat."

"The boat..., not Lonnie?" Ben asked.

"The Coast Guard found the *Dreamboat* drifting with the current,

183

almost smack in the middle of the Gulf. Nobody was on board, nothing was missing. No signs of a fight.... The engine didn't run out of gas. It had been shut off. In fact, they cranked it up and drove the boat back to Biloxi."

"What the hell?" Ben muttered.

"All the life jackets were still on board. His gun was still in the wheelhouse. The radio worked fine."

Each man had a theory, expressed in their own mind—silently— not daring to say it aloud. They had all seen and heard too much. Dan and Lucky were in the hospital, one crippled, one fighting for his life. Lonnie didn't just swim away from his boat. Someone, something had come for him, and it was not done yet.

"What did Fischer say about Duprez? Did he say to wait?" Bill pushed the issue.

"Not directly. I think he was under the impression we were going to."

"Lucky is his man," Ben added.

"We've got the book, we found the place. I say we do it now." Bill was adamant.

"You found the Indian town?" Jim started.

"Who the hell made you boss?" Ben interjected.

"I did," Bill practically shouted. "I read the book. I know what we're after."

His declaration was met with silence.

Bill continued, "The expedition members who moved inland were eventually captured and most of them killed, except for the ship's commander and the guy who wrote this journal. The Indians butchered the leader. They cut off his feet. They roasted his body. But before that, while he was still alive, they cast his head in pure gold. His face was covered in it. His mouth and his throat were filled with it."

"A golden head," Jim shuddered.

"So where is it?" Ben asked. "How do we find it?"

"They dumped the head, the rest of the gold—everything into a lake."

Bill paused and looked both men in the eye.

"I know where that lake is."

"All right," Ben said finally, crushing out a cigar butt underfoot.

"Let's do it."

"What about Lucky?" Jim stood his ground. The man had been decent to him. "When they cut him loose, he's gonna want to catch up to us."

Ben nodded. It was only fair.

"Okay," Bill decided. "We leave the Jeep, the keys, and a letter with directions at the hospital. All we need is the truck and the gear."

Ben hesitated. "I still think we oughta clear this with Fischer."

"Fischer is wherever he is. We're here. He doesn't know what we know. Every day we hang around out here, we're drawing attention to ourselves. We gotta move now. Hell, Duprez would tell you the same thing."

Ben threw his hands up. "It's your world. We just live in it."

***

Alachua General stood in the heart of Gainesville, a few blocks from the university. Bill started talking football the minute they set foot in the parking lot, but Ben had never been a Gator fan. He left Jim to suffer Bill's yapping and wandered the halls in search of Duprez's room. The bloated figure he found looked nothing like Lucky. His skin was a patchwork of ruddy blotches, and his eyes appeared sunken in a puffy face.

"You look like hell."

Lucky nodded weakly, his breathing still labored.

"How long they say you gotta stay here?"

Lucky held up three, then four fingers. He might have meant days or maybe weeks.

Ben eased into a chair opposite the bed.

"Bill and I found Potano. No doubt about it."

Lucky nodded, closing his eyes.

Ben hesitated a moment.

"Bill says he already knows where we gotta go. Something about a lake at the other end of a ravine we spotted."

Lucky's eyes fluttered open again. He reached feebly for a pad and a nearby pencil. Scratching laboriously, he wrote "Did he tell you about the gold head?"

185

Ben nodded. "Yeah. We got the campfire story."

Lucky scribbled out another brief note "The real thing is out there."

"So he knows as much as you do now."

"More, probably," Lucky wrote.

Ben realized now where that nagging sense of distrust had been born. Bill had been trying to figure this whole thing out before anybody else, ever since they were at Horseshoe Beach. He had been studying the book and the maps for days on the QT.

"He wants to jump on it. He brought us down here to leave you the Jeep." Ben laid a small manila envelope with the keys on the nightstand.

Lucky stared at the envelope for a minute then gazed out the window. His face was inscrutable. Finally, he nodded slightly.

"He said you'd agree with him."

Ben stood up to leave. Lucky wrote two words: "Watch him."

***

As Ben, Bill, and Jim rode in the cab of the deuce and a half, Lucky's warning kept bubbling to the front of Ben's mind. Rolling down a sandy track into the woods, they were so far into the boondocks the locals had given up naming the roads. Ben repeatedly stole sidelong glances at Bill, watching for some break in his friend's poker face. For his part, Bill was engrossed in studying the topo map that was their link to the gold, checking and re-checking every feature. There was no talking—none of the wisecracks they were used to serving each other— not even an idle comment passed between them. Jim just stared out the windshield, occasionally looking off into the trees, as if expecting to see something. The place, the whole situation was beginning to ratchet up the tension between them, making it tangible. Nerves and circumstance, greed and suspicion were all conspiring to warp their character. Each wondered who actually lived behind the eyes set in familiar faces.

At the end of the road was a large clearing. In the mid-afternoon sun, it looked deceptively peaceful, even beautiful. A six-acre lake sat eerily still, its surface smooth and shiny as polished glass. Reflecting back at the azure sky, it looked like a hole in the earth, cut through to the other side. Halfway around the lake rose a low bluff that sat back from the water's edge. Beside it loomed a borrow pit big enough to swallow a two-bedroom house. Bill seemed a bit crestfallen when he realized at some time in the recent past, a portion of the hillock had been excavated. Apparently, the top layer of clay had been carted off, leaving the limestone base partially exposed. He was still convinced this was the place.

There was no road to the hill, only a narrow footpath along the lakeside. Jim pulled the big truck as deep into the trees as he could to camouflage it as much as possible. From here on out, it was a covert operation, not just low profile. They had less than a week to locate the gold, recover it, and leave undetected.

Bill was ready to get in the water then and there, but they settled for a hike to the top of the mound to scout the dive. The entire lake was a shallow bowl from five to fifteen feet deep with a clean, sandy bottom. A relatively small area near one end boiled with springs that invisibly pumped out cold, clear water at fifty degrees. It would make the bottom layer of water and the deep sink dangerously cool. Even in the slanting sunlight, the clarity of the water revealed a depth that was unexpected.

"It must be thirty, thirty-five feet out there at the sink," Ben mused.

"Check out the shadow near this side. That must be a cave or a spring head maybe." Bill pointed.

"Glad we brought the wet suits. It's probably cold down there." Without their wet suits, they could expect to experience hypothermia within twenty minutes.

Bill eased up to the edge of the mound, testing his footing as he went. The drop wasn't bad, but the crumbly phosphate and limestone aggregate soil seemed unstable.

"It's about ten yards from the base of the hill to the lake. I guess half a century of erosion made most of this stuff slide forward. I just hope it didn't wash all that spoil on top of the search area."

***

Halfway around the lake, a giant blue heron stood in the weedy shallows like a silent sentinel. The pastels of sunset colored the water, echoing the skies above. It was eerily quiet. Ben couldn't help but feel as though something was out there, something in the water, something besides the gold. Evidently, Jim sensed it, too; Ben could see it in his eyes and furrowed brow. Only Bill seemed to be oblivious to the setting's spookiness. He was probably already spending his money. That's why they called him "Dollar" Bill. He never could keep a dime.

There was a lot to do. The rubber raft had to be unpacked and inflated, dive tanks checked and gear gone through. Sleep would be hard to come by tonight. The trio ate a cold supper from cans by flashlight. They couldn't afford to be discovered now. Eventually, they hunkered down silently in the dark. The night was suffocating, the air thick and moist. The faint glow of some distant, small town hung on the horizon, imitating moonrise. Beyond that, pitch blackness surrounded them. Only the immutable stars glittered overhead, each one distinct and brilliant. In four hundred years, the land may have changed, but these were the same stars that bore celestial witness to the last chapter of a tale of violence, greed, and revenge. This was the place. It looked right; it felt right. The treasure was out there, waiting for them.

27
~~Alachua County, Florida~~
June 24, 1959

In dawn's pale light, the lake lay mostly hidden under a smoky haze. Ben was up early, restless, and ready to get into the water. Walking the edge of the pond, he watched schools of minnows streaking along the weedy banks, hunted by shiners. In turn, the shimmering bodies of the little fish occasionally seemed to vanish under the lily pads as larger fish, bream mostly, ghosted through. Once, he spotted a banded water snake half in and half out of the water, trying its best to be invisible. The morning dew still glistened from enormous spider webs draped over the tall reeds. Where the forest came down to the banks, bay laurels and willows stood guard. He came across an anemic rivulet flowing out of the adjacent ravine, but that could not be the source of the lake's water. Because of its clarity and sheer volume, this had to be fed from a second magnitude spring at least, maybe even part of an underground river.

Anxious or not, Ben had to wait for Bill to finish a cup of coffee before they could get started. Bill refused to do anything before his morning brew.

"What are you in such a hurry for? If there's anything out there, it ain't going anywhere."

"You telling me after all we've done, you're not the slightest bit excited that it might be out there and all we gotta do is just scoop it up?"

"I'll believe it when I see it."

"Me too," Jim muttered over the rim of his coffee cup.

***

They launched the raft from the beach while Jim took a walkie-talkie around the edge of the lake and climbed the bluff. Arriving over the drop-off, they could tell that some sort of current was creating a slow eddy. That meant there was an outlet for the water down there somewhere, which explained why no high or low water marks were apparent along the shore. They anchored over the center of the sink and the line payed out thirty-five feet before it hit bottom.

Ben was the first over the side, his breath quickening as he took in the chasm below. The clarity of the water showed every rock, every feature in sharp relief. The warm white light of the sun near the surface cooled to the palest of blues near the bottom. Descending slowly, he scanned the walls of the sinkhole. Inexorably, patiently, nature had put down layer upon layer of sediment, concreting them into limestone ridges, trapping shells and their inhabitants hundreds of millennia ago. Often, sinkholes produced the teeth of prehistoric sharks or the bones of mastodons. They were windows into the deep past, but maybe this one held something more recent.

Once on the bottom, it was easy to spot a blue-green opening on the wall closest to the bluff. Disguised from the surface by a slight overhang, the cavern was definitely draining water out in stasis with the volume of water flowing in from the springs. The entrance was fairly small, but still accessible with an air tank. It was too dark to see more than a few feet, but it seemed to continue, maybe even opening up a bit.

Shortly, Ben was aware of Bill swimming next to him. He motioned for the two of them to start scanning the bottom. Waving away the sand and mud a bit, they looked for color. With their military-grade tanks, they could work at depth for about fifty minutes. The problem was they only had twelve tanks filled. Racing against the clock, they had to find what they were looking for in less than six hours before they needed to resupply. Even if they were at the right spot, time was against them.

***

From his vantage point on top of the hill, Jim followed the divers's bubble trail as they scoured the bottom. As far as he could tell, they were in roughly the right spot. Easing up to the edge of the bluff, he stepped a bit too close and a clod of earth broke off, causing a miniature landslide. His eyes followed the cascade of dirt, extrapolating the line and it confirmed his hunch that the guys were close to where the original promontory used to be. His attention was diverted by an odd root or stick exposed by the slide. It wasn't large, but something about its shape looked interesting. Dark, smooth, and symmetrically shaped, it just didn't look natural. Jim lay on his stomach and reached over the edge to tease it out of the bluff face. Once he felt it—cold, light—he knew it was a bone. Getting to his feet, he studied it for a minute, then put it in his pocket. He'd show it to the guys at lunch.

***

By eleven a.m., their tanks exhausted, Ben and Bill climbed back into the raft, slightly discouraged. They were going to have to work smarter. Limited to two dives a day per man, they had three days to snatch a fortune from the lake. To leave the spot and get the tanks refilled might mean discovery. They had no idea who owned the place, but by working covertly, they hoped to avoid any unwelcome inquiry. With any luck, anyone who came across them would assume they were recreational divers, enjoying the clear water.

Sitting on the beach, they munched gritty sandwiches as they fought off flies. Ben drew diagrams in the blindingly white sand as he tried to explain a back-up plan.

"When we get down to that last set of tanks, why don't we try relay breathing? We could drop a couple of rigs to the bottom, free dive down to them and relay breathe from that supply while we prospect. It's risky, but we might be able to get another thirty minutes from each tank."

Something Ben learned during rescue training: if it wasn't done right, both rescuer and victim could drown. It required a lot of discipline. Suddenly, he realized how much he missed Dan. Depending on your dive partner for your life, where seconds mattered, was the ultimate test of trust. It was a little gut-wrenching to acknowledge he was going to have to trust Bill that completely. He wasn't sure he could.

"Hey, take a look at this," Jim interjected. "I found it near the top of the bluff."

He offered the others his peculiar find. Bill took it and examined it closely, scraping its surface with his fingernail.

"It's bone. Looks human. Maybe an ankle bone?"

"It's been burned," Ben added. It took a few seconds to comprehend what they were looking at.

"I think that's probably the remains of the Spanish commander. They burned his body in a fire." Bill cradled the object in his palm, like a talisman. "Did you see any other bones where you found this?"

Jim shook his head. "Nope, but I wasn't really looking for that one. I just kinda came across it."

"You know what this means, right?" Bill looked at each man in turn. "This could be proof that we are in the right spot. That gold is probably here. It's gotta be."

***

Shortly after one o'clock, the men headed back out in the raft. A breeze made the water slightly choppy. No sooner had they gotten situated over the sink when Jim hailed them on the radio. He was on top of the bluff, waving his arm and pointing to the west.

"Looks like a bad storm, comin'." Small crackles of static on the walkie-talkie confirmed his assessment.

"Let's go back in and try it later. Tomorrow if we have to," Ben agreed. Lightning was too unpredictable to risk being in the water when it approached. If you were under when a storm came up, you might not hear it until it was on you.

Bill was clearly pissed, but consented. "All right. Let's head back."

Paddling against the rising wind became hard work. By the time they made the beach, the storm front had become a long black line on the horizon. The preceding overcast blocked the sun, making it cool. It was going to be a vicious squall.

"Better ride this one out in the cab," called Bill

Thunder pealed as they stashed the raft under the truck. As they settled into the front seat, huge raindrops rattled the roof. The wind gusted to near-hurricane strength, showering them with leaves, small branches, and pine cones from the treetops. Lightning popped like flash bulbs with an audible sound that signaled a proximity too close, seconds before the cannon-like thunder roared. The impact of the celestial artillery shook the ground. Unconsciously, they huddled together on the wide seat, not in fear but for protection.

"Damn, that shit's close." Ben looked at the roof as if he expected it to be ripped away any second.

"Don't touch anything metal," Jim warned. He held his hands up, trying to avoid the steering wheel.

Bill laughed. "Ha! The whole goddamn truck is metal. Metal doors, metal dash, metal roof..."

Ben looked at the metal shift lever between his legs and cautiously maneuvered around until both his knees were on the right side of it. That only made Bill laugh harder.

A brilliant pulse of white light stopped him. A pine tree twenty feet away exploded into splinters, blowing debris through the windshield and shattering it. Immediately, the wind and cold rain slapped them in the face. The smell of ozone nearly took their breath away. Despite the storm, the pine stump was smoldering, adding the reek of wood smoke to the miasma choking their lungs.

"God damn!" Bill shouted, "Everybody okay?"

"What?" Jim's ears were still ringing.

Ben was still too stunned for words and just sat blinking. Bits of glass and debris had cut his face, leaving small rivulets of blood. It took a long time for his senses to return. He flinched at every thunderclap like a shell-shocked soldier. In fact, it took all of them nearly half an hour to recover. They sat quietly with the rain drizzling in, soaking their pants legs, listening for the wind to die down and the lightning to leave.

Eventually, some semblance of tranquility returned, even though the sun failed to penetrate the residual clouds. A dismal afternoon quickly disintegrated into a somber twilight. Bill pulled Ben aside while Jim scrounged something to eat.

"I been thinkin' about something."

"Uh oh."

"Hear me out. This team is down to just the three of us. Noble

193

Fischer has no idea where we are or what's going on right now."

"What about Lucky?"

"If Lucky is as bad off as you say he is, he won't be out of the hospital for another three or four days. Now look, if we can bring up this haul, we can split it three ways and disappear. Nobody would be the wiser."

Ben looked hard at his friend for several minutes.

"Even if we find it and if we could get away with it. What makes you think a man like Noble Fischer wouldn't hire some thugs to track us down?"

"By the time he did, we could be long gone. With this kinda dough we could get us a boat, a big boat and go down to the Caribbean. It's easy to get lost down there. Think of it—girls, sun, sand, surf, and all the booze you can swallow."

"And how are we gonna get the money? You can't just go into a yacht dealer and offer them a gold skull for a cabin cruiser."

Bill waved his hand as if he was waving away smoke.

"I got that worked out. I know a guy that'll cash it in for us."

"And where is this guy? Sounds shifty."

"Don't worry about who he is. He has the connections for this kinda thing."

The two men stared at each other.

"Ben, we been shipmates for a long time. I've looked after you. Come in with me on this."

"How much are you into this guy for?" Ben finally spoke. Bill looked for a moment as if his feelings were hurt, then turned and looked away.

"Fifty G's. It was at a casino in Havana. I don't know what happened."

"A mob casino."

"I guess."

"Bill!"

"Okay, yeah. I didn't know. I shoulda guessed."

"How did you walk outta there?"

Bill dropped his head. "I told 'em about this deal."

"You told them you had a gig to make the money to pay 'em back?"

"No, I told 'em about the gold."

"Jesus," Ben whispered in disbelief. "Wait, how long have they known what we were in on? I mean, for sure."

"Ever since Horseshoe Beach."

"Brother." Ben shook his head. "You don't give me much to hold onto. Lemme guess, Jim doesn't know anything about this…plan."

"Of course not. I wasn't going to cut you out. I mean, I didn't know if you were gonna go for it."

What went unspoken was that Bill did have every intention of cutting Jim out. Ben was convinced that if he acted as if he wasn't going to go along with it, Bill would find a way to cut him out too.

"Yeah, okay," Ben finally nodded. After all, they still had to find something worth cheating for, lying for, something worth stealing. Even so, Ben had a nasty feeling he had just made a deal with the devil, and those never ended well. Out in the wet and dewy darkness, dozens of frogs sang bass and tenor to a moonless sky. The lake lay still again, its secret intact.

***

After a cold supper, Ben lay down in the back of the truck, nursing a growing headache. It was early, but without lights, once it got dark, it didn't seem to matter whether it was nine o'clock or midnight. He wanted to be up early anyway. With any luck, the morning dive might bring up something. As he rubbed his forehead, he noticed that he had light flares that persisted even with his eyes closed. Like the residual glare left by a flashbulb, the lightning strike must have caused a retina burn. Hopefully, it would repair itself overnight.

His dreams were a pastiche of old regrets and subliminal terrors. His brain regurgitated all the bad decisions he had ever made. He saw the shark attack on Dan over and over again, like a horror film that played in an endless loop. Falling deeper into sleep, his nightmares became more allegorical. He wandered an apocalyptic cityscape, hunting an invisible evil that was hunting him. By daybreak, he awoke nearly as tired as when he went to sleep.

***

195

Restless and cranky, his mood dissolved to complete calm the minute they hit the water. Below the surface, there were no irritating distractions; he could live in the moment. Even though runoff from the storm caused a slight murkiness that obscured his long-range view, the water in the hole was still crystal clear. Unlike the open ocean, there was nothing to fear out beyond the blue curtain. No predators here. Instead, it gave him a womb-like feeling of security as they descended. The limestone walls rose up around them, a sunken fortress, shielding them from all else. Nearly weightless, he floated downward, reveling in the silence. Only the regular hiss of air and the busy stream of bubbles when he exhaled kept him from the illusion he had gone deaf. After a while, it became an extension of his normal body functions, like the soft sound of the pulse in his neck.

On the bottom, bright sunlight rippled across the sandy surface. They worked the slopes of the sink, Ben to the left of the cave and Bill to the right. Ben stopped every few yards and dug his hands into the loose sand, letting it sift through his fingers. Bill stabbed the sediment with his dive knife, hoping to hit something that wasn't rock or mud. Trying to keep the silt from making clouds around their heads, they moved slowly over the search area, methodically checking every likely place they might find a clue.

A small flash of yellow caught Ben's eye and he held his breath, retracing the patch of bottom where he thought it came from. His fingers closed in on something hard, cold, and spherical. Bringing it close to his mask to study it further, the thing in his hand was unmistakable. It was a marble-sized blob of gold. He was about to swim over to Bill when he saw his partner waving excitedly. Bill had a similar find—a gold teardrop about two inches long. He pointed for them to surface. Alongside the raft, the men laughed simultaneously.

"We got it, buddy!" Bill roared. "We've hit the debris field! When they poured all the gold over the rim of that bluff, it spilled out here. The hill must have extended out a lot further back then."

***

Atop the hill, Jim saw the two men gesture excitedly and could hear their voices, but not what they said. He started to call them on the walkie-talkie, but hesitated. He wanted to see if they would call him. If they found something, it was beginning to look like his darkest suspicions were true. A scowl furrowed his face. He was angry about what he thought was happening, and he was even more angry that he had begun to trust Ben. He couldn't let his guard down. He had known whites like this all his life. Token talk—they would use nice words, smile at you, but when the chips were down, they would leave a nigger high and dry. They were always gonna be white, and he was always gonna be black. Segregation had been the only hard and fast rule he ever kept. It was law. Even now, two decades since he was a boy growing up in Montgomery, he could be sure that nobody would ever be charged for killing a black man.

***

Back on the bottom, they raked out more and more of the misshapen gold as they dug toward each other and the cave mouth. Nodules, flakes, nuggets, and even baseball size rocks of pure gold popped out of the sand. Once they knew what to look for and where to look, it seemed to be everywhere. By the time the air ran out, they had filled a half-dozen, quart Mason jars and a small cotton sack. The only thing they hadn't come across was the gold head. If the treasure was here, then the plated skull had to be somewhere down there too. Before coming in, they packed everything into a canvas duffel bag and left it on the bottom. Neither of them could think of a safer place to stash it.

Jim met them on the beach.

"What didya find?" he asked.

Ben grabbed his hand and slapped a gold disc the size of a fifty cent piece in his palm.

"This."

"You found the treasure?"

"Some of it."

"We only scratched the surface." Bill dismissed their enthusiasm.

"Then I can't wait till we hit the jackpot. There must be over one hundred thousand dollars down there now." Ben was clearly stoked.

Bill shot him a look clearly meant to make him shut up. Jim started to hand back the gold in his palm.

"Hang onto it. It's a souvenir," Ben insisted.

***

Trudging back up to camp, Ben veered off and climbed in the truck bed. He needed to get out of the wetsuit before it got any warmer. Searching his duffel for a T-shirt, he suddenly noticed his gun was missing. Several explanations raced through his mind, but he tried not to settle on any one of them. Bill joined him to change out of his gear.

"Did you borrow my gun?" Ben tried to act nonchalant.

"No. Why would I need to borrow your gun?"

"I can't find it."

"I don't have it. Maybe Jimbo took it."

"Why would Jim want it?"

Bill shrugged. "Maybe he doesn't trust us."

"Would you? I'm at the point where I don't know as I trust anybody."

***

Over Spam sandwiches, they tried to piece together the way the debris field lay and where the head might be. Bill drew diagrams in the sand as Ben and Jim looked over his shoulder.

"So the closer we got to here," he said, indicating the mouth of the cave, "the more we found and the bigger the pieces were. I think the bluff used to extend out to about here." Bill tapped a spot on the diagram representing about a dozen yards offshore. "When they threw all that stuff over the edge, I bet most of it landed in front of this opening. It may even be inside. There's a bit of a current."

"I don't know," Ben interjected. "If the bluff extended out that far originally, I think the head might be right in the middle of the sink. The reason the gold is up along this shelf is because they had to dump it. They *threw* the head over the cliff."

Bill shrugged a bit, "Well, we have a day and a half to figure it out." He inhaled the last of his sandwich and stood up.

"By the way, Jimbo, did you borrow Ben's gun?"

Ben almost choked.

"His gun? What do I want with a gun? Why do you need a gun?" Jim's brow furrowed in anger. "You sayin' I stole it?"

"No, he's not," Ben tried to intervene.

"I don't need a gun to take care of you." Jim clamped his steel-gray eyes directly on Bill's face.

"Nobody needs a gun for anything right now." Ben leaped to his feet and stepped between the two men. "I just couldn't find it a little while ago. I'm sure it will turn up. It's probably in my gear somewhere. Maybe it fell out of my duffel bag, and it's on the floor of the truck."

Jim turned abruptly and walked away.

Ben looked back at his old friend. "What the hell were you thinking?"

"I just thought I'd ask. I didn't know he'd get so sore."

"How did you think he was going to act? He barely trusts us as it is."

"Does it matter?"

Ben shook his head in disgust. "Never mind. Let's suit up and get in the water before we lose any more daylight."

***

Once under the water again, Ben struggled to regain his composure and concentration. It irritated the hell out of him that Bill had gotten him into a corner. Trying to focus on the hunt, he picked a new area to dig around in. Bill poked around the entrance to the cave, seemingly obsessed with his latest theory. Ben watched as half his partner's body disappeared into the dark opening. A moment later, Bill backed out holding something in his hand. As Ben swam over, he could see it was a hatchet head, corroded but still recognizable. From the design, it was at least two hundred years old. Bill pointed back excitedly to the cave and handed the relic to Ben. Bill immediately swam back to the opening and ducked inside before Ben could stop him.

They had been inside many a sunken ship, but they always knew what to expect. Ships were built a certain way, and a lot of the time they had seen blueprints of the vessel they went down to work on. Caves were different. They could collapse, and if the silt was stirred up, visibility could drop to zero. Passages could double back on themselves

199

and become disorienting. Divers had been known to confuse up and down in narrow spaces. They needed as much air to get out as they did to get in.

Ben knew Bill couldn't get too far. He would run out of light in the first fifty feet. Ben feared he might set off a slide or cave-in. They had no idea how structurally sound this siphon was. It had survived years, maybe centuries, undisturbed in the depths. That didn't guarantee that one solid impact on the roof by a metal air tank wouldn't cause it to fall in on itself.

Shortly, Bill re-emerged with a handful of gold nuggets that ranged in size from grapes to golf balls. After depositing them in the canvas stash bag, he motioned to the surface.

"We need a couple of flashlights and something to make a guideline with." Bill sputtered as he spit out his mouthpiece.

Ben shoved his mask up on his forehead and wiped his face. "I got a light. I think we still have a few underwater flares, too. Maybe there's some cord in the truck. Are we gonna have enough air?"

"I think so. The cave seems to go straight back, so we shouldn't have a problem with having to stop for decompression on the way back. If it's level, then we won't use any more air than we normally do."

"You really think that's where it is?"

"Yeah, I do."

Climbing back into the raft, Ben noticed two figures on the beach in the distance. One of them was Jim, but he couldn't figure out who the other person was.

"What is it?" Bill looked back over his shoulder.

"We got company."

"Shit," Bill growled.

As they paddled back toward camp, Ben suddenly caught a glimpse of a gray Navy Jeep.

"Hey, it's Lucky!"

For once, Bill had no comment.

***

Duprez seemed more gaunt than usual, almost frail, as he walked down the beach to greet them. He was all business, though.

200

"So you found it." His voice was gravelly from the breathing tube he had worn for three days.

"Not all of it," Ben started to explain.

"We haven't located the gold head yet," Bill interjected.

Lucky nodded. "Jimbo's fixing dinner. I brought some supplies with me."

"Bring any cigars?" Ben was hopeful.

"A whole box."

Bill might have thought Duprez was still debilitated and out-of-touch, but Ben noticed a caginess in his demeanor. Jim must have briefed him before they landed. No doubt, he already knew what they had and where they had it. He also had to feel the growing tension among the three of them.

"We'll get out of our gear and meet you by the fire." Bill smiled. "Hot food sounds pretty good to me right now."

***

The divers climbed into the back of the truck and shucked their wet suits.

"Now whattya gonna do?" Ben hissed to his partner.

"I don't know. I didn't count on Lucky making it back so soon. It kinda screws things up."

"You got a plan B?"

"Not yet."

"You gonna let me in on it when you figure it out?"

"Of course." Bill got changed first and hopped down.

"I'll save ya a beer," he threw over his shoulder as he walked off.

Ben struggled with his suit, trying to pry his legs out. He wound up sitting on the floor to get enough leverage and suddenly spotted a familiar shape under one of the benches, the place where Jim usually stowed his kit. The gun was still in its canvas holster. Ben retrieved it and checked the clip. It was empty. He always had a full clip in his gun. If he had to use it, he didn't want to have to fumble with stacking seven stubby rounds with potentially shaky hands. He also always had one round in the chamber. It was still there. Whoever unloaded the gun didn't check that. At least he had one cartridge.

Why was it over by Jim's stuff? Had he taken it, or did it just get kicked over there in the dark one night? Someone had deliberately unloaded it, thinking if he didn't have any more ammo, the gun was useless except as a bluff. Ben wondered if Bill had taken it and then planted it in Jim's bag to throw suspicion on him. All he knew is it wasn't where it should have been, and somebody went through a lot of trouble to make sure it wasn't going to be a threat.

***

Duprez sat in the back of the Jeep under the canopy to avoid the sun. While physically he acted weak, his attitude was one of somebody very much in charge. With Jim in attendance, the gathering took on an almost judicial feeling. Bill sipped a lukewarm beer, listening to Lucky as he took command again.

"The first thing I want you guys to do is bring up what you've already found. I have a strongbox we're going to lock it up in. We have to be ready to bug out if something happens. What's the plan for trying to find the head?"

Bill burped quietly and explained. "We found an artifact near the mouth of the cave." He handed over the metal object. "I think it's a hatchet head. According to the journal, Hernandez wrote that he threw the hatchet over the bluff right after they threw the head into the lake. I'm thinking they landed pretty close together."

Duprez showed no surprise that Bill had been able to interpret the book. He turned the hatchet head over in his palm.

"Looks like seventeenth century at least. I don't know where else it could have come from."

Lucky caressed it with his thumb, as if trying to coax the history from it. In his hand was an item that had crossed four and a half centuries to tell an amazing story. To him, it was much more intriguing than the gold.

"Ben and I figured out a cave-diving set up. I'll go in and try to locate the head. Ben's going to be the safety diver. I'd be willing to bet that what we're looking for is less than ten or fifteen yards inside."

"Ben, you okay with that?"

"Yeah, it should be all right."

"Then let's do it tomorrow morning. We'll bring the gold up this afternoon." Lucky decided.

"We need a couple more tanks of air apiece."

"I'll send Jimbo into Gainesville tomorrow."

***

It took several hours to transfer the gold from the bags on the bottom of the lake to the strongbox onshore. Heaped into the beefy wooden container, three hundred thirteen pounds of gold rubble looked like much more. For the first time since Gregorio had buried it on the beach so long ago, the treasure of the *Mano del Rey* was all together again. The only things missing were the gemstones, which had long since disappeared, and the gold that had been cast around Gregorio's head.

A long and restless night lay ahead. Ben wrestled with the changes that had made each of them someone different than when they had started. Jim had withdrawn again, not speaking or interacting much. Whatever inroads Ben had made with him had disintegrated. The wall was back up. Lucky's presence seemed intrusive now. He had come back from the hospital a changed man. He was trying too hard to make it look like he was still in charge because he felt sick and vulnerable. If Jim had sided with Duprez against the rest of them, he wasn't showing it. And ever since Bill spilled his plan to make off with everything, he hadn't let Ben out of his sight. In each of these situations, Ben felt stuck in the middle. The camaraderie that had been built between them all, since that first day in camp on Dead Man Bay, was just about gone. It had been replaced with fear and suspicion born of greed and anxiety.

***

At daybreak, Bill and Ben silently collected the gear they needed to dive the cave. A small spool of light hemp rope, two waterproof flashlights, a walkie-talkie, and the last two full tanks of air went into the boat. Until Jim got back from town with additional tanks, they would be diving with the last air they had. There was no room for accidents. Everything had to go right.

They didn't bother to wake the others when they made a pot of strong coffee and ate huge chunks of buttered Cuban bread. They kept the feeling of anxiety and excitement, the promise of the day, the danger they would have to chance to themselves. Ben had more wreck-diving experience, but Bill insisted on working the cave first. Ben didn't trust Bill's judgment like he once did, but there was no way he wanted to see his friend drown.

Once the sun hit the water, they were ready to go. When they paddled away from the beach, Jim was hunkered down by the coals of the breakfast fire, ignoring them. A slight breeze from the northeast wrinkled the surface of the lake, breaking the sun's reflection into long, sparkling bars of dazzling white. The raft cast a soft shadow on the sandy bottom through the clear water, eventually diving over the lip of the big blue hole as they approached the dive site. Riding at anchor, Ben checked and re-checked the regulator gauges and his dive watch. Again and again, he made sure both flashlights were working. Bill entered the water first, taking the hank of rope. Then Ben followed. In the silent world of aquamarine, they became synced, acting like one.

Swimming shoulder to shoulder, they approached the cave's black mouth. It seemed smaller, more forbidding than before. Bill tied off the rope to his weight belt and gave Ben a thumbs up.

Hesitating only a moment, Bill wriggled inside. He could feel the push of a current at his back, indicating this was an outflow, probably the mouth of an underground river. He tried to gauge the speed as he paused to let his eyes adjust to the semi-darkness. Switching on one of the flashlights and easing forward, he tried not to contact anything that would stir up silt. The rock making up the roof seemed pretty soft and fractured in a lot of places. The walls were sound enough, thick slabs and blocks of ancient limestone. The cave might have once been an open slit that was slowly bandaged with layers of sediment that solidified overhead. The floor was carpeted with beige silica sand, probably swept in from the lake bed outside over millennia.

Ten yards in and the cave curved slightly to the right. Bill noticed to his chagrin that the passage narrowed considerably before opening up again. To clear it, he would have to take off his tank and bring it in after him. Shining the flashlight through the portal, he strained to see anything of interest.

204

A flash of bright yellow caught his eye, and he swept the area with the light more slowly. Lying on the cave floor, nearly obscured by sand, was definitely something unnatural. He thought at first it might be the reflection of his torch off the mica in the sand, but this was something bigger, almost the size of his fist. In spite of himself, he felt his heart rate quicken and his breathing deepen.

Shrugging off his tank, he bundled it into a sling, pushing himself deeper into the cave and dragging his air with him. The small chamber clouded a bit from his exertions, but he sat still and let the current clear the room. Lying quietly a few inches from the bottom, he gently wafted sand from the object. He breathed in a huge lung-full of air as he recognized what it was. A horribly disfigured human face stared up at him in a silent scream, every inch of it cast in gleaming gold. Digging gingerly into the sand with his fingers, he slowly lifted the head from its resting place. A huge gold loaf the size of a hoagie roll lay against the base of the skull, the residual of all the molten gold that the victim was forced to swallow. Slipping from his grasp, it fell heavily onto the cave floor. Bill decided to pass the gold head out first, and then he come back for the loaf.

***

Ben checked his watch for the fifth time as he waited for his partner either to emerge from the cave or to signal on the rope. Only twenty minutes had passed, but it seemed longer. They were approaching the halfway mark on the air supply. Suddenly, he felt a tug on the rope, and Ben started pulling. Immediately, he realized he wasn't just bringing in slack, he was actually dragging his partner out. He was a little alarmed to see how much line had actually paid out. Bill must have gone deeper than either of them had expected.

Bill finally emerged from the overhang, clutching something in one hand and his tank in the other. He dropped to his knees and waved, pumping his fist over his head like he just made a touchdown. He held out the head to Ben. The gold gleamed even brighter in the sunlight, bringing out more detail. They could see wispy remainders of facial hair contained in and emerging from the metal. Gold had puddled in the orbital sockets, creating new eyes. Like the marbles of antiquity, they were opaque, blind. Stumps of teeth in the upper jaw had been completely capped in the brutal procedure, while the tongue was frozen in mid-scream, overlapping the lower teeth. The ears were still visible, although burned into a demonic shape by the heat of the ordeal.

Bill pointed to the cadaver head and made a stroking motion on his own neck, eventually conveying to Ben that there was more in the cave. Setting the head down, Bill turned to go back in, but Ben grabbed his arm. Ben pointed to his tank and then to his watch. Checking the regulator, he spelled out twenty-five minutes to his partner. He gave Ben an OK sign and ducked back into the darkness.

***

Visibility inside had dropped a bit due to their activity. Bill felt along the walls, measuring the distance mentally. At the squeeze, he stuck his arm and head in, searching the bottom for the loaf. He found it just beyond his reach, so he set down the tank and sling, taking a couple of deep breaths. Then he spit out the regulator and swam through the narrow pass, holding his breath. Grasping his prize, he rolled back toward the squeeze.

The current in his face seemed stronger than before, which didn't make sense. Maybe it was the weight of the metal bar slowing him down. It had to be twenty pounds by itself. Finally, within reach of his air supply, Bill paused to greedily suck a fresh lung-full of oxygen from the tank.

He breathed once, twice, before something grabbed his legs as he floated half in and half out of the small passage. He panicked, kicking blindly. The close quarters made it impossible to get a light on whatever had him. It felt as if two incredibly powerful hands or talons were gripping his ankles. The pain was intense. He flailed around trying to free himself. The silt completely obscured everything. One swim fin worked its way off and Bill used his bare foot to gain some leverage against the cave wall. Working his other leg out of the wrenching grasp holding him, he shot forward, slamming into a limestone shelf. Between oxygen starvation and the impact, he began to feel woozy. He jerked on the rope three times and felt himself move forward, floating like a dreamer.

***

Ben found the limp body of his friend at the other end of the rope. His aqualung was nowhere in sight. Using the buddy system of rescue breathing, he climbed toward the surface and the raft.

Climbing first, he man-handled Bill's barely conscious body into the boat. Bill coughed a bit, spitting some of the lake back out, then lay back.

"Man, I thought I was dead."

"You nearly were. What happened?"

Bill pointed to his legs. In the sunlight, he could finally see the tattered bottom half of his wetsuit. It looked as though he had been in a tiger attack. Where the rubber suit had been clawed open, long red scratches streaked down his calves.

"What the hell did that?"

Bill pointed with his chin toward the golden head as it lay in the stern of the boat.

"Whatever was guarding that thing."

***

Lucky came to meet them on the beach.

"What happened?" he asked, appalled at Bill's ripped up suit and wounds. "You run into a gator?"

"Maybe, I don't know. I thought whatever it was had me for sure." Bill winced as he rolled out of the raft. "My legs are burning."

"I'll get the first aid kit." Lucky turned to walk back up to the truck.

"Wait. Lemme show you something." Bill smiled through the pain. "This is what we came for." He lifted the head out of the stern of the boat.

"Jesus, Joseph, and Mary," murmured Lucky.

After everything, all the work and sweat, fear and suspicion, it was anticlimactic to realize this was it. From myth to reality, it had taken ten days and two lives to put their hands on more money than any of them had ever seen. The gold lying in the wooden chest took on a life of its own. It was the body of the murdered Spaniard, now capped and made whole by the recovery of the gold head. It wasn't a treasure or a campfire story. It was a real thing, embodied in hard, cold gleaming metal. It had more power now than ever.

"What else ya got?" Lucky pointed to the oblong bulge inside the top of Bill's wetsuit.

"Oh, this? This is what nearly got me killed." Bill seemed overly nonchalant as he reluctantly handed over the gold loaf. He arched his eyebrows at Ben in a sideways glance.

"Nice chunk of metal." Duprez hefted the bar, studying the dimples made by the Spaniards vertebra on one side. "I figure by now we must have nearly a quarter million dollars in gold."

The silence that fell on them emphasized the disparity of their desires. Secret greed had become nearly blatant.

"Where's Jim?" Ben asked after a minute.

"Still in Gainesville getting a couple more tanks filled."

They followed Lucky to camp and watched from a distance while he locked away the final treasures.

"You gonna be all right?" Ben lit a cigar. It was meant to be a double-edged question.

"Yeah," Bill grumbled.

"So what now? You're kinda up shit creek."

"I really don't know. If those mooks in Miami don't hear something soon, we won't have to worry about it. They'll find me and it ain't gonna be pretty."

"Speaking of which…" Ben nodded over his partner's shoulder, seeing Lucky coming toward them. What drew attention was the fact that Duprez was now sporting a shoulder holster in which the butt of an automatic pistol was in plain view.

"What's going on?" Bill demanded.

"Better safe than sorry," Lucky murmured.

"Christ on a crutch," Bill swore. "This job gets crazier every day. You have that all along?"

"Yep. When money is involved, I don't like to take chances. It's just a little nine millimeter." Lucky showed them the palm-sized handgun.

"Walther PPK." Ben recognized the model.

"Yeah. A little souvenir from the war. I got it from a friend of mine in the French resistance." Duprez was satisfied with the impact his display had on both of them. Better they know now.

"We're pulling out in the morning. Bill, you gonna be okay?"

"Sure. I'm fine. Where we going?"

Lucky started to walk away again, speaking over his shoulder. "That's on a need to know basis." After a few steps, he added, "And don't bother asking Jimbo when he gets back 'cause he doesn't know either."

In the distance, they heard the clanging of metal on metal and the vigorous growling of the Jeep as Jim rolled back into camp. Duprez met him out of earshot and said a few words. Ben saw the big man nod quickly and then hop out, clutching a first aid kit.

"Lucky says Bill got chewed up by somethin'," Jim said.

"That's an understatement." Ben pointed to his partner.

"Help me off with this suit, Ben." Bill was beginning to shake a little as if his knees were getting rubbery. A pair of shears from the first aid kit made short work of the remainder of the wet suit leggings. Hobbling to the Jeep, he climbed painfully onto one of the front fenders and leaned back.

"I'm gonna go get changed," Ben announced, disappearing into the back of the truck.

Jim started working on Bill's leg with antiseptic and gauze.

"It's not a gator bite, 'cause he wouldn't have let go. Those bad boys go into a death roll and you're done for. These are some deep gouges."

"Yeah, well they sting like hell." Bill tried to change the subject to take his mind off the fire in his legs. "So what did you do with Ben's gun after I went through the trouble of taking it from him."

Jim's eyes locked on Bill's for a second as he continued to bandage the man's wounds.

"I unloaded it and I was gonna put it back, but he must have found it first."

Bill laughed a little. "Wonder if he knows he doesn't have anything in the clip?"

"It's all about the gold now, isn't it? Damn the paycheck, you want it all, don't you?"

209

Bill was blunt and for the first time, truthful. "I gotta have that gold. If I don't, I'm a dead man."

Jim exhaled forcefully. "You probably got it comin'. I just want what's mine from the big man. I don't give a damn about you, the gold, or that fucking head."

"I don't believe that."

Jim hesitated. "Believe it or don't, but let me tell you, boy. Don't screw me over."

Bill eased off the Jeep and stomped off, stiff-legged.

Ben had just finished changing when his partner made it to the tailgate of the truck.

"Want to hang onto my gun?" Ben asked. "I found it in Jim's gear."

"You know it's not loaded."

Ben smiled, "Yeah, I just wanted to hear you say it."

"Well, there you have it," Bill shrugged.

Jim came up suddenly with an air cylinder on each shoulder. Ben helped him offload the first one but it was clear the man didn't really need or want help. He tried a lame attempt at small talk.

"Guess we won't be needin' those now."

"A waste of time," Jim agreed.

"If Ben hadn't been able to get me outta that cave in time, they might have been real important."

Jim turned to look at Bill. "If you were runnin' outta air, I reckon these would have come in handy. But I guess I woulda probably been too late. It's a good thing you got a friend to help you out."

"Kiss my ass."

Ben jumped down from the truck in between the two. Bill spun around and limped to the truck cab. Jim stood motionless.

"Hey," Ben said to him. "Forget it. He's got his knickers in a twist about somethin' else. It's not you."

Jim assumed one of those thousand yards stares only military men seemed to be capable of.

"Did Lucky tell you we're leaving in the morning?" Ben asked.

"Yeah."

"Did he say where?"

"No." Then Jim added, "He said y'all were gonna ask." He glanced downwards and chuckled softly.

***

Nightfall arrived more peacefully than usual. A glancing storm front blew in cooler air without raining, taking with it most of the buzzing insects. The breeze occasionally moaned through the tops of the tall pines but not strongly enough that it disturbed the leafy oaks growing lower. The stars were mostly invisible behind a high cloud bank, with only the brightest shining through occasionally as the weather steadily moved east.

They sat around a low fitful fire, staring into the coals, each deep in his own reverie. Light wisps of wood smoke circled them, adding the wild perfume of burning oak to the air. Surrendering their individual animosities for the evening, they were almost relaxed.

Only Bill remained restless, still trying to get some relief from the searing pain in his legs. Even in the dark, he could see that his feet had swollen into fat buns.

"Ben," he said in a low voice. "Whatever happens, don't let 'em cut off my legs."

"I won't, bud."

"I was thinking about Dan. I wonder if he's out of the hospital yet."

"He got transferred to a hospital in Miami," Lucky interjected, yawning slightly. "I checked before I left."

Ben nodded.

"When were you going to tell us?" Bill groused.

"You didn't ask."

Jim grunted, underscoring the statement.

"Well, while I'm not asking things, I guess they never did find Lonnie," Bill said.

"Nope."

"Lost at sea," Ben mumbled.

For a sailor, the phrase was equivalent to the Army telling the next of kin their loved one was missing in action. It was worse than getting a telegram that they had been KIA. For the missing, there was always a small ray of hope they had survived somehow. Maybe they were out there, wounded, left behind, slowly starving to death or dying of thirst.

211

Hope was the nightmare, wishing both that they might return and that they might be released from their misery, wherever they were.

***

Lucky got up without saying a word, climbed into the Jeep, and pulled a tarp over himself. Ben wondered if sleeping on top of a box containing a quarter million dollars in gold would bring him sweet dreams, but what he knew about the golden head suggested those visions might quickly become night terrors. He lit a cigar, momentarily blinded by the lighter's glare. It was odd that after all they had done, everything they had been through together, there was nothing left to say to each other. The four of them were as much a gathering of strangers as they were at the beginning. Mutual trust had grown and dissolved. Familiarity counted for little. They were a team of individuals, but he was afraid what was coming was going to fracture even that.

Jim wandered off to take a leak, then climbed into the truck cab to lie down.

"You get the feeling that everybody in this outfit has a chip on their shoulder?" Bill mumbled.

"Maybe." Ben took a long draw on his cigar. "Hey, whattaya say we just take the money we got coming and get lost? If we pool our dough, we can get a boat and head over to the Bahamas like you said."

"It's a good plan, but I'm not that lucky. The boys won't let go that easy."

"You really are hooked, aren't you?"

"Yeah." Bill groaned a bit as he tried to get comfortable, putting his back against a small pine. "That night in the casino, they worked me over pretty good. They got a goon named Antonio, only they called him Angel, like the angel of death. He's one of the worst. Got this tattoo on the back of his right hand—a skull with wings behind it. I remember it because I saw it every time he punched me in the face."

"But how are they going to know if and when we found the gold?"

"They're watching Fischer. For all I know his phone's tapped."

"So when he knows, they do; and when he shows up to collect, so will they."

Bill nodded, almost in shame.

"It's okay, buddy. At least I know what we're up against."

"It's not your problem. I got myself into it. I can take what's coming."

Ben climbed stiffly to his feet and retrieved a couple of wool blankets out of the back of the truck. Dropping one in Bill's lap, he spread the other one out next to him.

"Holler if you need something," he said as he put his back to the dying fire.

***

Daybreak caught them by surprise, stealthily arriving in small degrees under a high, solid cloud deck. The sunrise was muted, gray, without fanfare. Ben rolled over and checked his partner's breathing. It was deep and regular, but the shocking thing was the bright pink his lower legs and feet had turned. Ben could see the infection growing in the long gouges, and pus stained the gauze wrapped around the worst places. Angry red streaks flared upwards from his knees, indicating blood poisoning.

Ben stumbled down to the beach to wash his face. As he splashed water over his head, he noticed a strange set of footprints coming out of the water, leading toward camp. They were barefooted human prints—fresh, probably made last night. He checked to make sure it wasn't one of the guys, maybe left yesterday when they beached the raft, but these prints were in a completely different section of the beach. With a chill, he remembered the footprints they had found on board the *Dreamboat*.

Slightly skittish now, he went back up to check on Bill. The man was nearly cold to the touch and didn't respond much at all to Ben's attempt to rouse him. Ben walked back to the Jeep.

"Lucky."

"Mmfph," a muffled response came from under the tarp.

"Lucky! I need to ask you something."

The tarp whipped back and Duprez lay blinking at him.

"We going anywhere near a hospital today?"

"We can."

"We need to. Bill's in trouble."

Lucky climbed out of the back of the vehicle, walking up to check on the prostrate man.

"Get Jim," he said without hesitation. "We got to get him to the hospital now."

***

It was just a quarter mile back down the trace, but it seemed much farther to Bill. There was another mile and a half of hard-packed, clay road to the highway. He tossed and turned on the pallet in the back of the truck, grimacing with every bump. The roar of the wheels on the macadam echoed in his head, blocking out everything but the pain. It felt like something was eating him from the inside out. He tried to remind himself it was less than five miles to Alachua General, in traffic, maybe fifteen minutes. He could hold out.

By the time they got into town, he was less lucid. He imagined they were in a parade. He was dying. Why was he in a float in a parade? There was a sudden stop and several faces peered in at him. Someone came up with a gurney and they all lifted him onto it. All he could see were receding doorways and a bland, white ceiling. Light fixtures shone down on him, alternating with shadows overhead, like landing beacons on a runway. Installed in an empty bay of the emergency room, Bill lay almost comatose on the thin mattress.

***

Ben stood at the foot of the bed, wondering if his partner would make it. Dan had been in bad shape, too. He made it. Bill was a lot tougher. Funny how things turned out. Ben had made it all the way through the war without losing anybody close to him. Now, he had been in that position twice in one month. It didn't take a war to make bad things happen. People died in miserable ways every day. There was nothing you could do about it. If you made it through life without it happening to you, well, you were just one of the lucky ones. Instead of wondering why fate spared him or why it wasn't him in that bed, Ben now knew that if the worst happened, his responsibility was to remember. The only reason to feel guilty about still being alive and in one piece was if he wasted what had been given to him—another chance. That would be unforgivable.

Soon a flurry of doctors, nurses, and technicians elbowed Ben out of the way. In their white togs, they appeared like a team of angelic phantasms, flitting around on all sides, trying to keep Bill's soul from escaping. Ben backed off and waited.

Before too long, a doctor with a clipboard approached. "Are you related to the patient?"

"Shipmates." Then Ben corrected himself. "Co-workers."

"What's his name?"

"Bill. Bill Walden. How's he doing?"

"He's definitely in critical condition. How did he get the scratches on his legs?"

"Diving accident. We were doing some cave diving close by."

"Well, Mister—"

"Wheeler."

"Mr. Wheeler, I'm not sure if we can reverse his condition. He's got a severe case of blood poisoning from those wounds. The infection in his blood could kill him."

Ben nodded, and the doctor rushed off. The rest of the team burst from behind the curtains surrounding Bill and wheeled him somewhere. Already there were a couple of IVs in him and an oxygen mask across his face. An orderly anticipated Ben's next question.

"We're taking him up to the top floor, the critical care ward. Somebody will let you know which room."

Bill disappeared around a distant corner with everyone in tow. Then all was still again. The newly fallen quiet was surreal. It was almost as if they had never been there to start with. Just that fast, lives changed, things began and ended.

Ben slowly made his way out to the emergency room door and the sidewalk beyond. Feeling for a cigar, he remembered he had left everything in the Jeep. Wait. The Jeep—where had Jim and Lucky gone? The Jeep, the truck, the gold, everything had evaporated into thin air. Those bastards, he swore mentally. He didn't even have his wallet on him.

Back at the nurse's station, he waited for someone to give him Bill's room number. Looking around the ER, he wondered how many more of them might come in the way Dan, Lucky, and Bill had. It was beginning to feel all too familiar, a thing hospitals should not be. What were the odds that three people from such a small group would all end up here? There was a reason, even if he didn't want to admit it. Maybe it was just a matter of time.

He heard a phone ring, then a nurse finally handed him a slip of paper with a three-digit number hastily scribbled on it.

"Can I go up and see him now?"

The nurse shook her head. "He went into a coma. The doctor doesn't want anyone in there right now. They're still working on him. Is there any next of kin?"

Ben hesitated a minute.

"No. No one."

A shadow at Ben's elbow made him realize someone was standing beside him, waiting silently. It was Jim. They walked outside the lobby together without saying a word. As Jim slid behind the wheel of the Jeep, he finally spoke.

"I heard what that nurse said. I hope he pulls through."

"Bill is about as close to family as I got down here."

Jim nodded and started the engine. There was nothing left to say about it all. In that short exchange, apologies were tendered and accepted. Trust was restored and sanity recovered. They were a team again. The threat of imminent death had that power.

Skirting the edge of the university campus, Jim drove north, slowed by city traffic and sluggish lights.

"Where did y'all go? I thought you ran out on me."

A small smile crossed Jims face. "Nah, but we didn't think it was smart to sit in a public parking lot with a shitload of gold in a wooden box on the back seat. We didn't have any idea how long you guys might be."

Ben kept other questions to himself, like what would they have done if Bill died? Instead, he finally asked, "Where we headed?"

"Lucky has us holed up at the airport. Fischer rented a hanger out there."

A couple blocks past the police station, they turned right, receiving the early morning sun on their faces. Ben studied the foot traffic around the Greyhound station as they went by. He and a thousand other soldiers and sailors shared indelible memories of bus trips during the war. Whether the leave was for holidays or funerals, they all wound up sitting at the window of a Greyhound bus, watching the world go by for hours on end. Just after he enlisted, his folks had moved to Valdosta, Georgia, and the nineteen-hour trip from Valdosta to Key West became something he had to endure at least twice a year. The last time he came back off leave, he saw the sunset in Lake City and the sun rise in South Miami. They had to hang around in Orlando waiting for a connection in the middle of the night. He remembered tiptoeing around and over a dozen exhausted fellow travelers sleeping on the floor of the depot.

Crossing over Main Street, Jim picked up State Road 24 a couple miles south of the airfield. Already they could see planes in the air, coming in and out of the hub, circling, jockeying for position. Most of them were small private craft, and they all dispersed whenever a commercial flight approached. Even at this distance, Ben could identify the livery of the major airlines on the tail of each DC-4 and Connie.

Passing the terminal building, Jim drove to a darkened hangar at the end of the runway. Inside sat two huge machines, the deuce and a half and a new Beechcraft twin-engine plane. It had to be Fischer's. No one else could afford it. There were no markings but the tail number. Ben wondered who the pilot was. Jim parked the Jeep behind the truck. Apparently, they were going to hitch the Jeep to the back of the big rig and tow it. It made Ben a little uneasy, since that meant they were going to have one less man. Maybe Fischer was here to pay them off and cut them loose. Jim hadn't said a word on the ride over.

Lucky suddenly stepped from the plane.

"How's Bill?" he asked, his voice echoing slightly in the rafters.

"Critical. They say he has septicemia."

"Blood poisoning. That makes sense. Came up awful fast."

"Where's Fischer?"

"He's not here yet." Lucky walked to the back of the truck where Jim struggled with an old ammo crate.

"Give us a hand, willya? I want this on the plane before anyone else gets here."

From the weight, Ben knew the gold had been transferred from the strongbox, which still sat in the back of the Jeep. He wondered if any

217

had been left behind. Did someone take a personal share? Only Jim and Lucky would know. As they struggled to get the box into the cabin of the plane, Ben hated himself for his thoughts. It had come to this. He trusted no one anymore.

"So who's the pilot? Where is he?"

Lucky glanced at him with the faintest of smiles.

"I'm flying us out. Me and Fischer. Once he gets here and pays you guys, we're outta here."

"How are we supposed to get home?"

"Jimbo's taking the truck and the jeep back to Montgomery with him. I figured you'd want to hang around here until Bill got out of the hospital."

"Well, yeah."

"Don't worry. You'll have enough money to go wherever you want."

Ben realized what Lucky was saying was true. He couldn't go off and leave Bill here, not after what happened to Dan and Lonnie. Everything was changing so fast. He would feel better when he had his pay in his hip pocket. He decided he better take Bill's to him personally. Nobody was gonna beat him out of a nickel.

***

It was mid-afternoon when Southern Airways Flight 12 lumbered in for a rough landing and taxied toward the only gate at the terminal. The twin props on the DC-3 had barely stopped turning when the ground crew chocked the fat balloon tires and pushed a weather-beaten stairway up to the fuselage. The first passenger down the steps was a plump figure in a light gray suit and a Homburg fixed on his head. He paused at the bottom to mop his brow, the only concession he made for emerging from the relative comfort of the plane into the heat. Gripping a leather attaché case as he walked toward the concourse, Fischer glanced around furtively. Flagging down a skycap, he managed to convince the porter to commandeer a motorized baggage cart to drive him the length of the airport.

They rolled slowly past a series of nearly identical barns sheathed in oxidized sheet metal. Inside were planes, parts, and the shadowy superstructure of an avionic underground. At the edge of the property, they stopped in front of a hangar big enough to hold a three-ring circus.

The back of the hanger was closed and locked, so Fischer walked down the side of the building toward the flight line. His gait suggested a certain anxiety, and his knuckles were turning white from the death grip he had on the case he carried. Clearly, he was more accustomed to hearing the heels of his wingtip shoes echo off the polished marble floors of five-star hotel lobbies than the trash-covered perimeter of a backwater airfield. He peered through the safety glass on a door near the front corner, hesitating like a man visiting the proctologist's office. Not until he saw Duprez approach did he seem to gather enough courage to open the door and walk in.

"Mr. Duprez, good to see you again." The man finally doffed his hat, wiping the inside band with a linen handkerchief without releasing his hold on the attaché case.

"We've been expecting you."

"Of course." Fischer replaced the Homburg on his balding head and walked slowly toward the plane with Lucky in tow.

"Is everything arranged?"

"The artifacts are onboard. Wheeler and Carter are here. Walden is still in the hospital."

"I'm sorry to hear that. I was hoping he would be out by now. What's his condition?"

Lucky shook his head. "Not good."

Fischer pursed his lips but stayed quiet.

"Let's pay these guys off."

Fischer finally set down the attaché case and opened it.

"I'm prepared to meet my original obligation—five hundred dollars per man, cash."

"You realize we lost one man, had another permanently disabled, and a third near death."

Fischer continued to fumble with the contents of the case and never looked up.

"The collateral damage was to be your concern, Mr. Duprez. That was the arrangement."

Lucky took a step closer, invading Fischer's personal space.

"You also realize that this whole recovery project was completely illegal."

Fischer straightened up and blinked like a mole in bright sunlight.

"What are you implying? Are you saying I should now give them a cut of what was recovered? That was not our deal, Duprez."

"I don't welsh on a deal, Mr. Fischer. I'm suggesting that these guys deserve a bonus."

After a minute, the doughy little man nodded.

"Do you think eight hundred each would be appropriate?"

"Jimbo! Ben!" Lucky called over his shoulder, "Come here! It's pay day."

The two men were in the middle of unloading the truck, stacking the gear beside it. Lucky waved them into the middle of the hanger and each one of them dropped what they were holding. Jim propped the air tank he was holding onto the pile of tents that was growing on the floor. Less than secure, the cylinder slowly tilted until it clanked noisily onto the concrete, rolling easily until it stopped directly under the cab of the truck.

"Murphys Law." Ben smiled. "Anything dropped in a garage will roll directly under the vehicle you are working on."

Jim shrugged. "I'll get it in a minute."

Ben ambled to where Lucky and Fischer stood.

Fischer counted out fifty and one hundred dollar bills with the ease of a bank teller. He passed a wad of cash to Lucky, who passed it over to Jim.

"Eight hundred bucks, Jimbo. Thanks for all your hard work."

Jim grunted, a sound that said more than words. He folded the stack and shoved it in his front pocket.

"Ben, here's your eight hundred and eight hundred more for Bill. You're gonna stay here till he gets out, right?"

"Yeah. We'll leave here together."

***

Trying hard to appear nonchalant, Ben still couldn't shake the feeling they were being cheated. They had signed on for the cash, but the gold seemed so much more now. It wasn't just what it was worth. It was what it represented, what they had gone through together. Mostly it

220

was what it had cost. Maybe it was petty of him, but he suddenly realized Lucky was about to fly out of here with the gold and the cash. What kind of deal did he have with Fischer on the side?

Evidently, Jim was feeling something similar. He walked back toward the truck, and then paused as Ben came up behind him.

"I gotta take a dump," Jim abruptly announced and headed for the john stuck in the back corner of the hangar.

With everybody else otherwise occupied, Ben decided it was a good time to stash his money somewhere. Lifting his duffel bag out of the back of the Jeep, he knelt down with it to find a pocket in something to hide the cash. A slight noise near the front of the hanger made him hesitate and listen intently.

"Noble Fischer, I presume." It was a voice Ben had never heard.

"Who are you?"

"You don't know me, but we are going to become very good friends."

Ben got on all fours and peeked under the Jeep. He could see the new voice's feet, but not his face. After a minute, he saw a second person walk into view. The unmistakable sound of a revolver being cocked suddenly made the interruption ominous.

"Where's the gold, Fischer? I'm not in the mood to explain everything."

Ben heard Fischer clear his throat nervously, trying to stall the intruder. There was a sharp slap and Ben saw Fischer's wingtips shuffle, as if staggering under a blow.

"It's in the plane," Lucky's voice came through.

"Joe, take his gun and go check the plane."

"You're gonna need a pilot if you plan on flying out of here," Lucky continued.

"You mean I'm going to need you?"

"It's here, Angel," the other man called from the door of the plane. Angel—Bill had said they called him the Angel of Death.

"All right. Escort Mr. Fischer to his seat and get this bird fired up. You see, I brought my own pilot."

"What do you need Fischer for?" Lucky wanted to know.

"Oh, didn't he tell you?" Angel chuckled, "We're partners now. Mr. Fischer has some important connections in South America we want to do business with."

There was a stomach-churning pause. Ben suddenly remembered his gun, lying right on top of his stuff in the duffel bag. Easing it out, he cocked the hammer as quietly as he could and lay flat out on the floor. He still couldn't see the entire scene. His hand was shaking enough that he might miss if he tried to shoot the man's leg. Then he saw the air tank, still lying under the truck. That would be a lot easier to hit. Where was Jim? If he came out now, he was as good as dead. Feeling sweat trickle down his face, Ben tried to figure out if Lucky would get hit with shrapnel when the cylinder exploded. Angel might be getting ready to kill him anyway. The sound of first one of the plane's engines turning over, then the other, made the choice for him.

***

In ten seconds, it was all over, but the action seemed to expand into ten minutes. The crack of the forty-five was immediately drowned out by the enormous metallic clang the slug made as it penetrated the metal tank. A deafening rumble shook the walls, accompanied by a sound that resembled the hiss of a dying dragon. An enormous white mist obscured everything, the prop wash curling it into long tendrils. When it evaporated, Ben could see two bodies on the floor. Metal shards had partially shredded the plane's fuselage near the tail, but the pilot was gunning the engines. Ben stood up as the aircraft slowly taxied out onto the apron, the blast of the exhaust sending dirt and grit into his face. Jim was suddenly beside him, shielding his eyes from the flying debris. As the plane rolled down the taxiway, they emerged to check out Lucky and the man called Angel. Lucky was still breathing, knocked senseless from the blast. Ben studied the tattoo on the mob man's hand before realizing that his face was nearly sheared off by a piece of heavy-gauge steel embedded in his skull.

"He's dead," Ben replied to the question on Jim's face.

"Let's get Lucky outta here before anybody else shows up."

By the time they got Lucky into the Jeep, they could hear the twin-engine Beechcraft winding up at the end of the field. Headed toward the hospital one more time, they glimpsed the plane's shadow as it passed overhead. Fischer had his gold, if he could keep it.

28
~~Gainesville, Florida~~
June 27, 1959

The bar had only been open an hour by the time Ben sequestered himself in a back corner where no hint of daylight could ruin the illusion of a place where time might stand still. He needed to stop the world and get off awhile, let the spinning images in his head slow down and settle into place. Two weeks ago, he was a bored, broke-ass ex-sailor with no prospects. What was he now? Not broke, at least. He took a big slug of the cold draft beer and stared into space. He could go back to Cedar Key, but there was nothing there for him except his scooter. Bill might be in the hospital another month. He probably needed to find a place close by until Bill was ready to travel. Jim was on his way back to Alabama and when Lucky got out, who knows where he was headed. Lucky probably still had an itch up his butt to check on Fischer, but nobody else cared any more. It was all over. Everybody made a little money, got some scars to show off, and had a few stories to tell.

The tiny TV on the corner of the bar was broadcasting the last few minutes of "Queen For A Day." The midday news would be on soon. The porter was still trying to vacuum up part of the lounge, and Ben could only hear snippets of the TV. The station's news logo splashed across the screen as Ben watched absent-mindedly. Finally, the vacuum shut off and he could hear the announcer.

"At this hour, authorities are still searching for a
twin-engine aircraft that disappeared off ground control

radar at approximately seven thirty last night. The private plane, with an unknown number of people on board is presumed to have crashed during a thunderstorm over Lake Okeechobee. So far, no wreckage has been found. Police say one of the passengers may have been Noble Fischer, a Miami financier listed as a person of interest in the investigation of a fatal accident at the Gainesville Airport yesterday. Fischer has been missing since June twenty-sixth, when he flew into Gainesville on a Southern Airways flight. Anyone with information on Fischer's whereabouts is advised to contact their local sheriff's department."

Slowly, a faint smile played across Ben's face. It was more than irony. It had to be fate. The gold head had returned to its watery grave. Jim was right. That thing should never have seen the light of day.

About the Author

Jaeme Haviland is a native Floridian from Jacksonville. His travels have taken him to such diverse places as NYC, San Francisco, Toronto and Key West. He has had two songs published and recorded: "Stay Away From Planes" and "The Ferris Wheel." He is a photographer and his photos have appeared in books such as *Smokey Mountain Mysteries* and magazines like *American Legacy*. Two self-published travel anthologies—*Carolina Blue* and *From The First Coast* as well as a novella, *Groundfog*, are available on Amazon. Currently, Jaeme lives in Palatka, Florida, with his wife and four cats.

They say the sins of the fathers can be visited upon the sons through seven generations. The sins of the mothers know no such bounds. They are nurtured, protected, and handed down from generation to generation, world without end. They are inescapable and liberating, choking and cathartic, tomorrow and yesterday. These sins are an unspoken blood legacy, and though they may be forgiven in the eyes of man—and perhaps even those of God—the daughters are never truly cleansed. Their blood is tainted, an earthy rot just this side of perception. The sins remain across oceans, across time, across life, across death. As palpable as a heartbeat, as quiet as a still-soft voice, they are as present as a soul. They abide. They bide.

Available at www.syppublishing.com and other on line outlets